KAT'S NINE
Lives

Laina Villeneuve

BELLA
BOOKS
2018

Bella Books, Inc.
P.O. Box 10543
Tallahassee, FL 32302

Printed in the United States of America on acid-free paper.

First Bella Books Edition 2018

Editor: Cath Walker
Cover Designer: Judith Fellows

ISBN: 978-1-59493-608-1

Other Books By Laina Villeneuve

Return to Paradise
The Right Thing Easy
Such Happiness as This
Take Only Pictures

Acknowledgments

I am so grateful to my colleague Eric, who said just the right thing when I posed my dilemma of revising a finished draft of one book or starting this new book. Many thanks to my early cheerleaders, Roberta and Diane, who encouraged me chapter by chapter. I am also indebted to my Bella colleagues for their keen suggestions: Jaime Clevenger for her insights on writing a first page that grabs a reader, Rachel Gold for her tutelage on description, and Blayne Cooper for advice about pacing. Ruth, thank you for sharing all you know about commas!

I'm so lucky to have been able to work with Cath Walker on this fifth book. She had a special knack for leaving suggestions with me and patiently waiting through the drafts for me to figure out she was right. I may not have learned my lesson about certain verbs or rules of capitalization, but I have learned a lot about deleting details that detract from the plot. This is a tough story for me to launch, and the confidence I have in it now comes a lot from the faith Cath had in the story and in me.

My friend Heather has been my best fan from before I even started publishing. She and her wife Samantha gave me great reader's perspective before I sent in the final draft.

Thank you again to my mom, who read pieces of the draft when she could and answered all sorts of questions to help me understand my characters better. My dad filled in factual details, especially in terms of the legal vs the religious response to the legislation of same-sex marriage. My wife and kids graciously accepted the eighties soundtrack delivered by warbled mix tapes I dug out of the garage to help find the right songs for this couple. My wife has weathered a lot of emotional turmoil in the working of this book and has been especially gentle with me during each step. She also deserves all the credit for Wendy's culinary backstory, graciously filling in when I left [some cooking thing] in the draft.

When I was a kid, there was a commercial that ended with the line "Big sisters always make things easier." My big sister has done just that from day one, and this story is my attempt to say thank you.

About the Author

Laina Villeneuve is the baby of three. She and her brother and sister grew up with the handprint of a famous silent-movie star in their backyard, a fact her own three children have yet to appreciate. In real life, her sister has never kissed a girl. Her mother has. The AIDS crisis in the '80s significantly changed her father's dating habits, and her parents celebrate fifty years of marriage this fall.

Dedication

For my sister, Katherine
Who deserves a happily ever after.
I wish hers had come sooner
And lasted longer.

Author's Note

By 2015, thirty-seven states in the USA had made same-sex marriages legal either by state action or federal ruling. Because Ohio was not one of those states, Jim Obergefell and John Arthur flew to Maryland to marry. John Arthur had Lou Gehrig's disease. They sued the state of Ohio when they learned that the union would neither allow them to be listed as married on Arthur's death certificate, nor recognize Obergefell as his surviving spouse.

The case was reviewed by the Supreme Court of the United States, and on June 26, 2015, with a 5-4 decision, the court legalized marriage for gay and lesbian couples in all fifty states. Justice Anthony M. Kennedy wrote, "No union is more profound than marriage, for it embodies the highest ideals of love, fidelity, devotion, sacrifice and family. In forming a marital union, two people become something greater than once they were."

The ruling did not, however, end all conflict. In many states, couples continue to be denied services from many in the wedding industry, such as bakers, florists and photographers. Liberal churches celebrated the opportunity to officiate weddings for gays and lesbians. Though many conservative churches authorized clergy to perform these weddings, the decision is ultimately left to individual clergy.

Step by step, the LGBTQ+ community continues to move toward true equality.

CHAPTER ONE

"Guess who's getting married!"

Kat looked up to find her favorite couple in her doorway. "Married?" she said. She knew the couple refused to wed until marriage equality was available throughout the United States.

"The Supreme Court's ruling is out, and it's time to celebrate!" Evan said.

The volunteers in the outer office squealed with delight. Kat joined them and rushed to the pair to give them both a tight squeeze. She had only ever seen them in their Sunday slacks and ties. Seeing them in baggy cords and sweaters made them seem more like friends than parishioners. "I hadn't heard!" she said.

"The news just broke," Evan gushed. Years had done nothing to minimize his strong jawline with his cleft chin, and his pale blue eyes shone brightly. "I was still glued to the news report, and this one was already popping the question!"

Jeremy's salt-and-pepper beard almost hid the smile on his rounder face, but he was clearly emotional when he took Evan's hand and said, "We have a big anniversary coming up, and we want to talk to Reverend Thorn about making it our wedding day."

Kat clasped her hands over her heart, a surge of happiness lifting her. A wedding! Even though her own fifteen-year marriage had ended in divorce, weddings still thrilled her to her core. She loved every detail of a couple's plan for the ceremony and the reception: the music, the food, the favors! While her official duties at Kindred Souls Church did not extend beyond managing the facilities, she got pulled into many of the other details since she had the keys and alarm codes for the buildings. She had worked with so many photographers, florists and caterers that she often knew what couples needed before they did.

The phone rang, and a volunteer reached across the desk to answer it while Jeremy reflected on the Court's decision. "It's exciting news for the country," he started to explain, but emotion tightened his throat. "We've been waiting so long for this day."

The volunteer, phone to her chest, leaned over. "Kat, it's for you." Hating to step away from Jeremy and Evan, Kat was about to ask the caller to leave a message. "It's your mom. She says it's an emergency."

Pushing away her irritation, Kat stepped back into her office and picked up the phone. "Mom, this is the church line."

"I know. You didn't pick up your cell."

"What's the emergency?" Kat groused wondering why her mother couldn't have had her drama some other time when Kat needed an excuse to get away from the Altar Guild ladies and their fretting over new stains on the linens.

"I'm out of donuts."

Kat sat at her desk and closed her eyes. She pulled her blond hair over her shoulder and ran the soft ends back and forth over her lips, searching for serenity. She took a deep, even breath.

Her mother, Millie, must have heard her. Resigned, she said, "You're right, I'll survive."

"I can probably make a run between closing the office and bells."

"Oh, no. You don't have to do that. I'll be fine. I can make some sugar toast. I don't think the bread is that old."

"I just bought the bread last week."

"Yes, exactly."

"I'll see you at five twenty," Kat said. "*If* I get my work finished," she added, disappointed to see that Reverend Thorn was already shaking Jeremy and Evan's hands and ushering them into his office. She returned to preparing the Sunday bulletin, trying her best to ignore the volunteers' chatter.

"I don't think we have enough hangers or bags," one said.

"Have you seen the huge pile of donations? There's no way we have enough."

"Of course it's much easier to pull in some hangers than it is to pull in volunteers."

"How about Suzy?"

"Are you kidding? Suzy is such a gossip!"

"Suzy? I don't think I've ever heard her say more than two words."

"Oh, but she listens. She's the one who told Reverend Thorn about the Heyman's daughter."

"No!"

Though it was tempting to insert that they were gossips themselves, Kat finished proofing the order of service and printed the final copy. She carried the original from her small office to Verna, the most technologically savvy of the volunteers, to run the copies.

The door of the priest's office swung open. Reverend Thorn wore the self-satisfied look that always followed an opportunity to explain the Bible. He smoothed his tie, his hand pausing at his soft middle, a disingenuous smile on his pasty face.

Disappointment radiated from the men. They barely glanced up. Kat shot an angry look at the priest's closing door. "What's that about?" Kat asked.

"He refuses to marry us," Evan said. Time had diminished some of the musculature on his tall frame, but he always carried himself with dignity. Now his shoulders slumped forward and the muscles by his jaw rippled as if he was trying not to cry.

"But the law!" Kat exclaimed.

Jeremy wrapped an arm around Evan's shoulder. "It's okay. We can go to the courthouse."

"I want a church wedding," Evan said. "All these years, I've been waiting…" He swallowed hard, fighting tears.

Kat opened her mouth, but no words came. Verna rescued her. "Why won't he marry you?"

Forming air quotes, Evan lowered his voice and said, "While I recognize your excitement, you have to understand that the Bible forbids such unions."

Kat tried to bite her tongue but failed. "His interpretation of the Bible. That isn't the church's official stance. It's my understanding they have left it to the discretion of each individual priest."

Verna nodded vigorously, the reading glasses strung around her neck bouncing against her ample bosom. "Yes, that's true. My sister's church in Massachusetts has performed weddings for same-sex couples. But Reverend Thorn takes the Bible very literally. You might have better luck with Reverend Munson. She has a more progressive interpretation. Perhaps she could perform the wedding."

"We asked about that. He said no same-sex ceremony would take place anywhere on campus."

"Ceremony?" Kat said. "You're planning a wedding, not a ceremony."

Evan threw his arms around her. "Oh, Kat. I knew you would understand. I just knew it. What can we do? I've dreamed about our wedding, the garlands, the flowers at the end of each pew. I wanted the organ. The choir. Timpani. I wanted to be Maria Von Trapp in The Sound of Music."

"She wasn't Von Trapp until she got married. What was her last name before?" Jeremy asked.

"Don't try to distract me," Evan answered.

Jeremy turned pleading eyes on Kat. If she didn't shut him down, Evan was going to cry. "And handbells?" she offered.

"Of course the handbells. That wonderful peal you do! You're the sun itself when you swing those bells."

Kat blushed at the compliment. "Well there you go. The bells are portable, and we've provided music at all sorts of venues."

Jeremy searched Evan's eyes. "And we could probably still have someone sing?"

"Absolutely!" Kat chimed in. "You could hire a soloist. I know a couple. He plays the harpsichord, and she is a lovely soprano."

"Keep talking." Evan sat on the edge of the desk, tilting his chin and closing his eyes.

"So much of what you had planned can be done just about anywhere. Maybe you have a favorite park?"

"We love the Huntington. Or Griffith Park."

"There's no way we're getting one of those in a month," Jeremy said.

"One month?" Kat asked.

"Next month, we will have been together for fifty years. We want to get married on the anniversary of the day we promised to spend the rest of our lives together. It's mid-week, so we were sure the church would be free."

"So you want a place that is grand but private and available in a month."

"I want a sanctified wedding." Evan returned to the problem.

Kat shared his disgust at how appallingly Reverend Thorn was treating them. Frankly, she was surprised that he would risk upsetting two of their largest donors. Her mind spun for a solution and stopped on a tenuous alternative. "Have Reverend Munson consecrate a space."

Some of the sparkle she always saw in Evan's eyes returned. "She can do that?"

"She declares that people are gathered in the name of the Lord, and it becomes holy ground. Verna's right. I bet she'd be happy to perform your wedding. Shall we call?"

Jeremy took Evan's hand. "Would that work for you?"

"Where would we do it?"

"Let's call Reverend Munson and see if I'm right because I have a spot in mind."

Kat led them to her office and dialed. She handed Jeremy the phone and linked her arm with Evan's while they listened. Her grip on Evan's arm tightened as Jeremy's smile widened. Finally, he handed back the phone and wrapped his arms around Evan. "She'll do it!"

Verna whooped from the outer office, and Kat hoped that Reverend Thorn was getting an earful of their shared glee. "Okay! I have the perfect location!"

"Where?" Jeremy asked.

"How about a beautiful historic home with space in the backyard for fifty to a hundred guests?"

"Sounds nice," Evan said. Kat could still hear resignation in his voice.

"You know Rock Hudson?" She almost laughed out loud at their twin expressions of confusion.

"She asks the man who swoons at anything he's in," Jeremy said.

"The former owner of my parents' house once dated him."

Evan's eyes lit up, illuminating the dashing man Kat was accustomed to seeing at church. "How do you know?"

"His handprint is in the cement of the patio. Come check it out and see if you can picture getting married there."

"An outdoor wedding in March?" Evan sounded doubtful. "What if it rains?"

"It's Southern California. It never rains. Last year, by mid-March, we were in the high eighties. And Rock Hudson! We have to see this!" Jeremy said.

Kat had suspected she could capture the interest of the retired stage manager with the history of her parents' house. She glanced at her office. She still had work to do, but then she looked at her boss's closed door, and fury coursed through her. Their church had no moral right to deny this couple their dream, not when so many sanctioned marriages fell apart. "Let's go right now. Verna, hold down the fort. We're going on an adventure!" Kat ducked into her office to grab her purse. She fished out her keys and held them up like bait as she passed the guys. "Ready?"

"You can leave work, just like that?" Jeremy asked, falling in step with her.

"I am working. An important couple in our congregation needs help making their dream wedding come true. As far as I'm concerned, that's top priority." She clicked the remote to unlock her car. Though she had initially balked at getting an SUV, she loved its shade of maroon and how the black roof gave it the style of a smaller car.

"How many kids do you have?" Evan asked, peeking inside.

"Just one, but I chauffer him and his friends." Not lately, she realized. Since the divorce, she could count on one hand the number of times she had driven Travis and his best friend Leo to one of their band events or parkour. Once his father started dating her best friend, Ember, they had completely taken over the drop offs and pickups.

She belted herself in and, out of habit, made sure her passengers did the same before putting the SUV in reverse. She snapped off the sound system before the Trevor Hall CD could engulf the space.

They filled the drive with wedding dreams, Kat's favorite topic. When she had married at twenty-two, she'd spent half her life planning her own wedding, and nothing pleased her more than working to make someone else's dream come true.

She took city streets. One, she knew the 101 was a nightmare even in the early afternoon, and two, without detouring she could stop along Ventura at her son's favorite burger joint and the donut shop her mother liked best. Twenty minutes later, she parked at the bottom of the long drive next to the twin palm trees in the front yard of the house she now called home. She looked at the two-story white Colonial through Jeremy and Evan's eyes. "You could have the ceremony here in the front yard. Come look."

They climbed out of the SUV and followed her across neatly manicured grass taking in the grand porch of the almost one-hundred-year-old structure. To the left, steps led to a balcony.

"Whether you have the ceremony here or in the back, you'd have to get a picture of your wedding party from the balcony," she said.

Evan rested his head against Jeremy's shoulder. "At our age, it won't be that big of a gathering."

Jeremy put his arm around Evan. "You're the one who told me a party is made up of the people gathered."

"Come see the back." She led them past an aviary with parakeets and love birds. A red brick path ran the length of the house.

"It's magical," Jeremy whispered under the canopy of towering ficus trees. A fountain gurgled into a basin of smooth black rocks next to a white metal lovers' bench.

A smile stretched across Kat's face. She had known they would love it. "Explore the yard, please. Imagine what you can do with the space. I have to get this food inside before the natives get restless."

She climbed the back-porch steps and pushed the door open with her hip. "Delivery!" The house was quiet. She walked through the kitchen to the stairs. Back in the kitchen, she opened the door to the basement and hollered again, "Delivery!"

From below, she heard her son call, "Coming!" and from above, she heard her mother respond, "I thought that sounded like you in the drive."

Kat unloaded the food and listened to the footfalls on both sets of stairs. Travis's lanky frame emerged first. "I paused my game. Do you care if I eat downstairs?"

"No. Not this time."

"Thanks, Mom!" He kissed her cheek and disappeared.

"Why are there old men creeping around my house?" her mother asked. She leaned her cane on the table and sat, pulling the pink donut box closer.

"They're not creeping. I have a favor to ask." She sat across from her mother at the old scarred wooden table. They had spent innumerable hours in this position through many of what she thought of as her mom's various Barbie editions. She'd been Church-Goin' Barbie when Kat was a girl. In her teens, Kat enjoyed Athletic Barbie more than Baby-Talk Barbie. Shoppin' Barbie was fun for the two of them, but not so much when her dad had taken away the credit cards. She now worried about her mother's significant weight gain with the new Donut-Lovin' Barbie.

Millie bit into a glazed donut and lifted her eyebrows in question. Her thick white hair was tousled, a result of her advanced gift in napping.

"Reverend Thorn won't let them get married in the sanctuary, so they're looking for somewhere to hold their wedding."

Her mother kept chewing until Kat's words and the couple's presence connected for her. "Wait, you want a gay couple to get married here?"

"Is that a problem?"

"It might be for your father."

Kat paled. "I wasn't thinking about that at all."

"Weren't you?"

"Should I tell them no?"

Millie leaned back in her chair, plucking crumbs off her purple shirt. She looked at the men standing in the driveway, bright smiles on their faces. "Could you?"

Kat followed her mother's gaze. "No."

"When do they want to do this?"

"In a month."

Millie set her donut down and picked up a napkin. She slowly wiped each finger. "A month?" she said dubiously.

"I know it's a lot to ask, but they were so upset."

"If I were them, I'd be looking for a new church."

"They love Kindred Souls. And they love each other. I don't want them to leave just because Reverend Thorn hasn't caught up with the times."

"Someone has got to explain to that man what the name of his church means."

"Mom…" Kat didn't need another lecture about her ultra-conservative boss.

Her mother eyed her donut but didn't pick it back up. "It's already done, isn't it? You've never been able to say no, have you?"

Kat pointed at the donut box. "You really want to go there?"

Laughter filled the kitchen. "No. Fine. If they want to get married here, of course we'll support that. But don't expect me to do anything."

"Of course not." Kat rose and kissed the top of her mom's head. "I've got to get back. I'm going to have to stay after bell practice to wrap up what I didn't get done today."

"Fine with me if it's okay with Travis."

She trotted down the stairs loudly to warn her seventeen-year-old that she was coming. "I'll be late tonight. You're okay here with Gramma?"

"'Course. You want her in bed by ten?"

As she'd done with her mother, Kat kissed the top of his head. "Smartass. Are you sure you're not going to turn into a troll down here?" Through the tiny windows at the top of the wall, she could see Evan and Jeremy standing in the drive.

"It has crossed my mind to charge you guys when you walk over my bedroom."

"Hey, I fed you!"

"Which is why you got a pass." He smiled, and she saw a flash of herself. With his muscular build and dark complexion, she more often saw her ex-husband, Jack. Travis thumbed toward the window. "What's with the dudes walking the perimeter?"

"They're thinking of having their wedding here."

"Huh." He turned back to his game.

"Would you be okay with that?"

"Fine by me, especially if I can charge them for walking through the kitchen."

"Troll!"

"Ogre!"

"Love you."

"You, too," he said around a mouthful of food.

Back outside, she found Evan and Jeremy with their arms around each other debating which they liked better for the staging of their wedding—the porch between the regal pillars or the back patio with the wisteria arbor behind them.

"Does this mean it will work?"

Evan embraced her again, and she smiled at the look of relief on Jeremy's face. "You must be a fairy godmother in your spare time."

"Hardly," Kat said, but her heart felt warm.

"Speaking of time, we're feeling the crunch of planning all this with so little of it." He threw his hands in the air. "Less than a month!"

"I have a long list of recommendations for photographers, florists and a caterer. That should speed you up."

"How are we ever going to get all this done?" Jeremy asked.

"Don't worry about things here. I can get the chairs and tables from church, and the caterer is a friend of mine. I'd be happy to call her tonight to see if she can work her magic here."

"Oh, that would help so much!" Evan said. "Are you sure you don't mind?"

"I don't mind at all. Plus, it makes more sense for me to call since I can tell her what the kitchen is like. On the way back to church, you can think about what kind of food you'd like and your budget."

"Listen to you! You really do know what you're doing. I don't know how we're ever going to thank you enough."

"By not worrying about a thing," Kat said.

By the time they got back, she had a good idea of their catering needs and the office was clear. She'd managed to avoid her boss. She glanced at the clock. Street traffic had been kind to her, giving her some time before bell rehearsal. She pulled out her phone and scrolled through her contacts.

"Hey, sunshine!"

Kat smiled. It didn't matter when she called. Wendy always answered the same way. "Hey, I only have a minute, but I have a proposition for you."

* * *

Wendy Archer's stomach did the roller-coaster dip it always did when Kat Morehart's name lit up her phone. Though she'd come a long way from the wallflower admiring Kat from afar in high school, seeing her name still made Wendy feel like she was finally part of the in-club. "Anything for you." With how much Kat had helped her business over the years, she found it nearly impossible to say no to her.

"You might regret saying that," Kat said. A soft chuckle carried over the line.

"Try me."

"I've got a catering gig for you, off campus."

Almost three years ago at their twentieth high-school reunion's sit-down dinner, catered by one of the larger firms in the area, Wendy had complained to Susan, her girlfriend of two years, about the cold rubbery chicken. She'd been aware of their close proximity to the "cool kids", but she never dreamed they be listening to anything outside their circle. She was stunned when Kat pushed back from the table and asked why it was so hard to find a decent caterer. Kat was as vivacious as ever but seemed to have softened somehow, like she wasn't trying so hard. Wendy's professionalism saved her from turning into a stammering mess. She suggested a few common mistakes that may have been made in the kitchen and thought that would be the end of Kat's interest. Instead, Kat surprised Wendy by turning her chair to ask more of her.

The conversation stole her attention so completely that she and Susan had fought the entire way home. Wendy argued that her job required her to network. Her girlfriend complained that she never came first. Consequently, she had lost yet another relationship to her career, but as promised, Kat had begun recommending Wendy to cater church events. Wendy had started with staff gatherings, but she'd quickly landed huge weddings and funerals. Since the church had a congregation of nine hundred, she didn't regret that evening's networking one bit, especially when it meant receiving calls from Kat.

"That's no problem. You know I love any business you direct my way."

"You'll need to check your calendar."

"How far out are we talking and what's the venue?"

"That's the thing. It's in a month. But it's mid-week. And at my house."

"A month!"

"Yes. It's their fiftieth anniversary, and now with the Supreme Court's decision…"

"Isn't it wonderful?"

"For everyone without their head up their ass, sure," Kat said.

She had to laugh. "Is that targeted at a someone specific?" Wendy was touched by the passion in Kat's voice when she explained how she was trying to right what she felt Reverend Thorn had very much wronged.

"I'm sure we can make it work."

"Oh, I'm so glad to hear that. You just made my day!"

"That was easy."

"So do you want to come tomorrow?"

"What's that?" Wendy smiled wryly.

"To check out the kitchen. I thought you'd like to know what you are working with."

Wendy had a menu that would only need the final touches on-site, and could rent convection ovens or gas grills if necessary, but if the wedding party was small, she might be able to get by using Kat's kitchen. "Do you know how many guests they're expecting?"

"I told them our yard would max out at a hundred. Our plumbing wouldn't be able to handle more than that!"

"Sit-down or finger food?"

"Sit-down. I told them about some of the meals you've done at the church, and they're interested in setting up a tasting with you."

"Absolutely. We can do that. Text me your address. I should be able to swing by next week."

"Thank you, Wendy!"

"You're quite welcome!" The way Kat said her name… Wendy sighed like a schoolgirl. It was ridiculous how happy it made her.

CHAPTER TWO

Wendy grabbed a coat with "Key Ingredients" stitched on the breast pocket. Having her dream of running a catering business become a reality still filled her with pride.

When her mother left, she and her father had lived paycheck to paycheck. Eating beans and rice day after day had played a big role in her life and contributed to her desire to eat well and then to feed others. She didn't want to be tied down like her father, earning a minimal wage, caring for a kid and barely being able to pay the rent.

Over the years, she had enjoyed working on cruise ships, where unlike her father, she had called the shots. She chose her jobs, loving the freedom she had to move around. If she didn't like the job, she would switch to a new one. She wasn't stuck with an asshole boss who sucked the joy out of the carpentry her father had adored. It had taken time and the right business partner for her to settle down. She ran her side of the business and José ran his. They would have both gone under trying to do it on their own, but teaming up had given them stability and a better resource base.

Though Wendy had entered the event on the calendar, she hadn't mentioned it to her assistant, Cory Gutierrez, yet. Once he learned the location, she would not hear the end of it. He already teased her about how much work they got from Kat's referrals. His theory was that Kat was searching for ways to be close to Wendy, so she could work up the nerve to ask her out. While the idea held immense appeal, Wendy had known Kat for a long time and assured Cory repeatedly that Kat was as straight as an arrow. Still, he would have a field day if he knew she had a meeting at Kat's house. She'd kept the event a secret for now but revisited it like a smooth stone tucked away in her pocket that she could run her fingers over.

It was almost a week before she had an early afternoon and could meet Kat. She programmed the address into her phone and let the automated voice guide her from her restaurant home base in Sherman Oaks. It routed her along Sepulveda Boulevard instead of the 405, and in twenty minutes, she made it through the familiar neighborhood where she and her dad had shared an apartment. She remembered that her favorite house was only blocks away. Set far back from the street behind huge green hedges, it had always spoken to her as she walked home from high school. Every day, she had thought about the family that lived there. They had to be rich. What she would have given to have so much lawn to play on! She had always wondered what the backyard looked like and what it felt like to live in a place without shared walls. Without drug deals on the corner. Without gunshots.

You have arrived, her phone announced. *Your destination is on the left*.

The house. It couldn't be.

She pulled over and checked the address in Kat's text. It matched. She parked by the curb and tentatively walked up the long drive, her youthful self whispering that she was trespassing. Shoving such notions aside, she climbed to the porch and stood at a green door with a large oval of glass in the center. Looking inside was like looking into the past. An upright piano took up a small wall across the room. Upholstered chairs clustered in a sitting area next to polished wooden stairs. Kat lived *here*? She looked for a buzzer and found only a brass knocker. She lifted it and tapped as gently as possible.

And there, walking toward Wendy with a huge smile on her face, was Kat. She opened the door and pulling her inside as if Wendy had been there hundreds of times.

"Thank you so much for doing this!"

"You know I cater at a lot of private homes. I don't know what you're worried about."

"You haven't seen the kitchen yet. It's not exactly modern."

"Does it have electricity?"

"Of course."

Wendy leaned to the side to try to get a look.

"I'm so sorry." Kat ushered Wendy toward the kitchen. "It's straight through. Just keep walking."

* * *

Kat watched as Wendy took in the décor of her childhood home. She knew their living room didn't look like any normal family's with rocking chairs that had crossed the prairie in covered wagons, stiff-backed cane chairs and a small love seat next to a fireplace. Sheer curtains allowed light from the west and south-facing windows to fill the room. She remembered the family pictures on the mantel too late and hoped they didn't capture Wendy's attention.

What was she thinking when she invited Wendy to her home? Having Jeremy and Evan walk around the property had not panicked her, but Wendy in the living room had her sweating. Above them, she heard her mother get out of bed. She gave a powerful prayer that she would go to the bathroom and right back to bed as usual.

Thankfully, Wendy walked quickly to the large kitchen Kat's father had designed when he was a teenager and his parents remodeled. A range with six burners separated the kitchen workspace from the small table they used daily. She'd taken extra care to tidy the kitchen as if it were interviewing for the job. She was glad for the small bouquet of flowers her father had gathered from the yard. The mint he used offset the mustiness that crept up from the basement. She had emptied the drying racks and stowed them under the sink to leave as much free counter space in the cooking area as possible. Now she eyed the counter closest to them thinking she should have stored the bread box and napkin basket in the cupboard below.

"The table can be extended," Kat said to direct Wendy's attention away from the clutter. "There are two leaves that would give you more workspace," she continued, "and there's another table in the dining room."

Wendy followed where Kat was pointing through a doorway. "May I?" She inclined her head.

"Of course. Whatever you need to see. I see this as a nice staging area for the cake, plates and forks up on the sideboard and cake on the table. The French doors open to the porch."

"When was the house built?"

"Nineteen nineteen. My father lived here when he was a child and later ended up buying it back."

Wendy turned to her, surprise on her face.

"Your father?"

"I live here with my mom and dad. And my son." Recalling all the criticism her friends had delivered when she moved back in, she felt her defensive shield rise.

Wendy crossed her arms. "Your mom and dad?"

"I know how it looks. I really didn't want to move back home, but after the divorce…" She didn't want to say more. The last thing she wanted to talk about was the end of her marriage. Kat had told Wendy at the reunion that she was divorcing, but she'd never told her why.

"I get it. No need to explain. I just wondered how long your parents have lived here."

"They've always lived here."

"Wait, you grew up here?"

"Sure. Why?"

"I'm just…It's nothing," Wendy said.

"It's not nothing. Look at you…" She gestured to Wendy's crossed arms. "That made you mad. Why?"

"It's embarrassing."

"It can't be more embarrassing than moving back in with your parents." A flash of silver in the driveway caught her attention. "Just a moment," she said to Wendy. Back in the kitchen, she opened the door to the basement and hollered, "Travis! Your dad's here. Hustle!"

Luckily, he was ready, his flip-flops slapping the stairs as he bounded up. "See you later!" Kat called as the back door slammed. She worried that Travis probably appeared aloof to Wendy. She missed the boy who used to hug her goodbye and wore whatever she picked out for him rather than the shorts and T-shirts he wore year-round. She had given up those battles long ago.

Travis tucked his guitar into the trunk of Jack's midlife crisis before folding himself into the passenger seat. The car reversed out of the driveway as if the house was on fire. Did she have to explain anything about that whole exchange to Wendy, or could she simply move on?

* * *

Wendy stood looking out at the driveway wondering what to say. Kat faced the window as well, her shoulders rising and falling with her deep breaths. Her fingers found the rubber band that held her blond ponytail. She slipped the band off and ran her fingers through waves and waves of hair as sleek, thick and long as it had been in high school. Wendy had always been envious of Kat's hair, first of her French braids when they were freshmen and later the sophisticated buns she kept in place with a pencil. Her own chestnut-brown curls had never been tamed so easily.

"There. Now I can relax." Kat turned around and her easygoing smile was back. "I'm having a spiked lemonade. Care to join me?"

"Absolutely," Wendy said. She glanced around the spacious room split in half by the stovetop. A large bulletin board covered one wall. Almost half was home to business cards held in place by lady-bug push pins. A calendar, with reminders penned in purple marker on nearly every square, served as the centerpiece. Instead of envisioning how she would utilize the space for the wedding, Wendy pictured a teenaged Kat surrounded by her friends. No wonder she'd been at the center of the popular crowd with space like this to entertain in. Completely at home, Kat stood by an uncluttered yellow counter, popping tops off two bottles, handing one to Wendy.

"Cheers," Kat said, clinking her bottle to Wendy's before she took a sip.

Wendy sealed the toast with her own sip. "You have two refrigerators. This is a caterer's dream, unless they are packed to the gills already." A single cupboard stood in between them, just wide enough for the microwave. A fruit basket hung in front of a small window and held a few dried gourds. She looked for evidence of what kinds of meals Kat's family prepared. One counter had several cutting boards and knives hung from a magnetic strip on the end of the cupboard which suggested they did some cooking, yet no cooking smells lingered. She didn't pick up the heaviness of hot oils or any spices to give clues to favorite dishes.

"I couldn't share a fridge with my parents." Kat took another sip and studied Wendy. "Why did you want to know how long they've lived here?"

"I hoped you'd forgotten about that."

"I don't forget things easily," she said.

Caught, Wendy confessed. "I used to pass this house on my way home from high school. Sometimes I'd see you." Kat had done so many after-school activities that they almost never walked home at the same time, but Wendy distinctly remembered seeing Kat walk right by the house. "I never saw you walk up the drive. You walked all the way to Aqueduct."

"You were spying on me?"

"Everyone watched you in high school."

"Well nobody watching me would have understood." She disappeared into her thoughts.

"A house like this, I pictured you hosting all the in-crowd parties."

Kat's eyes met Wendy's. "Hardly." For a moment she seemed lost in the past. Then her expression cleared. She set down her drink and stepped toward the range. "Most of the burners only light with matches. We keep a box here." She reached into one of the numerous cupboards that hung above the countertops.

Business. Not pleasure. Wendy tested each of the six burners. "And the oven?"

"It gets hot. It's just that the numbers are all worn off, so we don't really know how hot."

"How do you bake?"

"We prefer to leave that to the professionals."

"Luckily, you know one." Wendy didn't want to talk business. As old as it was, the kitchen had generous workspace, and she knew she could make it work. She wanted to know what Kat thought people wouldn't understand and why she hadn't wanted to invite her friends to her house. "Why did you walk to Aqueduct if you lived here?"

Kat pulled her hair over her shoulder and started to lift the ends toward her face. Her eyes met Wendy's again, and she ran her fingers through it instead. "One time, I was walking with these girls, and they started talking about who lived in this house. They had this whole vision of how spoiled the kids must have been."

Wendy ducked her head, ashamed for thinking the same thing.

"I don't know why, but I agreed with them. And then I was stuck. I couldn't very well walk up the drive and wave goodbye to them."

"Why would you agree with them?"

Kat rolled her eyes. "Come on. You know that fitting in is the most important thing when you're a kid. It's hard to fit in when your parents live in a place like this. Even when they can barely afford it and put what little money there is into fixing it up."

"I'm sorry," Wendy whispered.

"You don't have to apologize."

"But I was one of those kids. I assumed whoever lived here was rich. And I was jealous. My dad and I lived in this shitty apartment on the other side of the freeway."

"Where does he live now?"

"He and his new wife have a place in Burbank."

"And you?"

"I'm in Eagle Rock. Cliché, I know."

"I don't follow. Why is that cliché?" Kat asked.

"It's where all the lesbians live."

Kat's hazel eyes widened just a little. If Wendy hadn't been watching carefully, she would have missed it. These were the things she would share with Cory to prove that Kat had not split with her husband because she'd finally realized she should have been dating women. She remembered Kat's curiosity after the reunion and how, though she expressed sympathy that Wendy's relationship had ended, she seemed more comfortable being around her once she was single.

"You said the couple has already toured the yard. Did you talk about where they'll set up tables?"

"Let me show you." She carried her empty bottle with her, so Wendy drained hers and followed Kat onto a wide white porch. Kat took her bottle and dropped it over the railing where it clinked against other bottles. "Recycling goes here," she said nonchalantly. Wendy stood mesmerized by the space. To her right, a patio stretched from the porch to the garage. To her left, lush lawn stretched back seventy-five feet or so to a large hedge. Trees that extended above the two-story house lined the edges of the property creating what felt like an oasis. It was hard to believe she was just a few blocks away from one of the major Los Angeles freeways.

"They said they're inviting thirty to forty. I thought if they use the church's round tables, they could fit everyone on the lawn." Kat stepped past her and walked out to a single tall swing. She sat down and kicked off, rocking gently. "But I'm sure you've got a better eye for space. What do you think?"

Wendy thought that seeing Kat in her native environment was messing with her head. Why else would she be contemplating how romantic it was to watch Kat swaying with the orange glow of the sunset behind her? It must have just been her high-school self reveling in the fact that she was at Kat's house, in Kat's yard.

Which she had asked her to assess. Wendy switched to professional and paced the lawn area, feeling out the space where the tables would go, how much room to allow for chairs for her waitstaff to pass through. "It'll be tight, but it will work," she said.

"I'm texting the guys right now to let them know!"

With Kat's attention on the screen, Wendy wandered to the patio. "Is the pool yours too?" she asked, peeking over grapevines that were just budding.

"Of course. And behind the garage is the turtle yard."

"I wondered where you kept your turtles," Wendy said. Then she burst out laughing. "Who has turtles?"

"We do. Actually, they are tortoises. Want to meet them?" Her buzzing phone stole her attention once again. "Evan and Jeremy want to know when they can choose the menu."

"I'm at Fairbanks all afternoon tomorrow. Can they meet me there?"

Kat's thumbs flew across her screen. Then she looked back to Wendy. "Did you want to meet the tortoises?"

"How can I resist?"

"There are some scraps for them in the compost bin inside. Let me grab it. More lemonade?"

The first one had gone down so easily that a second one truly tempted her. "I shouldn't on an empty stomach."

"Then let me feed you," Kat said. "We'll feed us and the tortoises."

"You don't have to do that."

"But I want to. You're helping me, and I'm sure you get tired of feeding everyone."

"You're sure?"

"I'm sure. Unless you have something better to do. I understand if you need to get going. I'm all loose-endsy now that Jack takes Travis to band practice. But it's nice not to have to sit there and make awkward small talk with the parents I used to call friends."

There were so many things Wendy wanted to ask. She wanted to know what had happened to Kat's marriage, why they'd decided to divorce, and why it was awkward being around her friends. And she wanted to know why she was doing so much to help a gay couple from her church. There were so many questions that she couldn't think of a single thing to actually say. Kat's phone buzzed, and she quickly read the message and passed her phone to Wendy.

"They're in. Want to text them the address?"

Wendy typed as she followed Kat back inside. She set the phone on the counter. "Why are you doing so much for these guys?" she asked.

As Kat pulled a few bags from her refrigerator, she started explaining about the church again.

Wendy interrupted her. "I know that part. I'm just curious about why it matters to you so much. Since, you know…"

Kat piled ingredients on the counter. "Since I'm straight? Come on, some of my best friends are gay."

"I'm sorry. That didn't come out right at all."

"It's okay. Even my mom wanted to know why it matters so much to me. It doesn't seem right that if I wanted to remarry, the church would happily let me stand at the altar, but just because Jeremy and Evan are both men, it's not allowed. It doesn't seem fair. It's not like people can control who they fall in love with."

"You really can't," Wendy said, loving Kat a little bit for understanding.

"I'm in a position to help take some of the sting out of how the church rejected them. Why wouldn't I?"

"True that," Wendy said. "But still. It's a pretty wonderful thing to do."

"I wouldn't go that far."

Kat was so kind and genuine. Didn't she know what a rarity that was? She had to know that most people just went along with the crowd. "You're amazing."

Kat rolled her eyes. "No more than you are."

"Not true. You're in a totally different position, like you were on Halloween, junior year."

"Was there something special that year?"

"I wore that gigantic heart, and everyone teased me. All day people threw mean comments about how dumb I was to confuse Halloween with Valentine's Day."

"That does seem like a weird costume."

"You don't remember it?" Wendy was surprised.

"Should I?"

"You were in a flock of your friends, all of you with your matching curled bangs, blue eye shadow and off-the-shoulder sweaters. They were dissing my costume, but you stopped. You plucked the cardboard glasses off my head and sang, 'Turn around bright eyes.'"

Kat's hand flew to her chest, and she dramatically continued, "'Once upon a time, I was falling in love. But now I'm only falling apart. Nothing I can say. A total eclipse of the heart!' Oh my god, I so remember that now! I loved that costume!"

"You were the only one who got it."

"Everyone else was laughing at your white tights."

"Can we forget about the tights?" Wendy cringed. "I had chicken legs back then."

"Are you kidding? You've always had great legs. And you've never had to worry about your butt being too big."

"I hope you never worried about that."

Kat laughed. "Worried, she says, like my big butt is a thing of the past."

"I wouldn't call your butt big."

Kat leveled her gaze on Wendy. "What would you call it?"

Wendy gulped, struggling to come up with the right adjective. She couldn't very well say nice, though it was the first one that came to mind. Or perfect. "Shapely?"

"Nice job, Bright Eyes!" Kat said, rewarding her with one of her perfect smiles. "You just earned yourself dinner. I live on bean and cheese burritos. Is that okay with you?" She held up a bag of tortillas and a block of cheese.

"Of course," Wendy said.

She was soon transfixed by Kat's dinner preparations. She watched in awe as Kat spread a thin layer of refried beans in the middle of a tortilla, grated some cheese on top of it and popped it into the microwave. When it came out a minute later, Kat quickly folded it into a burrito. Beans and cheese, warm in a tortilla. The woman was an amazing advocate, but not an amazing cook.

Perhaps, Wendy mused, *I could help with that.*

CHAPTER THREE

"Who was here earlier?" Millie traded Kat an empty Diet Coke for a new one.

"Wendy." Kat perched on the edge of her mother's bed. Across from her Millie reclined in her favorite purple cotton kaftan on the small sage-green sofa, her short legs propped on a matching ottoman and crossed at the ankle.

"The caterer."

"Yes. She said our kitchen is going to be great."

"She stayed a long time." Millie studied her cuticles and pushed them down with her thumbnail.

Kat couldn't help the smile that crept onto her face, remembering Wendy's fascination feeding the tortoises grape leaves one after another. "She was having a fun time with the tortoises."

"This is the friend from high school?"

"No. We barely knew each other back then."

Kat reflected on telling Wendy how she'd hidden where she lived from the girls. Wendy had never been one to conceal who she was to make or keep friends. She'd been the girl to petition the school to take her girlfriend to prom. When Wendy had asked her earlier why she was defending Evan and Jeremy, Kat should have told Wendy how she wished she'd stood up to her friends when they'd made fun of the story their school newspaper ran about prom. They had been critical of Wendy's dress, of her hair, of the fact that she didn't try to look like Molly Ringwald in *Sixteen Candles*. She had been herself.

And she'd been beautiful.

She still was, Kat realized. It had been a long time since Kat had considered a woman's beauty without it being a comparison to her own style or how she was aging.

"Well it's nice you're friends now. I still can't believe your Momzilla friends chose Jack over you."

"I'm a heartbreaker, remember?"

"Yes, I can see where they'd say it's all *your* fault."

"I'm happy, Mom, and I know you've been happier with me here these last few years."

"You deserve someone who worships you. You invested years of your life making everyone else feel special, and how do they repay you? Sleep with your husband and then guilt-trip you for not playing along."

"Jack only slept with Ember."

"Still, the rest have no right to pick on you for not following her slutty lead."

"Mom!"

"What? Out of all your friends, I think you and Jack were the only faithful ones. Well, until Jack talked you into that whole switcheroo thing."

Kat hid her face in her hands, wishing she had never admitted to her mother that the first thread in the unraveling of her marriage began with a full partner-swap with friends they'd made when Travis started kindergarten. Through her fingers, she said, "Do you need anything, or am I dismissed for the night?"

"Can you get the soft white throw from the hall closet?"

Kat fetched it. "Anything else?"

With the air of a queen, Millie waved her hand. "Your father will be up shortly. You're dismissed."

Kat walked down the hall to her childhood room and flopped onto her grown-up bed. The house was so quiet, much more so than her thoughts which had returned to Wendy and the prom. Did she still think about it? Was it easier for her after high school, or did she still experience pushback like Evan and Jeremy did?

Kat's phone buzzed.

Are you sure you're happy? her mother texted.

She tapped the phone against her thigh without answering. It buzzed again.

Because I wouldn't want you to feel suffocated.

Lol, she typed back. *Ironic much?*

You have a point, her mother responded.

Night.

It's been two years. You know you don't need our permission to have an overnight guest.

Gross. Not talking about this with you.

You could tell your dad and me if you need the house.

At this, Kat tossed her phone aside. She was not talking about sex with her mother. The phone rang. "I do not need you and Dad to leave the house, okay? Nobody ever died from not having sex," she said without checking the screen.

"Are you sure about that?"

Kat sat bolt upright. It wasn't her mother.

* * *

Wendy was startled. Kat's words had thrown her and now she was silent on the other end of the line. "Should I let you call your mom?"

"Let me give you her number, so you can call and tell her I died of mortification."

"I think it's better to die of mortification than lack of sex."

"I'm sure you didn't call to talk about my sex life. Or lack thereof."

"But this is so much more fun!"

Kat groaned in her ear, sending a jolt of electricity through Wendy's body. "I'm glad you called."

"You are?" Wendy grinned widely. Though Kat had seemed utterly relaxed as the evening wore on, Wendy had been anxious about overstaying her welcome. Now she was tickled to discover that she wasn't alone in finding ways to extend the conversation.

"Yes. Remember how you asked me why I care about Evan and Jeremy's wedding?"

"Sure." Wendy cringed a bit, worried that she had offended Kat with the question.

"I wanted to apologize."

"You're apologizing? For what?"

"For prom."

"Why in the world would you owe me an apology from more than twenty years ago?"

"I didn't stick up for you, and I should have. I didn't walk over and tell you how wonderful your gown was. Everyone was so surprised that you and your date both wore dresses, but they were so beautiful. I should have told you. So I wanted you to know."

Wendy was so overcome, she had to sit down. She stepped out to her living room and perched on the edge of her white couch. She didn't fully trust her voice not to crack when she said, "Thank you. For all of that." The line went quiet between them, and Wendy wished she could see Kat to read her. She wished she could reach for Kat's hand. The thought alarmed her. *Dial it back, there,* she scolded herself. *No falling for straight friends, no matter how nice they are, remember?* "They thought one of us was going to wear a tux, didn't they?"

"Yes. And I think you would have looked awesome in a tux, but I was glad both of you were in dresses."

"Why?" Back then, she was always met with either anger or indifference from the bulk of the kids. She had only ever talked about those days with friends who were on her side. She longed to know what the in-crowd thought.

"Because it made all my friends so mad not to know which one of you was the boy."

Laughter erupted from Wendy. "You have no idea how satisfying it is to hear that I boggled the minds of all the popular kids. If only I still knew Gretchen. It was her idea to wear dresses."

"You wanted to wear a tux?"

"I felt pretty uncomfortable in that dress," Wendy said.

"You didn't look uncomfortable, but I can see how you'd be more comfortable in a tux."

"You've never seen me in a tux."

"What you wear at work is practically a tux. Those pressed pants and the crisp white jacket. Don't lie. You know you look hot as hell."

Wendy covered her eyes with her arm. Kat actually noticed how she looked?

"Sorry. That wasn't professional, was it? Someone might have tempted me to drink more than I normally do tonight."

"You were the one who kept popping the tops on those dangerous lemonades."

"It's thirsty work feeding tortoises."

Kat's words reminded Wendy why she was calling. "That's in the ballpark of why I'm calling."

"Is it?"

"While I appreciated you feeding me tonight, I can't stop thinking about that oven and how I'm going to figure out the correct temperature. I want to do Brussels sprouts wrapped in bacon for the hors d'oeuvres, and they would be so much better cooked fresh than brought in my hot boxes. I thought I could maybe bring a thermometer and test it out, ideally by cooking something."

"You're smart," Kat said. "Smart and fun."

And hot, Wendy remembered. She also said I look hot in my catering duds. Would it be weird to ask if she could bring dinner tomorrow? Was that too soon? Did it make her look desperate? *Ask already before you chicken out! Just do it already before you chicken out!* "Would tomorrow work for you? Or is—"

Before she could even ask whether that was too soon, Kat had already said, "That's perfect!"

Relieved, she stood and did a little happy dance in her living room. "Any requests?"

"As long as it's cheesy, I'm easy," Kat said.

"You've got it."

They finessed the details, clarifying the number of people she would be feeding and when to arrive. Wendy was about to hang up when Kat pulled her back.

"And Wendy?"

"Yeah?"

"Thank you." She paused. "For not being mad about prom."

"Oh, you're welcome," Wendy said.

"My mom thought we were friends back then, and I felt really bad when I realized why we weren't. I'm glad we're friends now. My mom is going to be so happy to meet you tomorrow."

"I'll distract her from her worries about your sex life."

"You had to bring that back up!" Kat said. "I don't want to hang up because I know there will be fifteen more messages from her."

Wendy didn't want to hang up, either, but it was probably better that she not continue to talking about the problem of Kat's sexual inactivity—or thinking about how much she would like to be part of the solution.

CHAPTER FOUR

Her tan station wagon packed, Wendy stood in the kitchen at Fairbanks, ignoring the buzz of activity from those running through dinner service. She loved the flexibility of her job. As the chef for Key Ingredients, the catering side of Fairbanks, she was responsible for off-site events. Her business partner, José, was the primary chef. At least once a month she ran the dinner service in-house, but for the most part she did not have the late nights or a set menu night after night. She mentally sifted through the bins beneath the large steel countertop for anything she'd overlooked. If she forgot something instrumental, she would be able to make do in Kat's kitchen, but she wanted to present her best for Kat and her family. She was aiming to wow them all.

"Did we get a job I don't know about?" Cory asked. He stood a full head shorter than Wendy, but his Brazilian Jiu-Jitsu training lent a stance and delivery that demanded attention. When she had first interviewed him, the bold attitude, gravelly voice and baggy clothes had reminded her of the teenagers who used to hang out on the street corners in the rough neighborhood of her youth. He had impressed her with his skill and knowledge, but most of all, she knew that his street-style banter would keep her on her toes.

"No. Just a test run for the wedding we booked today."

"I loved those guys! What a sweet couple. The way they still look at each other after all these years." He rubbed his manicured goatee that countered his early-receding hairline. "That's the dream."

"And we get to be a part of it." Wendy stepped toward the door.

"Wait. They said something about not getting married at the church."

"Right. They're using a private home."

"Theirs?"

"No. A, um, friend of theirs."

Cory crossed his arms over his chest. His pastry chef background had given him forearms as muscular as Popeye's. "Why are you being all cagey about the location? Are they getting married in some sketchy place?"

"Don't be ridiculous. You know I wouldn't book a wedding somewhere unsafe." Wendy combed her fingers through her brown curls and tied them back in a bandana.

"So what gives?"

"It's Kat's house."

"Kat! You say it all casual, like it's no big thing, like you've been there before. Have you been there before? And now you're taking all this food. I thought the menu was already set."

"Did you actually want me to respond to any of that?"

He motioned with his fingers as if guiding a heavy truck into a driveway. "The whole story…"

"…will have to wait. The short of it is that the oven there dates back to the sixties or something, and the temperature dial isn't accurate. I'm taking a thermometer over."

A slow grin crept across Cory's face. "Is something heating up with you two?"

"Me and Kat?"

"As if that's never crossed your mind."

Wendy narrowed her eyes at him. "She's never even heard of the Indigo Girls."

"Keep adding to your list if it makes you happy. Doesn't make you right."

"Shut up. We're friends, nothing more."

"Be careful out there. If you ask me, you're stepping into a whole lot of unknown territory."

He said this without even knowing that Kat had called Wendy hot. He would love to add that to the evidence he'd collected proving Kat was interested in her. When he brought up the way Kat rested her hand on Wendy's arm, she argued that Kat was one of those straight women who didn't even realize where their hands were. Kat saying she was hot? That she couldn't explain away.

She sat behind the wheel with her eyes closed, briefly letting her imagination flutter around the fantasy version of the evening: Kat impressed by the food, Kat admitting that she looked forward to the events Wendy catered, Kat smiling at her and saying that she'd found herself thinking about what it would be like to kiss her.

Grimacing over the ridiculousness of the daydream, Wendy smacked her cheeks with her palms and then scrunched her face between them. She was just testing out the oven and having fun with her friend.

That's what this was, wasn't it? Becoming better friends. Sure, she found Kat attractive, but it wasn't like they were in high school anymore. Back then, she often imagined what it would be like to hold her hand or lean in for a kiss. Kat had always had someone on her arm, and Wendy would have loved to be that person. She envied the ease with which Kat walked the halls, her relationship on display for all to see. Wendy and Gretchen did their best not to attract attention, but there was no flying under the radar for them. They had decided they might as well go to prom together since everyone was talking about them anyway. And Kat had seen *her* there, not a lesbian. She had acknowledged *her*, the only one of the popular kids to hold Wendy's gaze when she and Gretchen walked in.

Wendy shook her head. That was Kat being nice the way she was with everyone. She'd said herself that she was helping Jeremy and Evan as an ally not because she was fighting for her own right to marry a woman in the church. She climbed the steps to the porch and tapped the knocker. This time, instead of seeing Kat through the large glass oval, a man approached and opened the door.

"You must be Wendy," he said, his voice was melodic and his smile revealed an incisor pushed past his otherwise straight teeth. His face had the same delicate features as Kat's and was framed by fine greying hair he wore on the longer side, slightly feathered back. He wore a plaid shirt neatly tucked into jeans that were dark blue and stiff.

"I am." She offered her hand, which he grasped lightly.

"I'm Kat's father, Clyde. She has been delayed by an unfortunate plumbing issue at the church. She will be along shortly."

The way he spoke and gestured grandly for her to enter made Wendy feel like she was talking to a butler. "I actually have a bunch of stuff to carry in," she said.

"Allow me to assist you."

His response made her realize how young she sounded. His posture and words were as formal as the furniture that filled the room, and she could not figure out the correct way to respond. He looked to her old beat-up station wagon and back again, a puzzled expression on his face as he waited for an answer.

Wendy closed her eyes and imagined that she was in a British film. What would the leading lady say if a gentleman offered aid? She smiled when it came to her. She opened her eyes and replied, "That would be lovely." Was she imagining things, or did he really smile more warmly after she matched his diction?

One bushy eyebrow lifted jauntily. "Let us get to our work, then. Although Kat did say that you would be providing the sustenance tonight."

"Indeed." Wendy hid her smile as she led the way to her car. No, vehicle. She found that she enjoyed pretending to be a lady, though Kat was much better suited to the role with her curvaceous figure and long hair. Wendy's lean, athletic build was more characteristic of a male romantic lead. Nevertheless, she allowed Clyde to carry the heavy bags and open the door for her.

Wendy set her things down on the yellow tile counter by the oven. Light filled the kitchen despite the fact that the window above the sink was surrounded on both sides by thin four-inch shelves. An antique soup can, faded Prince Albert tobacco tin, a faceless rusted iron man holding a steering wheel, old blue and green glass jars, a tiny replica of a mixing bowl: this was a collection of treasures, not clutter. On the sill above the sink, delicate plants grew in mugs the shape of women's faces, and a colorful top rested in the smallest of a hand-painted set of stacking bowls.

First things first, she twisted the dial to get the oven heating. The door was heavy, the glass obscured from years of accumulated grease. She placed a thermometer on the rack and set her timer for a half hour. "Do you mind if I put some things in the refrigerator?"

"Not at all. In preparation for the nuptials, I was tasked to clear out the refrigerator on the left. I hope it meets with your approval."

She opened the door and found it nearly empty, the shelves wiped clean. "This makes my job so much easier. Thank you."

"Do you need any help?"

"I did most of the prep in my own kitchen. I really just need the oven to heat up. I'll check it in about a half hour." She hoped that Kat would be home by then. She really had nothing left to do. "Kat said the oven was not the original. Do you know how old it is?"

"Indeed, I do. My parents had it installed in sixty-nine. I drew the plans for the kitchen. One day I hope to strip the ash cabinets and refinish them. The years have darkened them."

Wendy wouldn't have called the golden wood dark at all. For her, the cabinets added to the warmth of the space. "Kat mentioned that you lived here when you were a child."

"Did she also share with you the history of its famous inhabitant?"

"No."

"Did she not show you Rock Hudson's handprint?"

"The movie star?"

"The very one. Come this way." Just outside the back door, he pointed to a block of cement with several handprints. "Note the signature."

Wendy stepped from the porch and knelt down. "Rock." She placed her hand on the warm concrete. "He had huge hands!"

"Kat said the gentlemen she brought here said the same thing. Have you met them?"

"Yes, when they did the tasting to decide their menu." Wendy traced the smaller handprints in the cement. "Do you know who this one belongs to?"

"Rock's lover, who bought the house from my parents. They were scandalized by the thought of selling to a gay man, but when the gay man brought along the movie star, my parents were persuaded."

"Why did his lover sell it back to you?"

"My dear, he died. I happened upon the news when I was showing Millie the house of my youth. We bought it from his estate, before it went on the market. I tried to talk to the family to find out if they knew anything about Rock. Shame silenced them. It puts something right that this couple will wed here. We support such unions."

Before Wendy could respond, Kat rounded the corner, a large patchwork purse slung over her shoulder. "I'm so sorry I'm late."

"It's okay. Your father has given me a charming account of the house's history."

Kat wrapped her arms around Wendy in a warm hug. Acutely aware of Clyde's presence, Wendy could not truly savor the feel of Kat pressed against her. Her eyes closed, and she breathed in Kat's subtle perfume, a sweet floral scent that suited her perfectly.

To her embarrassment, Wendy's phone buzzed in her front pocket. Kat nudged her hip and waggled her eyebrows. "Happy to see me?"

Wendy hid the blush that rose to her cheeks by checking the message. Cory, of course, with a text asking whether Kat was wearing work clothes, date clothes, or no clothes made her blush even harder. "Time to check the oven," she said as a diversion.

Father and daughter went ahead. Kat climbed the back steps first, but Clyde stood for a moment. Wendy felt like he was sizing her up. She stood a little taller, wondering if he had read something in the hug she and Kat had shared. Was he the kind of person who supported gay people in theory but freaked if his own child turned out to be gay? Instead of delivering a warning, Clyde bowed slightly and once again extended his hand, ushering Wendy inside.

There she read her thermometer, impressed that she was only about five degrees lower than she wanted. "Do you mind if I mark the oven with a Sharpie?"

"Do as you wish," Clyde answered.

Kat startled Wendy when she placed a hand on her shoulder and fingered her V-neck tee. "I don't think I've ever seen you out of your slacks and pressed shirts. This is nice. I'm going to change too, if you don't mind."

"You'll never change," Clyde inserted, a suggestive smile on his lips.

Wendy was left to puzzle over what that could mean when Kat disappeared up the stairs with a bottled soda she'd pulled from the fridge. Wendy positioned her two pans in the oven and tried to avoid making eye contact with Kat's father. Thankfully, Kat returned quickly, having traded her skirt for pink sweats and a light long-sleeved gray shirt she was pushing up at the sleeves.

"It already smells so good in here," Kat said.

"You said cheesy is good, so I put together a small appetizer. Artichoke, mayonnaise and parmesan cheese. It won't take long to get bubbly, and then I'll put in the pasta and chicken."

"I have a new flavor of lemonade," Kat offered.

"Or I brought some artisan beer."

Kat pulled one of each from the fridge and used a church-key magnet to open them. She handed the lemonade to Wendy and took a sip of the beer. Kat made a face and passed the beer to Wendy. "Would you have hurt feelings if I had my black cherry lemonade?"

Wendy sampled Kat's lemonade, then handed her the bottle. "Would it hurt yours if I prefer my beer?"

"Not at all. It's nice to know you'll never drink my last hard lemonade."

Wendy toasted her comment, enjoying that Kat felt comfortable drinking from the bottle after she had.

"Evan and Jeremy sure had a lot of fun at your tasting. It sounds like a great menu."

"You already know the menu?" Wendy was surprised.

"They were excited to share every detail. First Evan and then Jeremy."

"I noticed that each one puts in his two cents. They both were talking about a cottage they want to decorate. I couldn't picture it."

"You didn't show her the stone cottage?" Clyde said, reminding Wendy that he was watching their exchange. How did Kat survive living under such parental scrutiny?

Wendy pulled her appetizer out of the oven and slipped in the pasta and chicken dishes to bake. She placed the dip in the middle of a platter, surrounded it with thin crackers and carried it to the table. Clyde helped himself and hmmmed his approval. "We should invite Travis and Millie to join us."

"Travis isn't home from practice yet," Kat said, "but Mom would probably like some." She dipped a cracker but did not scoop an artichoke as her father had. Wendy couldn't read her expression, but instead of having another cracker, Kat scooted behind her dad to grab a plate, then scooped a hearty amount of dip onto multiple crackers. "I'm going to take this up to my mom. Then I'll show you the cottage."

Another awkward silence. Wendy almost wished she and Kat had just planned to carry her simple bean and cheese burritos out to the tortoise yard again. The tortoises seemed much easier to please.

* * *

Poor Wendy. When Kat returned she looked as uncomfortable as a boy waiting for his prom date. Kat would have laughed out loud, but she knew it would hurt her father's feelings and confuse Wendy.

She grabbed her hand. "How long until dinner?"

"Half hour?"

"I'm going to finish the tour," Kat said to her father. "Mom wants more of the dip."

Once they were outside, Wendy said, "Does your mother ever come downstairs?"

"Only when we run a fire drill."

"I can't tell if you're serious."

"We don't actually run fire drills," Kat answered. Wendy looked so startled, Kat mercifully answered the question more truthfully. "My mom is agoraphobic. She gets overwhelmed easily. When it's really bad, she stays upstairs for days at a time."

"Is that something…recent?" Wendy asked.

"Nope. She's always been. When I was younger, it wasn't as bad. We could go grocery shopping. By the time I was learning how to cook, my dad and I went shopping, and year by year, her circle shrank. Sometimes she has a burst, like when Travis was born, but most of the time she's happy to be in her room."

"How does she eat? She depends on you and your dad to take food up?"

"She has her boxes of Pop-Tarts. She gets by."

Wendy started to say something but covered it with a cough.

"I know. Not the healthiest. To be fair, she usually has some bananas up there, too. And most of the time she comes down for lunch and dinner."

They walked side by side on the lush grass, past the swing, toward the hedge at the back of the yard. Kat guided Wendy to a tiny stone path next to the pool fence. Wendy gasped as they rounded the corner. Kat loved showing off the cottage, especially when people reacted as Wendy had.

"You didn't say anything about this last time."

"I got distracted," Kat answered.

"Considering everything you just said about your mom, I get it."

Kat was happy to let Wendy think her mom was the distraction even though it was really Wendy's presence. She'd had to take a minute at the top of the stairs before she gave her mother a fresh soda. And today, Wendy's hug had felt unexpectedly intimate, and she wasn't accustomed to seeing her in casual attire. What had compelled her to sample the soft material of Wendy's T-shirt? The action had flooded Kat with the image of Wendy reaching a hand over her shoulder and pulling the garment over her head.

Standing by the cottage, she feared Wendy would see and comment on her blush. Alone with Wendy, she was surprised to find herself imagining what it would be like to slide her hands under Wendy's tee.

"Can we go in?"

Wendy's words startled Kat. "Of course." She squeezed by on the narrow path, brushing Wendy lightly. She smelled sweet, like a bakery. Lightheaded, Kat wobbled on the path.

Wendy took hold of her elbow. "Whoa. Too much hard lemonade and not enough appetizer?"

"The stones are uneven," Kat lied.

"You didn't care for the appetizer." Her hand stayed warm and inviting on Kat's arm.

Kat had hoped Wendy hadn't noticed her reaction. "I don't like green things very much."

"It was white."

"Not the artichoke."

"I think you're the first person I've met who considers artichoke from a jar a vegetable."

"It is."

"No, it's not. It's a thistle."

"That sounds disgusting. Why would anyone want to eat a thistle?" Kat asked.

"Because they're delicious. Nobody ever ate an artichoke for the nutrients."

"I hope I didn't hurt your feelings." That was the last thing Kat wanted to do. She turned the antique iron doorknob and ducked through the doorway. She loved the smell of the stone and cool earth. The thickness of the walls insulated the small rectangle from the desert heat even in the dead of summer. As a child, before her parents had installed air-conditioning in the house, Kat would curl up here on one of the folded futons and read hour upon hour of her summer away.

"As long as you're honest, we're good. I have thick skin."

"I'll do my best."

Wendy bent to try the door of the tiny potbellied stove in the corner. She touched her way around the space, lifting the candle snuffer, opening the doors of a small wooden cupboard. "What's that supposed to mean?" she asked.

"I don't do well with honesty." Kat liked the way Wendy kept talking as she explored the place, and she tried not to let her eyes linger on how good she looked in her faded jeans.

"You're telling me you lie?"

Kat almost said no and then had to laugh at herself. "I don't lie, I just have a bad habit of not telling the truth."

"What kinds of untruths are we talking about? Do you even live here?"

"Of course I live here. You've seen my parents and my son."

"I've seen your dad and Travis. Your mom I'll see if there happens to be a fire drill?"

"She'll probably come down for dinner tonight."

"So…" Wendy looked like she was trying to do mental math. "You lie when you get uncomfortable?"

"Or to save people's feelings. Instead of saying I don't want to go out, I'll say I have to drive Travis to practice. Or if I don't get to the donut shop on my way home, I'll tell my mom they were out of the kind of donut she likes."

"What if you didn't like my haircut?"

"Don't be silly. I've always loved how you style your hair."

"Somehow I don't trust you anymore."

"I was honest about your appetizer," Kat pointed out. "You're different. With you, I can tell the truth."

"Why with me?"

"At the reunion, you said you were disappointed in how little everyone had changed. You said you had hoped that twenty years would have given people time to learn to be themselves."

"You heard that?"

"Of course. I was stuck at my table where my so-called friends were lying about how good it was to see each other. Air-kissing like they were still besties just to save face when they actually despise each other. You and your…" Kat hesitated. She knew that Wendy had been there with her girlfriend. Why did she find it so difficult to say the word?

"Girlfriend."

"Yes. You two were having the only honest conversation in the room. About how everyone looked old and unhappy. You said that the whole night was a competition that you refused to join. I realized I was doing the same thing, like life was some sort of game where being married beats being single and having kids beats that, but only if your kids do ballet or karate."

"Like I said that night, I don't compete," Wendy said. "I'm glad I never tried. All that sounds exhausting!"

"It is exhausting. Almost as much as keeping track of lies you've told."

Wendy laughed. "You say that like you've told some doozies."

Kat looked at the two glass windows cut into the door and felt a wave of sadness crash over her. "Do lies of omission count?" she whispered.

* * *

The quaver in Kat's voice told Wendy that what had started as fun banter had hit something far more serious. The sun had dipped low enough that the cottage had become dark, making it difficult to read Kat's expression, but her whisper conveyed a tone heavier than Wendy had ever heard from Kat. Until this conversation, she had believed Kat was the most genuine person she knew. She hadn't really believed Kat when she said she lied, but now she couldn't help but wonder what those doozies were. Unfortunately, she sensed that this was not the time to explore.

"You know what this place needs?" Wendy asked, gently redirecting their conversation. "Lights. You should hang small white Christmas-tree lights in here, along the rectangle of the roof. That way people could see the candy."

"What candy?" Kat sounded confused.

"Evan and Jeremy said it felt like a house right out of 'Hansel and Gretel.' Don't you see a multi-leveled counter here with little dishes of candy? Guests could assemble their own party favors."

"What a fun idea," Kat said. She sounded like herself again.

"As long as we're getting electricity out here, we might as well string lights on the outside." Wendy stepped outside the cottage, and the darkness that had seemed to wash over Kat stayed inside. Out on the stone path, her smile looked more relaxed. "We could loop the lights along the walk. That way, people won't trip on the uneven stones."

Kat smirked at her. "It's a marvelous idea, but I'm not sure how we'd run the electricity all the way out here. That's a lot of work and would involve climbing up on the roof. I'm not the one who…"

She stopped abruptly, but Wendy had heard her. "Not the one who what?"

"I'm afraid of heights," Kat amended.

"I could help you hang them. I'm not afraid of heights."

Kat took two full breaths before she said, "Dinner is probably ready, isn't it?"

Wendy wanted to press Kat's obvious skirting of the issue about the lights. She wasn't sure what compelled her to spend her spare time helping her help Jeremy and Evan, but she wanted to know what had dampened Kat's usual vivacity. Kat's elusiveness engaged Wendy's stubbornness. "There are some loose threads of conversation here." She looked around as if they hung on the bushes like spider webs.

"Leave them here. We'll pick them back up when you come back to hang the lights."

"When would that be?"

"Next week? Same time?"

Buoyed, Wendy followed Kat back to the house. It felt like an unspoken promise.

The herbs and spices she had rubbed on the chicken breasts had filled the kitchen with a rich savory aroma. On the other side of the range by the kitchen table three people stood in a huddle. Was she being oversensitive, or had their hushed conversation come to a halt when she and Kat entered? She recognized the men as Kat's father and son, and assumed the woman was her mother. Loose-fitting black cotton pants and a billowing long-sleeved purple shirt covered her rotund frame. Wendy was surprised by her size and searched for the resemblance to Kat. Though her hair was considerably shorter than Kat's, it had the same volume and luster.

The extended silence became uncomfortable, and Wendy was just about to introduce herself to Kat's mother when Kat said, "Mom! I didn't expect you to come down until dinner was ready."

"But I had to. Your father and Travis couldn't decide whether to take the food out of the oven or send out a search party. Or both."

"Wendy said we were eating in a half hour, and a half hour had passed," Clyde said, smiling widely enough to expose his crooked eyetooth. "But one doesn't want to presume."

"If she said a half hour, I don't see why you couldn't have taken it out," Millie said.

"Every time I try to take the initiative, I end up not doing it correctly and once again get criticized. It seems I can never do anything to anyone's satisfaction which is why I attempted to consult with you."

Kat held up her hands, silencing the bickering. "Does the chicken need to come out of the oven?" she asked.

"Yes, sorry!" Wendy said hoping food would diffuse the growing tension. "Do you have a trivet, or shall I set them on the range?"

"In the drawer on your left, there is a wooden trivet, but it is rather small. If you give me a moment, I might be able to locate the wrought iron…"

Millie interrupted him. "She didn't ask for an inventory of the kitchen."

"On the range is perfect. We never have formal sit-down dinners around here." Kat's tone was clipped. Wendy glanced at Kat who glared at her parents with a look that would put a toddler in its place.

"But what a treat," Millie said. "The house smells like heaven. And that artichoke dip! I'm going to need that every day."

Kat's son looked stricken. "What about your donuts?"

"This was so much better than donuts." She grasped the cane that had been leaning against the table and slowly walked over to the cooking space. She extended her free hand to Wendy. "Hi. I'm Kat's mom, Millie."

Wendy removed the oven mitt and took her hand. It was soft and strangely papery.

"And I'm Travis. Kat's kid. Is that mac-n-cheese?"

She took her hand back trying not to overthink why Kat's mom had held on so long. "Kat said everyone is a big fan of cheese. The foil packets have seasoned chicken breasts in them."

Millie smiled coyly and looked first at Kat and then at Wendy. Kat launched another glare at her mother, giving Wendy the distinct sense that there was a silent conversation happening with the family. There was no way she could sit through a whole dinner with Kat looking as uncomfortable as she did. She had to find a way out.

"I also brought a spinach and walnut salad with a raspberry vinaigrette. Are you the only one who doesn't eat greens or should I just take that back with me?"

"Are you not dining with us?" Clyde asked.

"Not tonight, I fear. Your oven passed the test with flying colors. I hope…"

"But your dishes," Clyde said.

"Stop interrupting her!" Millie chastised.

"It's fine. I hope you enjoy the meal, and don't worry about the dishes. I know where you live. And I'll be back next week, apparently." She gathered a few bags from the counter by the oven. "Very nice to meet you all."

"I'll walk you out," Kat said.

"You don't have to," Wendy said, not wanting to talk about her awkward exit.

"I've parked you in. Let me grab my keys." Wendy could hear the relief in her voice. "We can go out the front."

At the front door Wendy tried the knob, but the door didn't open. She tried the lock, but it wouldn't budge.

"I'm so sorry," Kat said, suddenly next to her. She grasped the handle and the lock below and swung the door open. "I thought you were going to have dinner here. They scared you off, didn't they? Because they are weird. My family is weird."

"Not at all. There's a bunch of stuff I have to get done at the restaurant tonight."

"I think you're lying to make me feel better about having a weird family."

"Not everyone is a liar."

Kat growled at her, but she smiled. "I'm going to let you get away with it because I really need your help hanging those lights."

"It will be my pleasure."

Kat cuffed Wendy's shoulder. "Quit talking like my father."

"He's a character." Wendy set her bags in the back seat.

"Go. I have to deal with them."

"I thought you had to move your car," Wendy said.

Kat seemed to study her as if she was trying to decide whether to call Wendy on her teasing. Suddenly, Kat's arms were around her. She tensed for a moment before returning the hug. Kat loosened her hold and said, "I do, but I wish we could have had dinner just me and you and the tortoises again. The mac-n-cheese looks delicious."

"I hope you enjoy it."

"If it didn't look so good, I might just jump in your passenger seat and avoid all of that." She waved her hand in the direction of the house.

"So I wasn't imagining that it got tense in there."

"No, not your imagination."

"I'm sorry I've put you in an awkward position."

"Funny. I was about to say the same thing. Do you really have time in your life to help hang lights?"

"I absolutely have time. We should probably start earlier, so we don't have to work in the dark."

"Works for me. See you next week."

* * *

Kat was certain that her family thought something was going on between her and Wendy. She hoped that Wendy had not been aware that her family had been talking about her. They were still talking, and they would keep talking as long as she was outside, and the longer she was gone, the more they would think that they were right.

The last of the sunlight angled through the trees bathing the backyard in a golden glow. She noted it to pass on to Jeremy and Evan. If they got married by the arbor at just this time, they would have a natural spotlight.

Time for Kat to be in her own spotlight. She bit the bullet and went inside. "You guys are all so busted."

"Because we started without you?" Travis asked. "Gramma said it would be okay."

Kat couldn't remember the last time she had seen more than one person seated at the kitchen table at the same time. The sight should have made her happy. The sturdy oak table with its four matching curve-backed chairs had been the center of her childhood. Family and friends had gravitated toward it and years of resting their elbows while they visited had worn the black and gold stenciling along the edge thin. Instead, she felt more frustrated with them than she had in a long while. "Because you scared off my friend."

"You didn't have to come in. You could have stayed out in the cottage doing whatever you were doing," her mother said.

"What were you doing?" Travis asked.

"Talking to my friend about Jeremy and Evan's wedding. She's the caterer."

Her mother took a bite of chicken and smirked. "These breasts are so tender."

Kat clenched her teeth so tightly her jaws ached. She refused to engage in her mother's innuendo. This was precisely why she kept her friends and family separate.

"Is she really a lesbian?" Travis asked.

So she'd been right about the topic of conversation. "Yes, she is."

"Do you like her?"

"Wendy and I are friends,"

"You were in the cottage for quite some time," her father said.

"Grandfather says she likes you."

Kat grasped at a way to divert the conversation. "Jeremy and Evan want to do a candy cottage." She couldn't help thinking about how, had she stayed, Wendy would have seen her gift for half-truths in action. "Wendy said it would be nice to have light out there. Do we have any Christmas lights that we can string in the cottage?"

"Inside or outside?" he asked.

"Both."

"You were quite flushed for talking about lights," Millie said.

"Mom!" Kat shot a look at Travis and then at her mother. "Why are you still downstairs?"

"I told you! Your father didn't know whether to take the food out of the oven," she said with exasperation.

"We tried to text you, but you didn't answer," Travis said.

Kat fumbled her phone out of her pocket. They had texted her? How had she missed that? She swiped her phone and frowned at the text.

"They wanted me to go out there, but I was like, you don't interrupt people in the stone cottage."

"Travis! What do you know about the stone cottage? No. Don't tell me what you know about the stone cottage."

"If that wasn't the rule, there would be no Travis," Millie said.

"I did not conceive Travis in the stone cottage. We are so not talking about this right now."

"You keep telling yourself that," Millie said. "Get some dinner. You're letting it all get cold, and it's delicious. If you're not kissing that woman, you should be."

Kat sent a *not in front of Travis* look to her mother as she grabbed a plate.

"What?" Millie said out loud. "Travis knows some women kiss women. Years ago, I—"

"We really don't need to go there!"

Travis looked from his mother to his grandmother and pushed out his bottom lip. "Leo's aunt is gay. Can you please spoon me some more mac 'n cheese?"

"There's a reason we stopped having family dinners," Kat mumbled to herself. She wished that Travis and her mother had opted to eat in their rooms. With them at the table, she couldn't get away with serving herself and leaving the room, so she dug in, accepting that there was no escaping her family.

CHAPTER FIVE

The week passed as slowly as 405 traffic on a Friday night. Kat left work early, securing a volunteer to answer the phones until the office closed at five. She changed into her version of work clothes—jeans and an old concert T-shirt—and sat in her pink bedroom where she'd spent twenty-two years before she'd moved out to play house with Jack and raise Travis. She had her wedding album on her lap fingering the edges of its thick pages.

An email from Evan about how to display the cake in the dining room prompted her to pull the album from the bookshelf. She stared at the happy couple on the cover. Jack had made a dashing groom in the classic black tux. His face had been thinner then, or his goatee had given his face more definition. As a bride, Kat had looked like a princess in her white lace dress her hair in banana-curl ringlets. The veil floated behind her as if caught in a breeze. The perfect couple. The perfect day. She smiled remembering the photographer's frustration with her veil. He was the one who wanted to catch it in motion, and it did give the photograph the magical air he had wanted.

Too bad the marriage itself hadn't been magical. Had it not been for Travis, it never would have happened.

But she was pregnant and had married the perfect man, a lawyer with the corner office that afforded the house and car all her friends envied. He was funny and patient, the very definition of a great catch.

She'd held on for as long as she could, ignoring the lack of chemistry. At first she had convinced herself that it was her inexperience that made her so uncomfortable when they had sex. Too soon, she could blame her morning sickness. But after years of feigning interest and pleasure, she had actually been relieved when Jack suggested they branch out with other sex partners.

If only he hadn't insisted that they both do so. She should have been honest with him about how she was perfectly happy to opt out completely. She didn't need sex to be happy. She had her family. She had Travis. He was her magic. She reached for his most recent class picture, a flood of pride and awe at how beautiful he was. The hair that typically flopped in his eyes was brushed to the side, and he'd smiled for her. How dare she wonder what life would have been like had she not gotten pregnant? She closed her eyes, yet the image remained clearly in her mind's eye. As hard as the photographer had tried to hide her baby bump, Travis was there, evident in the stretch of fabric across her belly and the roundness in her face.

And behind the trunk of the palm tree, Miranda, tucked safely out of sight. Kat's chest felt tight. She hadn't thought about Miranda in forever, yet she'd been hiding there every day. Nobody even remembered who tossed the veil for the photograph. It was Miranda. When the enlargement had hung above the mantel in their fancy house, no one recalled her part.

They didn't know about the kiss.

Kat hadn't allowed herself to think about that kiss for years. Thinking about it released butterflies she'd stowed away deep inside. They zipped about her body so viscerally that Kat felt dizzy. She shouldn't be surprised. Not with the way she enjoyed flirting with Wendy when she catered at the church. She couldn't help it. Wendy was such fun, so much herself. Her confidence was magnetic.

And she likes you, the butterflies whispered.

She can't, Kat answered internally. *She shouldn't.*

Then you have to stop flirting with her. Unless you're attracted to her.

I'm not, Kat snapped at herself.

Keep telling yourself that.

Hearing the tone of her mother's voice, the butterflies abandoned her, leaving her stomach as heavy as lead. Wendy was due any moment, and here Kat was talking to herself. No time to look at how she and Jack had staged their cake, she shoved the album back onto the bookshelf and scowled into the mirror on her bureau. She parted her hair down the middle and pulled half over each shoulder into farm-girl braids, letting her mind wander back to Wendy and her dark curls, now worn longer than in high school. A smile came to her face remembering Wendy's wild hairstyles, the way she'd shaved it close on the sides and left perfect floppy ringlets in the front.

Movement on the patio caught her attention, and she pushed back her curtain to get a better look. "Crap," she mumbled seeing her father heading to the cottage with Wendy. She jogged down the stairs to rescue Wendy.

"Hi," she said when she reached the cottage, breathless, she told herself, from her pace across the yard, not from the sight of Wendy in cargo pants and skin-tight spandex shirt. She looked good enough to eat. Ready to work, Kat corrected her thoughts, unable to afford such a distraction.

"Your dad said we can run an extension cord from the pool pump."

In fascination, Kat listened to the two of them plan to run the power through the trees to camouflage them and avoid tripping hazards. Wendy stood close to her dad, who was smiling, something she'd never seen with Jack. He had always found her dad to be "too intense," and she was used to him avoiding Clyde. Wendy and her father worked together as if they'd known each other for years. Suddenly, she was aware of how quiet it was, and expectant looks from both him and Wendy clued her in that she had missed something.

"You know where the lights are in the basement?" he repeated.

"Oh, of course."

"Do you require assistance?"

"Wendy and I can manage," Kat said, leading the way back to the house.

Wendy glanced back at the hedge that hid the cottage from view as if checking on the conversation they had left suspended the week before. Would she want to return to her lies of omission? She wasn't sure what it was about Wendy that compelled her to tell the truth, but she was in no way prepared to explore the things that Wendy had referred to as "doozies." She focused on the task at hand. "We have a ton of Christmas lights, and they are all white. White lights are classier, according to my dad."

"I am in total agreement," Wendy said.

Kat laughed.

"Why is that funny?"

"It's not really funny. Jack hated white lights and always had the exact same negative things to say about my father's decorations. Sometimes I thought they chose opposite of each other just to see who I would side with."

"I don't compete," Wendy reminded her.

"Pity you don't because you would totally be winning if you did."

"What's the game?"

"Competing to be the favorite, of course." By the kitchen table, she opened the door to the basement. "Lucky for us, Travis is at school, so it's safe to descend."

"What happens if he's there? Does he defend his territory in scary ways?"

"I just don't need to know what teenagers do in their own space."

"Got it!" Wendy waved her hands as if to say she needn't hear more.

"Lights," Kat said. She descended the stairs trying not to feel so aware of Wendy behind her.

"I can't believe you have a basement. Who has a basement in Southern California? I've never been in a house here that has one before. I still can't get over how you grew up here!"

"You're nice to focus on that instead of the fact that I'm living here again. My friends enjoy pointing out how depressing it is for a forty-year-old to be living with her parents."

"Your friends say that? But you get to live here. I don't see how anyone could pass that up."

"Pretty much everyone would pass it up. Living with your parents doesn't scream 'I'm a successful adult!'"

At the bottom of the stairs, Kat motioned to the right. "Past the shower curtain is Travis's domain. The lights are on this side." She stepped into a small room and pulled the chain on the above fixture for light. "Now we play shuffle the boxes until we find the one with lights in it."

"How does your son feel about living here?"

"It beats having to share a living space with his best friend since his dad is shacking up with his best friend's mom." She lowered her voice and leaned close enough to Wendy that their shoulders brushed. "He gets grossed out by their groping and kissing. Honestly, it's not fair to anyone the way they hang all over each other like teenagers. Gross. And he's almost as in love with this house as you are, so the transition hasn't been that tough for him."

Wendy was quiet for so long, Kat turned to look at her. "What?"

"Nothing…Everything you rattled off…That's a lot to take in."

"Oh, that's right. You didn't know about the whole best-friend-sleeping-with-my-husband thing."

Eyes wide, Wendy said, "Nope."

"Sorry. Somehow I forget to edit when I'm around you." Kat turned back to the boxes weighing whether to let the subject shift or say more.

"You shouldn't have to edit around friends."

Kat hmphed. "I lost my friends in the divorce."

"I can see where it would be tough to stay friends with someone who slept with your husband."

"I didn't care that they were sleeping together. It got awkward when they fell in love, and I felt bad for the kids, but by then everyone knew that Jack and I weren't happy, so there was no use lying anymore," Kat confessed, setting another box behind her. The stack grew as she checked the contents and moved to the next one. She glanced at Wendy. "TMI?"

"No, not too much. I didn't know whether it would be tacky to ask how you found out about them."

"Oh, I knew beforehand. We were all friends. Jack and I met Patrick and Ember when our kids started kindergarten. Our boys grew up together, and we knew each other really well. Then Jack wanted to know Ember better. My therapist had been encouraging me to come out of my shell, so I said why not and agreed to a spouse trade."

"How'd that work out for you?"

"Obviously it didn't! My therapist was aghast when I told him and said he had meant something like taking up a musical instrument. That ended up working a lot better. I bought the drum kit out there and started practicing with Travis."

* * *

Wendy stuck her head out of the little room. She hadn't seen a drum kit when they had descended the stairs.

"Do you still play?"

Kat looked sheepish. "Not for ages. What's fun for a thirteen-year-old is death by embarrassment for a seventeen-year-old."

"What does Travis play?"

"Guitar."

"It sounds like an awesome thing to do with your kid." Kat had rarely talked about her family during their brief encounters at the church. It didn't surprise her to find out that Kat was the kind of mom who got involved with her kid.

"I tried." Kat sounded wistful.

"It's super cool in my book. Play me something!"

Kat scrunched her nose and shook her head. "That was a different lifetime. I'm sure they're covered in dust."

"I think this is one of your lies and that you still rock."

Kat plunked two boxes on the stairs. "Can you get one?"

"Sure." She followed Kat up the stairs and out to the cottage.

"Travis is the one who rocks. I do my best to keep up. Where did my dad say he'd have the extension cord?"

"I've got it here," Wendy said. She tried to pull one string of lights from her box and came up with a huge tangle of wire and glass bulbs. "Yikes!"

"Let me see if this box is better," Kat suggested. She pulled on a strand and had the same result. She started to tease one away from the rest, shaking and tugging at it. "Once we get one free, you can hang it while I work on another."

"You think we can loop it on the bushes to get to the roof?"

"I'm just technical support. You're the one with the vision."

"And you're just doing your best to keep up?" Wendy said wryly.

"If you heard Travis play, you'd understand." Kat lit up. "You should hear him play. Wait! Are you busy tomorrow afternoon? He's playing!"

"Where?"

"A bar in Glendale."

"Your teenager plays in bars?"

"Just Aura. It's this little wine bar. Twice a year the owner helps the music studio with their fundraising. The whole audience is family who clear out long before the real bar crowd. But the kids love being on a proper stage."

"I can imagine. It's a great space."

"You know it?" Kat asked.

"It's right around the corner from Fairbanks."

"Then you have to come! Jack will be there with Ember, and I hate being alone because then I get stuck sitting next to Patrick, and he'll say something about how maybe we *could try harder*, like it's a joke, but it's not really. Do you know what I mean? I'm babbling because I'm nervous because I want you to go."

With all the ideas Kat was throwing at her, Wendy's mind was spinning to gain traction. "I could probably check it out."

Kat quickly replied, "You don't have to."

"I'd like to. I'm sorry. I realize it didn't sound that way. I was thinking…" She pushed stray curls from her face. It wasn't her place to ask. She handed the string of lights to Kat. "Do you have a ladder? We should go from the tree to the top of the roof and then run down to the bottom."

"You can climb up the side."

Wendy crouched to avoid branches and followed a path behind the cottage. She stared dubiously at the stone wall and its one square window set high.

"You put your hands on the window and climb the stones until your feet are there. Then you can hoist yourself onto the roof."

"You could show me," Wendy said.

"Afraid of heights, remember?"

"Yet you know how to climb up on the roof?"

"Travis used to go up there to freak me out. I think my dad showed him."

If a child could climb up, Wendy figured she could as well. It was easier than she thought and in no time she stood on the flat roof with her hands on her hips. "It's a great view from up here. You sure you don't want to come up? It's not that scary."

"Who will hand you the lights?"

"Good point." Wendy held out her hands. She wedged the strand between two wood shingles at the edge of the roof and did this several times along the roofline, accepting another set of lights halfway along.

"Are you still thinking about coming to Travis's show?" Kat asked, fiddling with the next set of lights.

"What time does he play?"

"Sometime between three and four."

"That should work. I have an event that evening, but I could get started early and step away for an hour. Catch this light at the corner on the bottom, would you? I'll do the rest from the ground." Next to Kat again, she ran the lights along the bottom of the roof. "We'll use that window to run some lights inside, too. I might need some finishing nails to hold them up on the ceiling. Would that be okay?"

"Sounds good to me."

While Kat was off looking for tools, Wendy ruminated on the spouse swap Kat had mentioned so offhandedly. She had said she started drumming at her therapist's urging. That was four years ago, and she'd been divorced for three years. Did that mean she stayed married to Jack for a year while he was sleeping with her best friend? Kat came back with a hammer, nails and a stepladder. "My dad said you'd probably need this."

"Worried I'd stand on one of those antique chairs?" Wendy unfolded the ladder and stepped up to look at the rough boards of the ceiling.

Kat didn't answer immediately.

"I'm sorry," Wendy said. "Did I say something wrong?"

"Opposite from that. It's so weird how you seem to know him so well when you've just met him."

"He's different, but in a neat way. He's so formal. Do he and your mom go to see Travis play?"

"Are you joking? My mother would have to leave the house, and drums are so not classical, so that's a 'no' for my dad. But maybe Patrick's sister will be there!"

"And that's a good thing because…"

"She's gay, too. After the spouse swap fiasco, Patrick said maybe I should go out with her. She's cute and fun, and she could be perfect for you." Kat's smile was as bright as the string of lights in front of her.

"Why would he say that you should go out with her?"

Kat shrugged. "Because if I don't want to sleep with men, I must be a lesbian, right?"

"I've heard it's an option." Wendy was relieved that Kat smiled.

"My friends say I should have just slept with Patrick, that it would have saved a lot of heartache."

"They don't sound like friends to me."

"Maybe not. You sound like my mom."

"Your mom knows about all this?"

"I know you remember the whole 'nobody ever died from not having sex' comment."

Wendy laughed and took the opportunity to tap in some nails. "I had actually forgotten about that."

"Ugh. I don't believe that for a second."

* * *

Kat waited for Wendy to press for more like everyone did. Jack. Patrick. Erin. They all wanted her to explain herself, to give a reason for not wanting to sleep with them. If she hadn't had sex with Jack, she would not have gotten pregnant with Travis. If she hadn't had Travis, she would not have married Jack. If she had not married Jack, she would not have spent so many years telling herself that she could learn to enjoy sex or that it was something that she could do to keep Jack happy and keep her family intact.

Lying to herself about whether her happiness mattered.

Miranda had called her on it. But Kat hadn't listened.

She had learned the consequences of pursuing what made you happy.

She had learned that you make sacrifices for your family.

But Wendy did not ask. She looped a set of lights around the nails, folded the ladder to set outside and stepped back to admire her work. The more time passed, the harder Kat's thoughts pushed to be heard. She was curious to hear what an impartial friend would say about why she didn't want to have sex. Maybe that was the problem, that she could not tell the whole story. Even now, even standing in the cottage that held so much history, she knew she could still not share what made her feel so vulnerable.

"I was in love with someone else when I married Jack." Absently, she rubbed the tips of her fingers down her palm, alternating her hands. Again she waited for Wendy to say something, but she didn't. She thought about her parents and how they had stayed together. She had already become her mother. She absolutely refused to be her father. "It was my true love, but I knew it wouldn't work. I slept with Jack and got pregnant, and I walked away from what I really wanted and married Jack. That was my chance, and I missed it."

She knew it wasn't an explanation. This was where everyone insisted that people got more chances in life. That's what Erin had said when Kat maintained they could not be more than friends. But she couldn't talk about it, especially not now that she was living with her parents again. She had her own family to look after, even if that meant only her and Travis. She wasn't sure what she expected Wendy to say, but she was not surprised that it took her a moment to respond.

"You're saying you couldn't sleep with Patrick because you're not in love with him."

"That's a big part of it, yes."

Wendy seemed to weigh this and then shrugged. "Sounds reasonable to me. No regrets if you sleep with someone you love, right?"

Kat held eye contact with Wendy thinking that regret was all she knew. But that wasn't quite true, since she had Travis. She didn't regret that. And there were many things she loved about Jack. Again she imagined what her life would have been had she accepted what Miranda offered. She thought she was doing the right thing. It didn't make sense to regret doing the right thing.

"Kat?" Wendy's voice was gentle.

"I'm sorry. I've only ever slept with Jack. I loved him, of course. Your question about regret got me tangled up."

"You don't have to explain."

Kat laughed nervously. "Honestly? I'm not sure I even could."

"That's not what I mean. You don't have to explain. To me or anyone. You're allowed to do what is right for you because it feels right to you."

"Not according to my friends."

"I think you need new friends," Wendy said. "Forget about them and put yourself first." A bright smile spread across Wendy's face surprising Kat.

"What's that smile for?" Kat asked.

"You play the drums. Do you know any Go-Go's?"

"Of course!"

Wendy sang, "Pay no mind to what they say."

Kat joined on the next line, "It doesn't matter anyway!" She kept singing and found her own throat tightening at the lyrics that urged her not to cry. She laughed instead. Nothing fixed her sadness as well as eighties tunes. "Come tomorrow. I'll get Travis and his boys to let me play with them and do that song."

"That would be something to see for sure," she said slipping into eighties lingo.

They shoved the surplus lights back into one box, Kat feeling lighter than she had in a long time. "You make a good friend. I don't know why it's taken so long for me to see that."

"Our paths crossed for a reason. I definitely felt that way at the reunion."

"And yet it took us years for us to talk about more than work."

Wendy shrugged. "This wedding is different."

"That it is. I hope I didn't make a big mistake offering my parents' house. Guess we'll see!"

CHAPTER SIX

"I'm confused," Cory said. "Is this a blind date kind of a thing?"

Though she hadn't known him when she hired him, with the long hours they had spent working together, he'd become a friend.

"I don't think so. Blind dates don't happen with a whole group of people, do they?"

"Depends on the group. Who is going to be there?" He asked as he headed into the walk-in fridge.

Wendy followed Cory to gather the ingredients for fajitas.

"Kat's ex-husband, his girlfriend, the girlfriend's ex-husband and his lesbian sister. And the kids, but they'll be on stage."

"You're not seeing any red flags in that list?"

"They're all there to watch the kids on stage. It'll be fine."

"Are you walking or driving?" Cory asked. He looked pointedly at the clock.

"Walking."

"Go already. I can handle the rest of the cleanup. It's mostly dishes."

"I don't have to be there right at three. Kat is the only person I know. If I get there too early, it'll just be awkward."

"She's introducing you to someone who wanted to hook up with her. It's already going to be awkward."

"Which is why I should check with José about the waitstaff for tonight."

"Go. I can check in with him. Your nervous energy is tying my stomach up in knots."

Wendy flipped through the catering supplies list and instructions for the desserts Cory was going to make later that afternoon.

"I got it, boss."

Grumbling, she washed her hands and went to change out of her chef's coat before grabbing a light jeans jacket and stowing her ID and cash. Hands deep in her pockets, she walked the three blocks packed with Saturday afternoon shopping traffic to the bar and paid the cover at the top of the stairs. The proprietor was still onstage talking about the budding musicians. Though the place was packed, mostly with parents, Wendy found Kat on her first scan as if drawn by a beacon. She sat at a crowded table at the front of the room to the right of the stage.

As she wove across the back of the room Wendy kept her eyes on Kat. She'd pulled her hair up into a ponytail and wore an off-the-shoulder gray sweater. Half-dollar-sized white hoops dangled from her earlobes, drawing Wendy's attention to how much of Kat's creamy skin was exposed. She was telling a story, her hands flying in front of her, and she had the whole table's attention. She was as cute as Wendy remembered her being in high school, and Wendy felt the same desire she had back then to grab one of those hands and pull her away from the cluster of people around her who were obviously trying too hard.

A couple sat with their arms wrapped tightly around each other, alternating between sipping their beer and kissing each other. The ex, Wendy guessed, wondering if he'd had more of a jawline when Kat married him. He looked as if he'd been shaped in clay by a child who added a smaller round ball to a larger one and called it head and torso, His slightly wavy hair fell over his ears and was just a shade or two darker than his pale skin. On the other side of the kissing couple was a taller man. He was dressed much more casually and kept bending over to talk to Kat. He rested his hand on the exposed skin of her shoulder, something that both Wendy and the last woman at the table noticed. The lesbian sister, she guessed by the similar megawatt smile that graced her lips.

The audience burst into applause and the first group of youngsters slinked on stage. Reluctantly, Wendy used the segue of the band plugging in to approach the table. The lead singer looked to be in her early teens. She nervously chattered about the songs they had chosen, but Wendy had her eyes on Kat waiting to see when she would register her presence.

Laughing about something the man on her arm said, Kat's eyes flicked up and found her. Without pause, Kat jumped up and ran to her, embracing her warmly. "I'm so glad you made it!" She quickly ushered Wendy to the table, one hand wrapped familiarly around her forearm. "Are you okay here next to Erin?" she whispered. "I'll introduce you after they wrap up."

Wendy nodded since the band had begun to play and talking was impossible. She smiled at the woman next to her and extended her hand. Erin accepted the gesture and appraised Wendy openly. She leaned in as closely as Kat, and Wendy was enveloped in her perfume. "Kat's told me all about you."

Wendy looked from Erin to Kat. Kat raised a thumb and her eyebrows. Wendy wished she hadn't, wished that she had made everyone scoot down a seat, so she could sit next to Kat. Erin was gorgeous, a pixie face framed by blond hair just long enough to sweep behind her ear which she did with regularity. She turned in her chair, long sleek legs extended out from a curve-hugging black dress that ended mid-thigh. An exaggerated swing of the top leg brought her gaze back up to Erin's smile, a smile that said that she was welcome to look.

They whispered in between songs, and when the first band left the stage, instead of Kat introducing Wendy to the rest of the table, Erin quickly did the honors, starting with her brother Patrick. "Patrick and Ember used to be together, and their son Leo is in Travis's band."

She delivered this information flippantly, but it still made Wendy feel uncomfortable to sit with a group of people who had made Kat feel so self-conscious. She was amazed by Kat's demeanor. Had she not said anything about the way she felt about Patrick's persistent flirting, Wendy would not have suspected that anything was wrong. Objectively, the group dynamic was amicable and seemed relaxed. Because of work, she had to decline Erin's offer to grab her a glass of wine from the bar but made no objection when she scooted her chair close enough that their thighs and shoulders touched.

"Kat said you work at Fairbanks," Ember said. It was cool enough in the bar that Wendy was comfortable in her jacket, yet Ember had a sleek sleeveless top that tied around her neck. The way she rested her arms on the table reminded Wendy of a praying mantis.

Wendy nodded.

"Does the restaurant do wedding receptions?"

"Stop," Jack said.

"I thought you were having your ceremony and the reception at that cute little hall in Long Beach," Kat said.

Wendy bit back the surprise. Kat hadn't mentioned that her ex was marrying Ember. She listened in fascination as Ember insisted that her wedding plans had been ruined by the rainstorm a few nights before. Both men at the table rolled their eyes as Kat expressed sympathy for Ember's fretting.

"The manager assured us that the damage is minimal and that they were confident they'd be able to honor their reservations," Jack said.

"But it's just a few weeks away, and they need to replace the roof and redo the flooring. What if they don't get it finished? We need a backup plan," Ember persisted.

Erin shushed them both. "Enough about the wedding. Here come Travis and Leo."

Four teenage boys appeared, three in dark jeans and sneakers. All had shirts with logos she did not recognize, but

Travis stood apart in his shorts and flip-flops. He took center stage and adjusted the mic. "I recognize Travis. Which one is Leo?"

"On keyboard. They're so awkward and so cute. You're going to love them."

After the beating her eardrums had sustained with the first band, she wasn't sure she would be able to appreciate anything, but she had to admit that it was fun to watch Travis and look for Kat in his movements and expressions. His comfort behind the mic surprised Wendy, and though she didn't recognize any of the songs, she found herself understanding and enjoying the lyrics. She was utterly absorbed when she felt Kat stand behind her. Wendy's belly erupted in butterflies as their drummer ducked offstage, passing his drumsticks to Kat. How could she have forgotten that Kat had promised to play?

Kat beamed at Wendy. She was looking at Wendy, wasn't she?

"What's she doing?" Erin whispered.

"Playing, it looks like." Wendy sat mesmerized as Kat situated herself behind the kit.

"Okay, so like when Leo and I first started our band, we didn't have a drummer. My mom learned, so we could do shows like this. She didn't complain when we kicked her out of the band, so I couldn't say no when she said she wanted to do our last song tonight." The house erupted into applause.

Leo started a keyboard intro that immediately transported Wendy back to prom. Then the low beat of the bass drum started in sync with Kat tapping on the cymbal. She leaned toward her mic and sang with a voice as sweet as honey the opening lines to "Head Over Heels" by The Go Go's.

Wendy was transfixed by Kat's muscular arms, exposed when she'd pushed up the sleeves of her sweater. Every beat from the bass drum reverberated through her body, a steady beat that was all Kat, Kat, Kat. Wendy tried to recall if she had ever seen her like this. Unapologetic joy radiated from her. The song and the athleticism brought high school to mind. Wendy recalled Kat the cheerleader and wished she could hold up that version to the one on stage. From what Kat had said about her friends, she guessed that a more careful observation would have revealed a veil of reserve. The person in front of her in this moment had none of that. She was utterly lost in the song with the boys and easily the most beautiful Wendy had ever seen her.

Warm breath graced her neck again. "Isn't she great?"

Wendy snapped out of her reverie. "She's amazing."

"It's hard not to crush on her," Erin said.

Why was she talking during Kat's song? Wendy wished she'd thought to record it, so she could watch again later. It was passing too quickly. They were already at the instrumental part, and Kat was adorable, encouraging Leo as he jammed on the keyboards and then the young man on bass. Even Travis had a huge smile as he encouraged the crowd to jump in on the clapping part. Wendy happily joined the boisterous crowd as the band repeated the chorus, Kat earning *woots* for her throaty delivery of the lyrics.

Wendy felt dizzy as she rose to her feet along with the rest of the room to give Kat and the boys a standing ovation as they left the stage. She felt her smile stretch as wide as Kat's as she returned to the table.

To Wendy's surprise, Kat wrapped her arms around her, the drumsticks clicking together behind her back. Her lips hovered near her ear, and she said, "Don't be mad I didn't do your song." She squeezed and then was gone, hugging Erin and Patrick before she sat down, glowing.

Wendy glanced at her watch and decided she should take this opportunity to slip out. She tapped Erin on the shoulder. "Very nice to meet you. I'm catering an event tonight and need to get back to my assistant."

Erin grasped her hand. "I wish we'd had more time to talk!"

"I'm really sorry I have to slip away early. Do you mind if I get your number from Kat later?"

"Please do!"

Wendy crouched next to Kat. "I wish I didn't have work. We have to talk about how truly awesome that was."

"We'll be here for hours. How long is your event?"

"It's just hors d'oeuvres. And then I have breakdown in my kitchen."

"Text me when you're through, and I'll let you know if we're still here."

"Deal. Thanks again for the invite!" She placed both hands over her heart. "That was really terrific."

* * *

After the boys had come around for hugs and congratulations and disappeared for burgers, Erin grabbed Kat before she could sit. "Come get the next round with me."

Kat saw that coming. She'd taken note when Erin scooted closer to Wendy and had seen the way she kept whispering in her ear during Travis's set. She remembered the way Erin used to drop her voice to a sexy timbre to whisper flirtations in her ear. She missed the playfulness without expectation that she had enjoyed with Erin before the divorce.

"Do you and Wendy have a thing going?" Erin asked after she'd ordered another wine for herself, soda water for Kat and a pitcher of ale for the others.

"I told you we're friends."

"And then you sang 'Head Over Heels'. It's not such a stretch to think you might have a thing for her."

"I don't have a thing for her," Kat shot back.

Erin put her hands up. "No need to get defensive. She knew you'd be playing today, so I thought maybe it was a message for her."

"I invited her here to meet you."

"You're sure? Because she's totally someone you could fall head over heels for." She began singing the chorus of the song, swinging her hips and clapping her hands in time.

Erin's theatrics annoyed Kat. She was reading too much into the song choice, wasn't she? Had she subliminally picked the song because of how she felt about Wendy? She shook the thought away. "She was singing a song by the Go-Go's yesterday. When I asked Travis if I could play, he pointed out that 'Head Over Heels' has a solo part for everyone."

"Fine. Fine. I was just checking to make sure I wasn't stepping on any toes if I asked her out."

"You're not stepping on mine." Kat gazed across the club at their table and felt tightness in her chest. Ember was relaxed into Jack's wandering hands. God, she'd hated sitting next to Jack at things like this, feeling the pressure and expectation of every touch. She should be happy for them to have found their compatibility. She'd read the same comfort in how Wendy sat next to Erin. They were a good match, both successful and full of life. They could be good together. For some reason, this thought brought a pang of jealousy.

They watched the table while they waited for the drinks. Suddenly she wanted nothing more than to leave. The anticipatory buzz while waiting to play and the high from being onstage drained away, and all she wanted was to change into her pajamas and watch *The Great British Baking Show* for the rest of the evening. Wendy had her hooked and was ahead of her in the series. She enjoyed teasing Wendy about her baked goods. But she had invited Wendy to come back later, which meant she had to stay.

The bartender delivered their drinks, and Erin paused, leaning slightly against Kat before they walked to the table. "You're sure? Say the word and I'll back off."

"Don't be ridiculous," Kat laughed. "I'm glad you like her."

Erin pulled out her phone. "Then can you give me her number?"

Kat hesitated. She had wanted them to meet, and Wendy hadn't offered her number before she left. Maybe she should wait and ask Wendy before she complied.

"She said she was going to get my number from you. I'm just saving her the trouble."

"Oh." Kat felt oddly disappointed. She pulled up her contacts and tipped the phone toward Erin.

Erin typed in the number and then leaned back, her finger sliding along the keys. "Just texted her about getting drinks after work."

Kat gave her a thumbs-up and felt a tickle of envy for her being able to simply text and ask about getting together. She was always happy to have an excuse to call Wendy when a catering gig came up. She couldn't imagine just texting Wendy to say she wanted to see her.

Erin did a little happy dance when her phone buzzed. "She answered!"

Kat tried to ignore her and the smile on her face as she concentrated on her phone's screen. "Do you know anything about her restaurant? It looks really nice." She held out her phone to show their website.

"I've never been," Kat said.

"They have a jazz ensemble there tonight!" Again, her fingers flew over the keys. The whole table seemed to be on pause as she waited for a reply. Finally, the phone buzzed. After she read it, she coyly pocketed her phone and said, "We're on for drinks!"

Patrick leaned against Kat. "Looks like we're the only ones not getting laid tonight," he said lasciviously.

She scooted her chair away from him and traced the lines on her palm.

"Unless, you know…The offer's still good. I don't see what it would hurt to fool around, let off some steam."

"Still not that easy," Kat said thankful the next band was finished setting up and starting their set.

"Nobody ever said you were easy," Patrick said loudly enough for the whole table to hear.

Though Kat kept her eyes lowered, she could feel everyone absorb his critique. She refused to look at anyone, refused to react to his childish outburst. She filled her lungs and held her breath as long as she could before letting her frustration out with it. If she left, he would think that he'd stung her. She wouldn't give him that satisfaction. She leaned back in her chair and sipped her drink thinking about her decision to sleep with Jack. The product of that night sat at the bar. Travis was the reason she didn't regret the decision her former self had made, but she had no desire for Patrick, period. She reminded herself that she was under no obligation to please him.

She tuned out the band onstage and replayed her favorite Go Go's song in her head. The audience response had been fantastic, and she savored Travis's nice intro. Like the song said, she'd been waiting a long time. She'd been playing the part of mom so long that she had, indeed, forgotten about her heart. She had been pulled into playing the part of wife and mother, and even though she was divorced, she wondered if she was holding on too tightly to the past. She sang again to herself, *One hand's just reaching out, and one's just holding on. It seems my weaknesses just keep going strong.*

Head over heels. She'd been head over heels for her baby, but he wasn't a child anymore. As he'd said, she had been a stopgap until they found a drummer. And in another few years, he'd be off to school. That was the way of parenting, she supposed. Who would she be when he went away to school, when he had a family of his own? A grandma? There was an idea she couldn't even fathom.

Tonight she'd head back to her parents' home to sleep in her childhood room. She'd pass her wedding album on the bookshelf and feel Miranda hiding there. Miranda who had whispered that she didn't have to marry Jack just because she was pregnant. Miranda who had insisted that they could be a family, the three of them. Miranda who had said it wasn't too late. They could run away together. She'd broken her own heart as certainly as she'd broken Miranda's when she said she had to marry Jack. We can be friends, she'd insisted. They had always been the best of friends.

Until Kat said no.

And Miranda had left.

She wasn't supposed to leave.

Kat closed her eyes and allowed herself to imagine a parallel life, one where she let herself be head over heels for Miranda. Miranda could have been Travis's proud other mom. They would be holding hands, and she would feel safe, content and happy. She couldn't remember the last time she had felt that way.

CHAPTER SEVEN

"This feels surreal," Wendy said, sliding onto a stool at the mahogany bar in the restaurant, the liquors displayed on the wall. She had broken down her kitchen as quickly as possible in order to join Erin, and it took her eyes a moment to adjust to the restaurant's mood lighting after the harsh fluorescent lights in the kitchen.

"Nice place," Erin said, looking around the main seating area. Wendy appreciated how José didn't overcrowd the space with too many tables. The cozy booth seating offered a view of the classic palm-tree lined street. "And I'm so happy to see you again tonight." Erin leaned forward and kissed Wendy on the cheek.

Wendy hesitated before leaning forward to hug Erin.

"Sorry," Erin said. "Was that too forward?"

"No. Absolutely not. It's nice. It's really, really nice. It's also so unexpected."

"But Kat told you that I'd be there, didn't she?"

Wendy reviewed the conversation when Kat had invited her to the club. What had she said about Erin? She hadn't even told her Erin's name. She had said the lesbian sister might be there. She said Erin was fun and cute and that she might be perfect for Wendy. Not a whole lot. She didn't even know what Erin did for a living, where she lived. "She did."

"I've been on her to introduce us forever."

"Really?"

"Ever since she ran into you at the reunion."

"She told you about that?"

"Of course! Our families have been close since the boys were five."

"I didn't realize you hung out with her that much."

"All the birthday parties, Halloween, Fun Fridays every summer. My brother always hauled me along, so he could drink and flirt with the moms. Nobody says no to having an adult around who actually enjoys children."

"Parents don't enjoy their children?"

"I'm sure they have their moments, but my brother was always happy to hand Leo off for an auntie adventure. I'd swoop in and swim with all the rug rats while the adults drank themselves just short of shitfaced."

"Even Kat?"

"Never Kat, which is why I like her best. She was always coherent enough to talk to. And she told me all about the hot lesbian at the reunion."

"She said that?"

"Absolutely. And she didn't lie. I'd yell at her for not introducing us sooner, but you were with someone at the time."

"I was."

"But that someone isn't in the picture anymore?"

"No." Wendy was glad that the bartender had appeared to take their order.

"Mind if I ask why?" Erin startled her.

Her thoughts were sluggish as she reached back in her memory. What had they fought about? Wendy put herself back at the reunion, climbing behind the wheel as Susan ranted about having been ignored for most of the evening. There were so many critical issues, but that night was the catalyst to her moving out. "We wanted different things. José had just brought me in as the catering chef, and I spent a lot of time networking. She wanted someone who could devote more time to a relationship, someone with a more static schedule."

"It wasn't that you wanted kids, and she didn't." Erin sipped her white wine.

"Nope. We weren't anywhere near that kind of conversation." Wendy glanced toward the stage and took a sip of her beer trying her hardest to appreciate the jazz group that José brought in once a month.

Erin turned her body to follow her gaze. Her foot bounced to the beat, and her smile grew wider as she listened to the musicians on a slightly raised stage. "I was so excited when I saw this on the website! I can't believe you can just walk out of your kitchen to a performance like this!"

Wendy nodded noncommittally.

Erin glanced back at Wendy. She frowned. "Unless you hate it."

Wendy chuckled. "I like songs to have words."

"You liked Kat's song?"

"Oh, I love eighties music, and that song was one of my favorites. Oh, shoot. I said I'd text her when I was back at the restaurant." She pulled out her phone, but Erin stilled her hand.

"I told her we were doing drinks here."

"She was okay with that?"

"Yes. She knew I was excited about the band." She held eye contact with Wendy and added, "and the company."

Wendy blinked in surprise. "Okay." Tentatively, she placed her phone on the bar. "If you're sure."

"Course I am. She looked pretty wiped out when I left. I'd be surprised if she was still there, honestly. It was fun to see her play, especially a song she clearly loved. Back when she was drumming for the boys, they chose all the songs. I always thought it was cool how into it she was, but she never looked like she did tonight."

Wendy thought about how much Kat did for other people and wondered how often she did what she wanted for herself.

When Wendy didn't immediately respond, Erin said, "I asked her if she had a thing for you."

"What?" Wendy said, trying to find her place in the conversation.

"You've known each other for a long time, and she never followed through on her promise to invite you to hang out."

"I don't really know her that well, mostly as a work contact."

"I thought you two knew each other in high school as well."

Wendy laughed. "No. Kat was way too popular. I was surprised she even knew we went to the same school, but what you said about the drums makes me wonder how much she enjoyed stuff like cheer back then. How much does she do because it's what people expect?"

"Back then or now?"

"All those years of being married and being a mom. I get the impression that she got married because people expected her to."

"That's a societal expectation. Don't you feel it being your age and single?"

"My age?" Wendy was surprised by her phrasing.

"At our age, I find that people want to know why I'm not partnered. That doesn't happen to you?"

"Does it matter? I'm not going to hook up with someone just to avoid being alone."

"I think you're in the minority there. Don't you feel sad if you're alone on Valentine's Day?"

"I care about Valentine's Day for one reason only. It drums up business. Personally, I could do without the holidays that add unnecessary life pressure."

"Are you always so candid, Chef?"

Wendy scrunched up her face in thought. "Yep, pretty much. It's who I am."

"Who you are is very appealing," Erin said, reaching for Wendy's hand.

They talked until the band packed their instruments and Wendy was unsuccessful in hiding a yawn. She promised it had nothing to do with Erin's law stories and everything to do with her own schedule. Wendy said her goodnights to the staff and escorted Erin to the parking lot.

"You don't have to stay?"

"When I'm on dinner service I have to, but not when I'm catering. Did you want to see the setup?"

"Not really," Erin said. Before Wendy could register the words, Erin was leaning forward, pulling Wendy toward her. Their lips met, first just a gentle brushing of soft full lips and then a bit firmer. The tickle of her tongue against Wendy's lower lip elicited a small gasp. Erin took advantage to assert her interest more boldly, delivering a kiss that said without question that she would very much like to be headed for either her house or Wendy's, and not the restaurant's kitchen.

Erin wove her hand into Wendy's curls and pulled her closer. Making out next to her date's car, Wendy felt like a teenager again, the thrill that accompanies the risk of being caught making her body tingle even more.

She didn't think anyone would bother them, but the idea of being watched made her feel vulnerable enough that she pulled away.

"You are an exceptional kisser," Erin said, her eyes still closed, a dreamy expression on her face."

Wendy stroked her cheek. "Thanks. So are you."

"Whew!" Erin exclaimed. "Thank you for saying that. The last woman I kissed did not agree with you. Kind of gave me a complex."

"Inconceivable!" Wendy said, channeling *The Princess Bride*.

"What?" Erin asked.

"I do not think you know what that word means," Wendy continued the movie dialogue. "*The Princess Bride*?"

"I never saw that."

Wendy leaned over and kissed Erin soundly. She kissed her until they were both breathless, and then she whispered, "Well, I definitely know what inconceivable means. I cannot see anyone not being moved by a kiss like that."

"Make sure to tell Kat what she's missing." Erin waggled her eyebrows playfully.

"Wait. You kissed Kat?" Wendy stepped back.

"Just once. My stupid brother and Ember had me convinced that she had a thing for me. Hell, even her husband fanned that flame. Probably just because he wanted to watch." She shrugged. "I always liked Kat, but she so did not like me that way."

"Huh," Wendy said. "But you kissed her?"

"She and I had flirted for years. Turns out she never saw it going past that. I on the other hand like to do a lot more than flirt with a hot lady."

If she hadn't mentioned kissing Kat, Erin's next kiss might have extinguished the notion of taking things slowly. This time, when they parted, it was Wendy who kept her eyes closed. She'd be a fool not to give this woman a chance.

"We could have a lot of fun tonight." Erin stroked Wendy's lower lip with her thumb.

Bodily, Wendy agreed. But mentally she needed more time. "You make me feel like I'm in my twenties, but I do have an early morning tomorrow."

"Even on a Sunday morning?"

"We cater all sorts of events, weekends especially. Sunday afternoons, Mondays and Tuesdays are my usual days off, when I can get them."

"Your work ethic is a huge turn-on. I'd like to see you again. Do you ride?"

"Ride?"

"Horses. We could go riding. Tomorrow afternoon when you're finished with your morning gig?"

"That sounds…painful," Wendy said.

"Serves you right for ending our night here in a dark parking lot."

Wendy leaned over to kiss Erin one more time. "You really are good at that. If I were twenty, I'd be following you home."

"Are you kidding? If we were twenty, we'd be naked in the back seat of my Mercedes, sweaty and satisfied right now."

"Good night, Erin."

"I'm glad I've met you, Wendy."

She walked over to her sleek red car, waving to Erin as she navigated back to the street. Wendy took out her phone. She scrolled through the flirty texts Erin had sent from the bar and was happy that she'd said yes to meeting for drinks. She sent a thank-you to Erin and reminded her to send her address for their afternoon ride. She hovered over Kat's name debating on whether to send a text to her as well. She leaned against her car. What was she thinking? Erin had said she told Kat. Why did she have the urge to apologize for not making it back to Aura? It wasn't like they were that close. She hadn't even told her that she'd kissed Erin once. Here she thought they were developing a friendship, but perhaps she had misread their conversation in the cottage.

CHAPTER EIGHT

Miranda wasn't supposed to leave. The thought invaded her brain like a worm. She was supposed to stay. They'd been friends for such a long time that she assumed they'd still be friends after she came home from her honeymoon.

First, she had been confused. Why wasn't her friend returning her calls? Kat gave her time, imagining that she was busy.

Then she'd been angry. Who did Miranda think she was? It was just rude not to return calls. She didn't need to be friends with rude anyway. Sour grapes, for sure. But a position from which she could justify not calling anymore.

But as the months extended to years, the sadness came. Miranda had abandoned her. Kat had never considered the possibility of a life without Miranda, and then she was living it. Until she'd seen Wendy at the reunion, Kat had successfully boxed all the messy Miranda emotions away. Wendy had forced that box open.

Speaking of women not supposed to leave…

Kat slammed the heavy door of her SUV as if she could trap her musings inside. The quiet church campus was nestled in a residential cul-de-sac at the base of one of the small hills that at least gave partial validity to the city being called Woodland Hills. Now that the hill was covered in homes, she couldn't help feeling as if she was being observed as she strode across the parking lot. Rosebushes lined a patio that separated the steepled sanctuary with stained glass windows where church services were held and the narrow flat-roofed utilitarian building that housed the kitchen, rehearsal space and her office. She did her best not to think about Erin's smile when she'd received Wendy's text last night. Or the text she had sent later saying thank you for the introduction. She'd spent a lot of time staring at the time stamp wondering whether she was in her sexy I'm-not-a-mom car about to follow Wendy home. Home where nightcaps were had, where clothes came off, where hands were allowed to roam more freely.

The office door bounced off the wall. She caught it before it smacked her in the face, remembering that she was at church. Regardless of where she was she had no right to be thinking of Erin and Wendy naked in bed, but she acknowledged how it was especially inappropriate on the campus of the conservative church and her place of employ. She glanced toward the priest's office, angry again. Had he not been so narrow minded, she would not be spending so much time with Wendy. Had she not been spending so much time with Wendy, she wouldn't be thinking so much about Miranda.

She settled herself calmly into her office chair, centering herself for the essential tasks before the Sunday morning service. While she waited for the computer to boot, she quickly pushed aside the stack of things others had left piled on her desk that she didn't have time to sort. She knew Reverend Thorn frowned on what he considered clutter, but the family pictures, awards, and wide assortment of tchotchkes on her desk, mostly glass angels gifted to her by members of the congregation, made the space feel comfortable. Too soon, she discovered that she would find no respite in her work. As quickly as she could, she put out email fires, including her least favorite, the "Sorry, I can't make it," from one of her bell girls meaning she'd either have to find a last-minute replacement or play the peal in the church foyer herself.

She took the easy route and just did it, annoyed with herself for not enforcing the rule that players find their own replacements. As she expected, more people than ever stopped, their memories jogged about some project or another that they wanted to talk to her about.

"I'll find you on the patio!" they mouthed.

Please don't, she thought, smile still plastered to her face. *Remember how I said the last fifteen times you approached me about garden club that it's better to ask me to schedule the planting workshop or seed selection or pruning party or whatever it was you need when I'm IN MY OFFICE and actually HAVE MY CALENDAR in front of me?*

She needed to get a grip, reduced to yelling at herself because she could not yell at the clueless. The Stechers wanted to order a rosebud for an altar dedication. Not her job. The health care committee needed to schedule a day for the fair. The director of the spring play wanted to book the auditorium for rehearsals and performances. It seemed there was no end to the questions, not one of which she could answer on the patio. And would anyone actually follow her to her office? Of course not. "I need to catch…" "I just found…" "I've got to…"

Absolutely finished with the whole lot of them, Kat skirted the main patio where the congregation had their coffee fellowship and marched past the rose garden and small playground toward her office to jot down as many of the things she had Post-it noted in her mind onto the actual calendar. She almost made it, had almost reclaimed her peace when a voice slipped through the tiny crack in the door.

"Kat!"

She could pretend that she didn't hear him, couldn't she?

"Kat! Just a moment!"

She heard Evan's dress shoes clicking on the sidewalk and pushed the door open.

Evan held his hand on his chest as he caught his breath. "I had a fabulous idea, but Jeremy said we had to get your approval before I proceed." When Kat said nothing, he paused. "You seem spent. Are you having a bad day?"

"Nothing. Everything. It's been busy." Kat felt badly for trying to escape to her office. She took a deep breath catching the faint smell of pipe smoke on his coat. She squeezed his shoulder in apology and then flicked her hands outward as if she was shoving all the irritations out of her way. "There. Better. What's your idea?"

Evan frowned. "Something's bothering you."

"I told you. I've had a busy morning, but it's already better. You know weddings are my favorite thing. Tell me what is going to make yours the best."

He hesitated, but only for a moment. Then he lit up, twinkling brighter than a Christmas tree. He clapped his hands together. "You know how we want to do the unity candle."

"Yes."

"Okay. Reverend Munson said that it's important after we light the middle candle that we leave our individual candles burning because they represent the fire that burns only inside of us. We liked that idea a lot, that we're both still individuals as well as unified by the middle flame. But there are so many people who support us. We'd like to represent that, too."

"How do you plan on doing that?" Kat asked.

"Everyone gets a candle."

"Sounds nice."

"Oh, and there may be more guests than we originally planned." He fussed with his tie.

"How many?

He took a small notebook from the inner pocket of his suit jacket with pages of names listed. "We may have fifty now."

Kat pointed to the pad. "What's with the list?"

"Jeremy calls it reverse invitation: all the people who have heard about Reverend Thorn's position and would like to celebrate with us. In protest, as well as in support."

"And you have to feed them?"

"We don't have to, but it will be our joy to have them for the full celebration."

"You've told Wendy?"

"Of course."

"So fifty candles. That's a lot of fire!"

"That's where the pool comes in! We could have floating candles. I found some shaped like flowers. So many colors. They're beautiful! After the ceremony, each guest lights a candle from our unity candle and floats it in the pool."

Kat could picture it vividly. "That sounds…" Her voice cracked.

"What? Dumb? Dangerous?"

"Beautiful. It sounds beautiful."

Evan hugged her tightly.

"Why did you think you needed approval for that?"

"I haven't gotten to that part yet."

"Oh."

"Remember how it looks in your mind, how beautiful all those flames will be."

"I've got it," Kat said.

"I want our photographer to capture that with me and Jeremy in the middle."

"How are you going to be in the middle of the pool?"

"On a bridge! Jeremy said he could design one. I want the picture to show how our friends and family help to hold us." His arms extended to illustrate the idea.

"But it's the bridge that will be holding you, not the fire."

"It's the symbol," Evan insisted, "You're helping my romantic dream come to light. See what I did there? Come to light?" He nudged her with his elbow.

He had to mention romance, reminding her of Erin's text about how well she and Wendy had hit it off. The image of them entwined in bed flashed through her mind again, and she pushed it aside angrily. She was unsuccessful in masking her feelings when she answered. "Sure. Do it."

Evan didn't look convinced. "I thought you'd be excited. Or concerned. Or hesitant. Or 'absolutely not.' Instead you're…I can't put my finger on it. Is everything okay? What's bothering you?"

What was bothering her? That Wendy had blown her off after talking to Erin for five minutes. She couldn't say that to Evan, yet he waited for a response. She rummaged around in her mind for an appropriate answer. "It just feels like there is so much to do before the wedding, but I want you to have everything you want, so tell me what I can do to help."

"Really? But you've already done so much for us! Wendy said that the lights are finished, and wonderful," he added, his twinkles brightening again.

"Super." Kat said her voice notably cooler.

Evan furrowed his brow. "Are you mad at Wendy? Is that what this mood is all about?"

"I'm not mad."

"Could've fooled me. What happened?"

"Nothing. Nothing happened."

He waited.

"I thought…I just got confused about something I invited her to last night." Evan still said nothing. She would not think about Wendy and Erin having drinks at Wendy's restaurant. She absolutely would not think about whether that was all they'd done. Her silence betrayed her mood.

"Okay. Out with it." Evan pointed to one of the visitor's chairs and sat in the other.

"What?" Kat sat next to him.

"Whatever is spinning around in your head right now. It's like you're watching a movie in there, one that you're not particularly enjoying. Tell me what it is."

Kat adopted the most offhanded tone that she could and explained the setup, Wendy and Erin having drinks together, and how Wendy hadn't even bothered to text her.

"Wait. I missed something. You like these women. You liked them enough to set them up, but now you're mad that they might have connected? Shouldn't you happy for them?"

"The way lesbians commit, they're probably planning their wedding, right?"

"It's a bit soon for that, but young people today do seem to move rather quickly."

"They're not so young."

"Still, there is a good chance one of them is moving in with the other today. Who has the better house?"

Kat's jaw dropped.

Evan slapped her shoulder playfully. "I was just kidding. Mostly. Why would that bother you so much?"

"No reason. Like you said, it's great they hit it off so well." But Evan was right about her not liking what she had been imagining. Ridiculous, she scolded herself. If I don't want to sleep with either one of them, why shouldn't they sleep with each other? "Enough about that," she said both to herself and to Evan. "You said Jeremy is designing this bridge. Who is going to build it?"

"Yes. Well. That does get a bit more complicated. Some of our reverse-invitation guests have asked if there is anything they can do," he said.

Kat's mind spun back to another time a bridge had spanned the pool. She remembered her father building a rope bridge one Halloween, and her breathing went shallow. Her palms started to tingle. Could she take an Ativan like she did when Travis wanted to swim?

"Kat? Are you okay?"

"I won't…" Kat started to say she wouldn't be home. She was already inventing errands that would keep her away from the house because she couldn't tell him no. Not without explaining. The conversation she'd had with Wendy about how white lying was a bad habit of hers rang in her ears. Her voice faltered and she offered vague honesty instead. "I don't know if I can help."

"Dave has offered his skills. He's young and strong. But he might need someone to help. Hey! Maybe Wendy would."

Kat breathed more easily when he didn't question her further. "Wendy?"

"She mentioned that she has Mondays off and to say the word if we needed help with anything else since we're squeezing in a year's worth of planning into a month. I'm sure power tools are involved. You know how lesbians love their power tools!"

"She's your caterer, and you're going to ask her to build a bridge?" Kat asked skeptically.

"Why not? She is such a kindred spirit. You know when you meet someone, and you just know you're going to be friends instantly? That's how it was with her. She's the kind who would do absolutely anything for a friend, like hanging the lights. She went on and on about how pleased she was to be able to do that with you."

"She did?"

"Of course!" he said. "She has all sorts of stories about how great you've been to her."

Kat wasn't expecting this. Sure, she had sent business Wendy's way, but that was something worthy of a sentence of thanks, not what Kat considered stories. She thought about her envy of Erin's ability to simply text Wendy without an excuse. She enjoyed supporting Wendy's business because it afforded her the opportunity to talk to and see her occasionally. Jeremy's bridge gave her another such excuse, and she seized it. "I could call her to see if she's willing to help."

"You sure? You seem upset with her, like you're uncomfortable that she hit it off with your friend."

"I'm the one who introduced them."

"I know, so why the grumps? Are you freaked out that they might have hooked up? Girl sex puts you off?" He was laughing, but he stopped abruptly at the look on Kat's face. "That's it? Girl sex puts you off?" He sat back, looking dumbfounded.

Kat looked away. His question had propelled her back to Miranda, and she could hear her voice as if she was sitting there with them. *Go ahead. Tell me that you don't want to sleep with me. Tell me that you are not burning with desire from that kiss, and I won't say another word about it.*

She couldn't imagine it. That was the thing, wasn't it? She had thought she wouldn't know what to do. The idea had terrified her. She could not find any words to explain it. She hadn't been able to answer Miranda, could not tell her why she was so afraid, and she'd taken it as a no. Now she had no words for Evan, and he took that as a yes.

"Oh, my." He drew out the words. "I did not expect that."

"Evan, please. You can't say anything. It's not like that, I just…I can't talk about it."

He waved her off. "Not my business. Sorry I asked. I'm on your side. I can't even begin to imagine what two women do in bed."

The problem was that since she'd started spending time with Wendy, Kat found that she absolutely could.

* * *

The name on her phone brought a smile to Wendy's face. "Hi there, sunshine!" she answered brightly.

"Hello." Kat sounded guarded. "Do you have a minute?"

"Of course!" Wendy had just pulled up outside Erin's house in Hidden Hills, but she'd been thinking about Kat all morning and was glad to have a chance to apologize for the previous evening. "Sorry I didn't end up seeing you after work. I wanted to hear whether you were happy with your performance."

"I was. Now I'm at work and Evan has a request."

Wendy was surprised that Kat said so little about her brilliant performance, but reasoned she was just preoccupied with work.

"What kind of request?"

"Evan approached me about a vision he and Jeremy have to build a bridge spanning the pool." Her voice went so soft Wendy had trouble hearing her. "I have the day off tomorrow. I should be able to help, but…I can't."

Wendy had been about to get out of her car, but the shift in Kat's voice gave her pause.

Kat continued, "Evan said that you'd offered to help with anything they needed."

Something about Kat's voice didn't sound right, and Wendy spoke quickly to try to put her at ease. "I did offer to help, and I am happy to. Is everything okay? You sound stressed."

"I am, honestly. I didn't realize how hard this wedding was going to be. I hate to ask for more of your time."

"It's okay to ask for help."

"That's about as easy as telling the truth."

"I'm glad you asked."

"You are?" Kat sounded relieved. "Thank you."

"I really am happy to help," Wendy said. "I'll call Jeremy to see when they need me."

The line went quiet.

"Yes. Good idea. And Wendy?"

She'd been about to hang up. "Yeah?"

"Thank you. Again. I knew you'd understand."

"Of course!"

Wendy tapped her phone against the steering wheel, reluctant to get out. Kat's call made her wish she was about to walk up to the now-familiar house she had always loved so much. With a sigh, she swung the door open and stood, only then taking in the full grandeur of Erin's place. Did she live here alone?

The house sat at the top of a sweeping drive. Perfectly manicured lawn and trees decorated the front yard. It was two stories and constructed of beige stone. The bell chimed a melody, and the door swung open to reveal Erin dressed in tailored jeans and a plum form-fitting mock turtleneck. "You made it!" she said.

Wendy stepped inside and absorbed her surroundings. On her immediate right a black sofa and coffee table looked like a receiving area, and on the left a den with a large table and bookshelves filled with decorative pieces. A huge painting of an orchid filled the wall in front of her, and a hallway led both left and right. Erin pointed to the right. "Do you need a drink before we ride?"

The shorter hallway to the right revealed a large living room with a built-in flat-screen TV. A bar separated the living room from the open kitchen. A motorized cleaning unit swept the floor. "How many square feet is this place?" Wendy couldn't help but ask.

"Downstairs is twenty-four hundred." She took a few steps into the living room and pointed to a stairwell Wendy hadn't noticed. "Upstairs isn't quite that much. Much of it is storage. I could give you a tour."

"That's okay." Wendy was feeling overwhelmed by what she could already see. She could fit her house into Erin's four times. She wondered whether Kat had been to Erin's house and what she thought of it. What would she think of her own tiny, quirky place?

"Hey." Erin stepped closer and pressed her lips to Wendy's. Hers were soft, uncomplicated and unquestionably lesbian lips. She really was an exceptional kisser, and someone who deserved her full attention. So why was Wendy thinking about Kat?

CHAPTER NINE

A feeling of peace settled over Wendy the moment she passed the hedge shielding Kat's house from the street. Walking up the drive, each step took her further away from the crazy loud world and closer to the quiet reflective space of Kat's home. Mid-morning, the sun was already high in the sky, shining directly on the front of the majestic house. She wondered if anyone ever sat on the balcony gazing out over the front lawn in the morning sun.

A truck was parked in front of the garage, and a young man was crouched over a board, a pencil in his mouth.

"Good morning!" she called.

He stood and brushed dirt from his rugged cargo pants before removing the pencil from his mouth. His red hair was shaved on the sides but long on top and had flopped forward on his face. He feathered it away before he extended his hand, the muscles of his forearms visible below the rolled-up sleeves of his denim shirt. "I'm Dave, the muscle in this project. Do you go to the church, too?"

"No. I'm officially the caterer but also apparently trusted with power tools."

"Jeremy's in the garage."

Wendy found Jeremy with a wet rag, bucket of sudsy water and a pile of dusty planks.

"Can you believe Clyde had an old bridge stored in the rafters from a Halloween party? His was rope, but the planks will work just as well on the supports Dave is putting together. You wouldn't believe how many in our congregation have offered their help." He paused and assessed her. "Why are you walking so funny?"

"I went horseback riding yesterday. My date said I'd be more stiff today but I didn't think it would be this bad!"

"Where did you ride?"

"All over Hidden Hills."

"Are you too sore for this?"

"No. I'm sure that the way to get my muscles to loosen up is to put them to work. How can I help?"

"Clyde offered these boxes and boards for the treat stations in the stone cottage. Can you carry them back?"

Wendy glanced at the house. Was Kat home? Still asleep?

"Kat said she'd be back soon."

Caught, Wendy turned back to Jeremy. "Sorry."

"She said something about needing a refill from the donut shop down the street."

Wendy was worried about Kat. Running to the donut shop sounded like the kind of excuse she would fabricate to avoid an uncomfortable situation. Perhaps she would have a chance to talk to Kat about whatever it was that was bothering her. For now, she would carry boxes. She grasped a crate in each hand. "Do you want to show me how you want these set up?"

"Sure. Sorry I can't help carry anything. Evan warned me to let everyone else do the heavy lifting, so I don't throw out my back again. I'm just not as strong as I used to be." He stood and brushed dust from faded overalls.

"You should absolutely let the people who care about you help out," Wendy said, following Jeremy out to the cottage.

He opened the crudely hewn door with two small glass windows staggered, one high, one low. "We are so thankful for all your help. The lights are perfect, I was here last night to do some measuring, and Clyde turned them all on for me."

She hadn't been able to stay long enough to see the party lights at night, and she wouldn't ask if Kat had been with Jeremy and what she had thought. "Romantic enough?"

"Absolutely. It's magical, exactly as I imagined. What I can't fathom is how you parent with the perfect love shack in your backyard. If I'd lived here growing up, I would have gotten into so much trouble! Isn't it amazing?"

"It is!"

"Did you know they built it?"

"Kat didn't tell me that."

"Clyde said he built it with his daughter. Did you know Kat's lived here her whole life?"

"Yes, but I didn't know she built this. Clyde gave me the history of Rock Hudson's handprint but he didn't talk about building the cottage."

"We almost missed it, too! We thought that hedge was the end of the property, but Evan's the biggest snoop. He saw the roofline and then found that little path. He immediately fell in love with it and had his heart set on using it somehow. He loved your idea to put treats in here. Kat's mom says we can use their china, and she'll write out tags to identify the chocolate treats. We're aiming for different levels to put treats on, maybe three different levels created with the boxes and boards Clyde pulled out?"

"I'm sure we can make something work. This is all coming together so beautifully for you! I've never seen beyond the catering table to consider how much thought goes into all these little details."

"We are so lucky to have Kat's help, and yours too. How about you? Will you be planning your own wedding someday?"

"Hopefully!"

"I'd be happy to help you with your planning when love plants a permanent seed for you. Does the horseback riding lady have potential?"

"We've only been out once."

Jeremy tucked his chin toward his chest and stared at her drolly. "I think you already know."

Wendy didn't want to say how intimidated she'd felt in Erin's house. The ride had been very nice. There was no need to calculate what it must cost to maintain a barn and two horses. "There are a lot of appealing things about her." Were she to make a list of Erin's assets, and by that she didn't mean her material wealth. Or did she? She pushed herself to think beyond Erin's grown-up stability and came up with how hot she was. "I'm not quite sure what we have in common. Our date was nice, but I don't find myself thinking about when I can see her again."

"That doesn't bode well."

"I don't want to be with someone just because it's convenient and comfortable. And I don't mind being alone until I find the right person."

They reached the driveway at the same time as Kat emerged from her car, carrying a pink bakery box. "Sorry I'm late! I had to get a refill for my mom. Be right back!" She scurried into the house.

"Donut shops do refills?" Wendy asked Jeremy.

He shrugged. "Not that I've ever heard of."

"The supports are all bolted. You want them over the pool now?" Dave asked.

"Good idea," Jeremy said. "Once they're in place, I'll be able to help more."

Dave and Wendy hoisted the first of three curved support beams.

"Looking good!" Jeremy said from his position holding the gate.

One after the other, Wendy and Dave walked the supports to the middle of the pool by a stack of three-foot lengths of redwood decking. Jeremy explained how he planned to keep them evenly spaced, but she listened with only half an ear, waiting for Kat to return.

She held the first beam on the railroad tie that would anchor the structure on each side. When Jeremy was happy with the beam's position, Wendy accepted a handful of screws and secured the beam to the railroad tie on one side while Dave secured the other. They repeated the process with two other supports.

"Dave and I can get started on the planks. Can you and Kat carry the rest of the materials out to the cottage?"

"Sure."

As she left the pool yard, Wendy spotted Kat standing on the porch staring out toward the pool. She waved and Kat crossed the patio. Kat's tension in greeting the two men was obvious. Though she was curious about why Kat couldn't help with the bridge project, now was clearly not the time to ask. She held a crate in each hand and motioned to two others for Kat to carry. She focused her greeting on something light. "Did I hear you correctly that you got a refill of donuts?"

"You did. My mother doesn't like the donuts to touch each other. The shop doesn't like to use a lot of boxes. I found a compromise. If I bring the box back, they'll lay the four glazed donuts flat like my mom likes."

Wendy was speechless.

"I know what you're thinking."

"Do you?"

"Everyone says my mom is unreasonable and that I only encourage her when I do things like take an empty bakery box with me to the donut shop."

Wendy did not want to agree. If she looked past what sounded like enabling, she could appreciate wanting a fresh donut not stuck to its neighbors. "It makes sense. They don't want the cost of a box without selling twelve donuts, but four in a bag get smooshed. It's a very clever compromise."

"One you'd make?"

Wendy hesitated.

"It's okay if you wouldn't. I'm used to it. Jack was always on my case not to 'indulge her oddities'."

"It's not my place to comment on how you cope with your mother."

"That's kind of you."

"Are you doing okay? You said on the phone you weren't going to be able to help."

"I can help with things on the patio." Again she looked out at the pool. "But I can't help with the bridge."

"There are still more boards and crates to carry out to the cottage if you want to lend a hand."

She agreed, and they worked in silence. After the last trip, Kat stood in the cottage with her arms wrapped around herself as Wendy worked. Her mind spun in search of a reason for Kat not to be able to work on the bridge, but she didn't want to pry. As she had done when they were hanging the lights, she kept working, trusting that if Kat wanted to talk, she would. But aside from giving her opinion about the cottage arrangements, she was quiet. Finished, they stepped outside, and Wendy shut the door to the cottage. "This is the coolest spot you have back here. Jeremy said that you and your dad built this."

"What? No. This was never my project." Kat's grip on her arms tightened.

"I must have misunderstood Jeremy," Wendy said, confused. She remembered that Kat had become upset before when they'd been in the house discussing how to hang the lights. She had started to say something about not being the one who could climb up on the roof. Maybe there was another daughter who climbed on roofs. Before she could enquire, Kat strode away, leaving Wendy alone.

* * *

Kat was completely beside herself. Unexpected tears pricked at the corner of her eye, and she struck them away with the heels of her palms. It had been bad enough to see Wendy after Erin had texted to say how much fun they were having. The way she was gimping along, she and Erin must have had a weekend-long sex-fest. And then to ask about building the cottage!

She couldn't have known. What in the world would give Jeremy that idea? She stormed along the side of the house on the brick path that led to the front yard where her father was planting alternating puffs of white and purple flowers.

He squinted up at her when she stopped next to him.

"What did you say to Jeremy?"

Clyde stretched his back, his face frustratingly neutral. "I am in need of some context. We talked about a myriad of things this morning."

"What did you say about building the cottage?"

The muscles in his jaws rippled before he said, "That I had my daughter's help."

Kat's body flooded with anger. "You had no right mentioning her."

"After all these years…"

He was still talking when she turned and walked away. She had heard it all before, and it fixed nothing. She prayed the front door was unlocked, so she would not have to pass Jeremy or Wendy to get to the back door. It was. She slipped inside and crept up the stairs to avoid her mother as well. Safely inside her room, she looked out the window. Wendy and Jeremy stood together on the patio talking. About her? Most likely. Why hadn't she lied and taken credit for the cottage? It was such an easy lie, and she'd once been so good at it.

Her throat constricted at the thought. That lie would have served to erase even more of Ava. Refocusing to see her room reflected in the window, she studied the pink chair behind her. It had been thirty years since her little sister had sat crossways, her long legs hooked over one of the chair's arms, her elbow propped on the other. She tried to remember when Ava had started watching her get ready for school, standing in front of her mirror to fix her hair and makeup. Her sister sat behind her, distracting her with the pop, pop, pop of her leg.

"What's the point of all that?" Ava had asked her once.

"A girl likes to look her best."

"Not this girl."

"You will, someday. And I'll teach you how to do your makeup and use the curling iron."

"I like my braids."

Kat had teased her that running wild like Laura Ingalls Wilder, she would end up a poor farm girl. She'd teased her about so many things. Teased her for reading too much. For licking the salt off her potato chips before she ate them. For singing in the church choir. For spending so much time sitting in her pink chair when she didn't have to wait for her to finish getting ready. She'd spent so much time pushing her away. Squinting through the tears that ran freely now, she imagined her sister sitting there again.

"I teased you too much."

I knew you were kidding.

"I miss you. You have no idea how much."

Then you should have told her I helped Dad build the cottage.

"I'm sorry." She turned to the empty chair and sobbed, seeing the truth in how much her not talking about her sister hurt. But could she tell Wendy about Ava and not tell it all? Only her family knew the scope of her loss. Jack and Travis knew that she'd had a sister, but not even they knew the whole story. Something about Wendy told her that if she said one thing, a dam would break inside her, and she would confess everything. Angry and alone, she crawled into her bed and clutched a pillow to her, so her mother wouldn't hear her crying.

* * *

"What happened to Kat?" Jeremy asked.

"She had to step away," Wendy said, surprising herself with the lie. She sent out a quick text asking if Kat was okay. "Great progress on the bridge, guys!" Each had only a small pile of planks on the sidewalk.

Jeremy stretched his back. "Did Kat happen to say anything to you about me and Evan?"

"We barely talked at all. I asked about the donuts, commented on the cottage, and then she had to go. Give me the drill. You promised I'd get to play with power tools."

Jeremy handed it over and glanced to the driveway. "She left?"

"She had to do something inside." If she wasn't so preoccupied by why the bridge was causing Kat such distress, she might have found the white lies slipping from her lips amusing. They were so out of character for her, but she found that they came so easily.

"Evan said that she was really distant at church the other day. He was wondering if she was regretting offering to host the wedding. Since you know her better, I thought maybe she'd tell you if we'd made her uncomfortable somehow."

"Why would you make her uncomfortable?"

"Because we're both men."

"You do realize that I'm gay, too. If you make her uncomfortable, then logically, I would, too."

Suddenly Jeremy was very intent on counting the remaining screws.

Wendy paused. "Wait, you're saying I make her uncomfortable?"

"That I never said. I'm sure I'm just being paranoid. We're stepping on a lot of heterosexual toes these days, and you know Kat. She wants everyone to be happy. Maybe she offered her home even though it makes her uncomfortable only because the church said no."

"What are you not saying?"

"Nothing." He stared at her a little too long, like what he really wanted to say was making it hard for him to think of something else to tell her. She shook the thought away. Just because Kat said she lied all the time didn't mean everyone did. "Maybe she is okay with it but her parents aren't. Maybe they pitched a fit about it, and she's in there trying to smooth it all out."

"Now you're making things up. It seems like Clyde is helping a lot. He pulled out all this stuff for your bridge and the candy cottage."

"Yes, that's true." Jeremy agreed, reaching for another board.

"What?"

"What nothing. Kat just disappeared so quickly. Like I said, it made me paranoid."

"How's it going?" All three of them startled at the sound of Kat's voice. Purse slung over her shoulder, Kat stood on the other side of the chain-link fence.

"On my last plank." Wendy caught Dave's eye. "How about you?"

"Got it!"

Kat peeked over the fence. "It looks lovely. And a bit dangerous."

"We got a lot done today, but the handrail will have to go on tomorrow. I've got to meet Evan at the florist."

"Dave and I could work on the handrail," Wendy offered.

"Unfortunately, Dave is my ride."

He snapped a few pictures on his phone before joining Dave at his truck. They both waved as they inched down the long drive in reverse.

"What a gorgeous young man."

"He is. He's with the majority of the congregation, outraged at Reverend Thorn letting his personal bias color his decision. You wouldn't believe how many people have come by the office to ask how they can support Jeremy and Evan. So in the end, Thorn's intolerance has demonstrated just how loved they are. There's some justice in that."

"That's the perfect consequence. Maybe all the love he sees in the congregation will make him reconsider."

"Or run with his tail between his legs. That would be okay with me," Kat said.

Wendy smiled. "I was going to mess around with the shelves in the cottage, but it looks like you're on your way out. I guess it can wait until another day."

Kat shook her head. "No. I was actually coming out to offer to pick up lunch for everyone."

"You don't have to do that."

"It's no bother. My mom asked for In-N-Out. It's the least I can do to pick something up for you, too. Will you still be here for a while?"

"Another half hour, I'm guessing."

Kat took her order, and Wendy returned to the cottage. She thought about the response of the congregation and how so many had stepped forward to support Jeremy and Evan. No other wedding had made her think about who would attend her own wedding ceremony, and it brought some sadness to realize that beyond her parents and Cory and José, she couldn't really picture much more of a guest list.

When she was happy that the shelving was stable, she returned to the bridge. She walked to the middle, precarious as it was without the handrails. Before she could puzzle out how they were going to be built, Kat arrived. Chagrined, she hustled off the bridge and jogged to meet Kat at her car where she accepted the take-out bags.

"Give me just a second to fish out my parents' food."

"We can sort it out in the kitchen. I need to wash my hands anyway."

Kat didn't answer right away, and Wendy noticed her eyes were puffy and red-rimmed.

"Are you okay?" Wendy asked gently.

* * *

Kat wasn't okay. Nothing about the day had been okay, including seeing Wendy standing in the middle of the pool. God, Ava would have loved it. She had adored the rope bridge that Halloween. She closed her eyes and clamped her tongue between her teeth. She would not cry again.

She took a deep breath. "I will be. I wasn't prepared for the memories this would bring back."

"Oh, were you and your husband married here?" Wendy asked, her eyes wide.

At first Kat didn't follow the question, but then she understood that Wendy was tying the weddings together, not the bridge. "We were married at the church. But we had the reception here. I'm sorry. I know it makes no sense. It's this bridge. It's the cottage. It's all these…my dad's projects. It brings back memories, and…" She swallowed. She couldn't say more.

"And there's no getting away from them."

Kat sighed gratefully. "How do you always know what I want to say?"

"I don't. Can't we tell your parents we prefer to dine with the tortoises?"

"That might work to deter my mom. The tortoises freak her out. But my dad would ask to join us."

Wendy handed the food back. "You can sort it out inside. I can scrub my hands in the pool."

If she didn't have her hands full, Kat might have hugged her for understanding. Inside, she grabbed two plates for her parents, grateful her mother had not descended yet and that her father was still outside. She left two drinks and carried the others out with the bag of burgers and fries.

"Lunch!" she called up the stairs and out the front door before escaping out back. She didn't feel like explaining that she was eating with her friend. She found Wendy already feeding grape leaves to the two desert tortoises. She dished out their meals, smiling when Wendy snatched her chocolate shake and took a long pull from it.

"You earned that today."

"And yesterday. I swear riding a horse feels like exercise even though Erin insisted that only the horse was getting a workout."

"Oh, is that why you are so stiff?" Kat blushed hard when she realized that admitting she noticed the way Wendy was walking would betray where her thoughts had been.

"Wait, you thought I was sore because I spent all weekend in bed with Erin?" Wendy said.

"I never said…"

"You didn't have to! The look on your face!" Wendy laughed. "Give me some credit. I barely know her!"

"I'm sorry." Kat tried her best to hide her embarrassment. "From her texts, it seemed like you two really hit it off."

"She's very nice, and we did have a good time."

"I'm glad it worked out. That makes me happy."

They ate in silence for a few minutes. Wendy fed the smaller tortoise some of her lettuce while she worked on her milkshake. "Not as happy as drumming that Go-Go's song."

Kat looked up to find Wendy's piercing dark eyes on her. She worried that she was going to ask her why she'd been crying.

"You didn't do 'Our Lips Are Sealed'," she noted.

"I hope you weren't disappointed. Travis liked 'Head Over Heels' better."

"I'm impressed you got teenaged boys to play The Go-Go's, at all, and you've got the perfect voice for it. You were amazing on the drums, too. Don't tell Erin, but I liked listening to the kids doing covers way more than our restaurant's fancy jazz band."

"I was so worried you hated being there!"

"Not at all! It was fun hanging out with you. A little bizarre with your ex and his girlfriend and everything, but fun."

"I hope you'd say if it wasn't because it was so much better having you there."

"As long as you promise to do the same, like if it was too hard to have Jeremy and Evan get married here."

Kat looked stricken. "What? Why?"

"Because maybe your parents have a problem with them being gay?"

"They don't think that, do they?"

"A little?"

"Wendy! That's ridiculous. My father's gay."

"What? But he's married to your mother." Wendy looked confused.

"Doesn't make him any less gay. You've met my father. You're telling me he didn't set off your gaydar? Didn't he give you the Rock Hudson spiel?"

"I thought he was…artistic."

Kat laughed. "He wanted a family, and back in his day, you got a family by marrying a woman."

"Did your mom know when she married him?"

"She knew but she didn't know. He told her he'd been in a relationship with a man, but she was nineteen. She didn't really understand. She'd been trying to catch my dad for a long time, so when he proposed, she thought that was it. She'd won."

"But somewhere along the way, he started to have boyfriends again?"

"After I was born, he began an affair that my mother didn't know about."

"And when she found out, she stayed."

"She did. I think it kind of worked for her that my dad had another person to go out with. We went to the zoo with him and his boyfriend. They took us to museums and to the beach, all sorts of places my mother wouldn't go. My mom isn't easy, either. But my dad has stayed with her."

"Your dad is gay," Wendy said like saying it out loud would help her understand.

Kat wadded up the burger wrapper. "My family is… complicated. How well my mom can cope with my dad and how much patience my dad has for my mom change day to day. So it's always been hard to have people here."

Wendy snorted. "You don't have to explain to me. I never wanted anyone to come to my house. I didn't want them to know where I lived. Didn't want them to know how little money we had or see my father who didn't ever seem to care how little we had. He used to say that all we needed was each other. Now I understand that he didn't want me to think that if I had stuff I'd be happy, but as a kid, it was really tough to be the one kid without new brand-name clothes."

"I agree with your dad. The stuff I had didn't make me happy. I had stuff, and I had them, but it was like they wanted the stuff to make up for what they couldn't be."

"Because of your dad's sexuality?"

"Partly," Kat said. How could she explain the void they were trying to fill without talking about Ava? There was nothing they could give her to replace what she'd lost. The vow her dad made that he would not date again did not replace the time he had spent with his boyfriends. Though her mother was physically present and bought her everything she wanted, she wouldn't talk about Ava. So Kat had learned not to mention Ava either. She put the past in a box that could remain closed if she spent time at her friends' houses with their normal parents, part of their normal life. Though she wanted to, she didn't know how to explain.

"I can see where that would have made it hard to bring your friends home. I can't get over how different your life is from what I'd pictured. I thought this was the perfect house. Who wouldn't have the perfect childhood living in a place like this? I even envied you for having parents who are still together…"

Kat laughed. "Before I told you about my dad?"

"Yeah."

She stuffed her trash into the bag. "You finished?"

"Yes." Wendy followed Kat out of the yard.

"Now I have to text Jeremy to tell him my parents are happy to have them get married here. This is all your fault, you know?"

"What's my fault?" Wendy face crumpled with worry.

"If I'd just lied and said I didn't think the bridge was a great idea, it wouldn't have come up."

"Sorry I'm such a bad influence."

"No. You're not. You're the best. I can't thank you enough for being here today." Before she chickened out, Kat stepped forward and wrapped her arms around Wendy. She closed her eyes and let her whole world just be that warm, safe hug.

CHAPTER TEN

Wendy tucked her phone back in her pocket and washed her hands.

"I thought you were going to lunch," Cory said.

"She couldn't get away after all."

"Hmm." He kept his eyes on the mini-quiche pastry he was rolling for the evening baby shower.

"What does that mean?"

"People have to eat," Cory responded.

"She had a lawyerly emergency."

They worked in companionable silence for a few minutes. She was mercifully busy with this last-minute event which had required an unplanned run to the local grocery store and doubling up on the usual prep work. Too busy to think about Kat and what she was doing and whether she had a Go-Go's song playing in her head. Wendy had reprogrammed her radio to an eighties station, and every song made her think of Kat.

"Are you going to see her tonight?"

Wendy almost opened her mouth to say that she hadn't talked to Kat since lunch last week. Then she realized that Cory was talking about Erin. "No. I'll be wiped out after this shower."

"I could handle the breakdown if you want to get dinner with her."

The right answer was yes. Wendy knew this, but she couldn't make herself say it. To be honest, she was relieved that Erin had flaked. Though the horseback riding had been fun, she found herself hesitant to set up another date. Erin had been trying to find a time to get together for the last week, and Wendy had been dragging her feet wondering how to say that she wasn't interested in getting together again. The phone rang, saving Wendy. Cory answered.

"Key Ingredients of Fairbanks Bistro."

She seasoned the spinach custard for the quiche, not really listening to Cory's phone conversation. She jumped when a pad of paper dropped in front of her. Wiping her hands on her apron, she read over the notes. Mr. Whitman. Unexpected death. Food for a hundred. Tomorrow. Wendy's eyebrows shot up. She pointed to the word. "Tomorrow?" she mouthed.

Cory pointed to the phone and then to Wendy. Already mapping out the hours of work added after tonight's event, she took the phone.

"Hello, this is Wendy Archer. My assistant says you'd like us to cater a funeral."

"A memorial," the speaker on the other end of the line clarified. "My brother died suddenly. We'd only just arrived for the Alternative Music Awards show. He was a record producer. The Mawling Screemies' latest album is up for the Progressive Pop Award but now…"

"I'm so sorry for your loss." She waited politely as the brother shared details about the number of family in town who would be flying out the following evening, necessitating the hastily planned memorial. "Where will you be holding the reception?" she asked. She smiled as she wrote the familiar address. She walked to her storage refrigerator and took inventory of what she had on hand. She ran through her standard luncheon menu options taking notes on Mr. Whitman's preferences for a Jamaican theme including jerk chicken sandwiches and several sides.

As she talked, Cory searched the producer's name on his phone, flashing pictures of the man with various celebrities. Each find increased his excitement to the point that Wendy had to turn around to tune him out. The financials were established and the deposit transferred electronically. When she'd ended the call, Wendy held the phone to her chest. "We're not sleeping tonight."

"As if you could. Look at this!" He flashed a photo of the deceased with The Absolites at his home in Beverly Hills. "Please tell me they're having food at his house."

"Sorry. Not this time."

"How in the freak did you get this gig?"

That reminded Wendy. Someone deserved a thank-you. She pulled up Kindred Souls on her phone and hit dial. "Is Kat Morehart available please?"

Cory smirked and crossed his arms over his chest.

Stop, Wendy mouthed as she waited to be put through. She motioned for him to take over the quiche, unable to hide the smile that lit up her face when she heard Kat's voice. "You have no idea how happy you've made my assistant."

Cory leaned toward Wendy and sang, "Thank you, thank you, thank you!"

"Why is he so happy?" Kat said, laughing.

Wendy loved that sound. "Apparently the dead guy was the man responsible for his favorite band."

"Say they'll be there! Oh my god. I could meet Bobby Desimone tomorrow." He spun in circles unable to contain himself.

"I'm glad to make someone happy."

Wendy heard ruefulness in her voice. "You make everyone happy."

Kat huffed into the phone. "Right."

"We're all excited about this job, and it's completely ruined your day?"

"Something like that. I'm sorry. I don't mean to take it out on you. I lined up help to load Jeremy and Evan's chairs and tables today, but with the memorial tomorrow, I had to put it off. Why didn't I tell them to rent tables and chairs? It would have been so much easier."

"I can help," Wendy said.

"What? No."

"They have to be put away after the memorial anyway. I'll help you load them up."

"You don't have to do that. After feeding all those people tomorrow, I'm sure you'll be wiped out."

Wendy could hear her typing as they talked. "Okay. I get it."

"Get what?" The typing stopped.

"You want all the glory. You want to be the one who works all day and then goes the extra mile. You want to be the white knight everyone counts on to save the day."

"That's ridiculous."

"Okay, then you're the only kid. Growing up, all the work fell to you and there was no one else for you to say, 'make her do it!' so you don't even realize you're pulling way more than your weight."

"No. That's not how I grew up."

There was something serious in Kat's voice that Wendy had never heard before, and it made Wendy hot with discomfort. She was trying to tease Kat into letting her help, but it had backfired. She searched for how to fix it. "There's only one other explanation."

"What's that?"

Her voice was tight, and Wendy wished they were talking in person. "That I smell bad." Finally Kat laughed again, so Wendy continued. "You've been looking for a way to break it to me, but you don't know how to, so you insist that you can take care of it on your own. I'll shower. I promise."

"You do not smell bad."

"Great! So we have a plan."

"We do?"

"I feed a bunch of famous people at the church, and then we take the tables and chairs to your place."

"You said you were helping me load them. You don't have to follow me home. I'm sure you have better places to be. I wouldn't want to stop you from hopping over to Hidden Hills to see Erin."

"We don't have any plans this week. I was swamped even before Mr. Famous died."

"Oh, I thought…" Wendy waited for her to finish her sentence, but she didn't. Instead, she said, "I'm swamped too," in a tone clearly meant to wrap up the conversation.

Wendy wasn't going to let her off easily, though, and said, "Exactly why you should accept my offer." She thought she was speaking softly, but Cory looked up. Why was he looking at her like that? She furrowed her brow at him, and he raised his and lifted his hands as if incredulous that she didn't see what he did. Wendy frowned and turned her back to him.

"Why are you so nice to me?"

"Because you deserve some niceness."

"You're so stubborn. If I didn't have so much work to do for this memorial, I'd convince you I don't deserve any kindnesses."

"I've got my own work to do, so thank you for giving up."

"I didn't say I was giving up."

"Thank you anyway. Especially for the referral. It means a lot. Especially to Cory."

"Always glad to help."

Wendy punched the phone to end the call and pressed it against her chest for a moment.

Cory popped a sheet of quiche in the oven and cleared his throat.

"What's that for?

"What about the perishables?"

Wendy frowned. She hadn't given thought to how she usually took home and sorted out what was left over after events. "You can take them home. The dishes can wait. I'll bring those."

"You'll be too wiped out to go out to dinner tonight, but you'll take on all that grunt work tomorrow?"

"I'm not up for a date. Helping with chairs and tables is hardly a date."

"If you say so."

"I don't date straight ladies."

"I've said it before, and I'll say it again: Kat's into you."

"Well you can stop saying that. She told me herself that she's straight."

"Wait, you asked her? How could you not tell me that?"

Wendy hadn't wanted to share that Erin had pursued Kat. Too many layers of weird. There was so much history between Kat and Erin, between Kat and all the people she'd met at the bar. She would rather not have divulged it all to Cory, but she'd forced her own hand. "I didn't ask her. Erin did. There was no spark."

"Just like you!" Cory said

"I'm attracted to Erin."

"Sure you are." Cory's voice dripped with sarcasm.

"Just because I'm not up for a date tonight doesn't mean I'm not attracted to her!"

"Okay!" Cory drew the word out in a sing-song manner. He pulled open the oven to check the quiche. He exchanged the cooked ones with another sheet.

"What's that supposed to mean?"

"My offer to break down tonight still stands. That's all."

Wendy ignored him and went to the walk-in refrigerator. Cory could finish the quiche, and she could slice pears and wash the spinach. She grabbed some butter. She'd get started on the candied walnuts as well.

None of this took her mind off Cory's suggestion that Kat was simply not attracted to Erin. Hadn't she thought the same thing when she was riding with her, wondering whether Kat had not liked kissing Erin because she was a woman or simply because she was Erin? Wendy shushed her inner monologue, telling herself that there was no purpose in thinking about Kat kissing women.

* * *

Kat tucked her phone back into her purse. She should have been texting Jeremy to let him know that the chair issue had been resolved, but she just sat, thinking about how easily Wendy had offered her help yet again. She was ashamed that when Richard Whitman's brother had called the church to arrange the memorial, she was happy to have a reason to call Wendy. Since Jeremy installed the bridge the week before, she had been pretending her days were what they normally were when they were anything but.

Somehow having this wedding at her childhood home had trip wired so many emotions, dredging up memories that she had boxed away long ago. Being married to Jack had given her years of training in the art of focusing on the present. She was a wife. She was a mother. That was enough, and for years she had been able to fool almost everyone. With her past flooding into her present, she waited for her volunteers to ask if she was okay. She waited for the priest to rest his hand on her shoulder and notice how tired she looked. She'd been doing the bare minimum work-wise, and so far no one had noticed.

Yet Wendy had known. After she'd said her father was gay, there was something in the way that Wendy had hugged her that suggested things would be okay. Kat tried to remember the last time that someone had held her like that, as if their arms alone could make things better. Had Jack ever held her that way? Her parents might have, once, before she pushed them away.

Miranda had hugged like that. Not when Kat had first joined cheer. All the girls hugged generously and with ease, and Kat had been full of self-doubt, judging herself for being shorter and less fit than the others. She had kept those memories at bay for so long that it took some time to tease out when Miranda's hugs had become different. At first she thought that it was her own insecurities playing tricks on her because Miranda was the prettiest cheerleader: tall, athletic and graceful. Everyone she knew, male or female, sighed when she drove up, her honey-brown hair windblown from driving her convertible Karmann Ghia with the top down.

First, she felt Miranda watching her. Then she noticed that Miranda's hugs had changed. They were tighter but less frequent. Kat noticed immediately and asked what she had done wrong, sure that Miranda considered her an impostor. They met away from school, away from practice, where Miranda could finally explain that she didn't want to upset Kat, explaining her attraction as if Kat had never heard of the same gender desiring another.

It was when she had hugged Miranda that things had shifted. She had meant to reassure Miranda that her feelings were not wrong. She had not expected her body to react.

And now Wendy's reassuring hug had had a similar effect.

She would see Wendy tomorrow at the funeral. If they embraced again, Kat honestly thought she might dissolve in her arms. It made her believe she could tell Wendy everything, even things she'd never told Miranda.

She drove home in silence that evening, memories wandering freely in her mind. She climbed the stairs stealthily and instead of turning right and heading to her room, she turned left. Her mother lay in her bed in the larger of the two south-facing rooms. Warm hues from the sunset spilled into her parents' room. Though there was at least an hour of light left, her mother was fast asleep.

Ava's room was darker at this time of day, having windows on the south and east walls. She crept in and perched on the edge of a straight-backed cane chair. Her parents had not kept a shrine. They added more comfortable chairs in the room and kept only a few of Ava's things. A picture she loved of a girl having tea with her stuffed monkey. The multicolored herd of wild ponies behind the glass of the secretary their father had crafted for her. Her mother's trinkets.

Kat shut her eyes and tried to imagine what her life would be like now with Ava. She took a shuddering breath and felt tears slip from her eyes. The pain of not having her sister with her broke through the foggy barrier she had erected long ago. Kat shut her eyes and let the tears come again.

She looked to the east-facing window and saw the prism her sister had hung in her now dark window. Ava had always made her own rainbows. Maybe it was time for Kat to make some of her own.

CHAPTER ELEVEN

Kat could not move. She was on her way back to the office to print the programs for the memorial service when out of the corner of her eye, she caught sight of Wendy wheeling a contraption that held trays of food. She had on her signature crisp white chef's coat that buttoned to one side, tailored black slacks and black clogs. Here, they were two professional women, yet Kat's body reacted as if she was about to meet Wendy in private.

"Kat!"

She tore her eyes away from Wendy to find Verna waving her toward the office. Reluctantly, she followed. Kat hadn't planned on telling Wendy about her father and was tempted to cross the patio to make sure that she wouldn't talk about it with anyone, but she waved instead. She felt certain Wendy wouldn't betray her confidence. She glanced back and found Wendy's dark eyes on her. She smiled shyly and the smile Wendy returned was just as cautious, as if she, too, felt like something had changed between them.

* * *

This was no time for Wendy to be distracted. She was already behind schedule. Wendy pushed Kat from her thoughts and reached into the warm oven to squeeze a French loaf to see if it was soft enough to cut and assemble into sandwiches.

Cory was preparing large bowls of fruit which they would set out first with the platters of sugarcane shrimp kabobs.

"We've got time. You could go talk to her," he said.

"That might have been an option if I'd pulled the bread out of the freezer last night like I was supposed to."

"How are they now?"

"Almost there. But I'm worried about drying them out." Twenty minutes before the service ended. Crunch time. She needed the sandwiches to come together. Out of the corner of her eye, she saw Cory set the fruit bowls aside and start pulling marinating trays of skewered shrimp and pineapple out of the cooler and lining the kabobs on trays to go in the oven.

Taking the bread out and cranking up the oven temperature for Cory, she grumbled to herself. She should have been finished with the sandwiches now, not just about to start. She swore under her breath. "I need another pair of hands."

"Should I call the main kitchen and have them send someone over?"

"By the time they get here, we'll be serving. We can do this. We have to do this." The catering was her responsibility. José had enough to worry about on his end of things than to have to spare one of his prep staff to bail her out. She said a little prayer for a long-winded eulogy.

"I see people on the patio," Cory said fifteen minutes later as he finished arranging a tray of sweet potato cakes with tartar sauce and garnishing them with scallions.

"You're shitting me." Wendy glanced up and confirmed what Cory saw. People were congregating on the patio, already eying the buffet tables.

"Get the fruit out there. Anything that's ready to go, move it."

Ready or not, she grumbled to herself, grabbing the tray of loaves off the stovetop. "Shit, shit, shit," she swore. The metal was much hotter than she'd anticipated.

"Fire is hot," an unexpected voice said.

Wendy flapped her fingers and grabbed a cold bottle of water. "Oh, no! Are they already complaining?"

"I haven't heard anything. You have everything under control in here?" Kat asked.

Wendy grabbed a loaf and sawed through it. She thumbed the middle. It had just enough give. She pulled a few more. "I've got it."

She felt Kat hovering. "Cory said something about wishing you had another set of hands."

Wendy growled. Here she'd thought Kat was only stopping in. She couldn't believe Cory would ask her to help. No, that wasn't true. It was exactly the kind of thing he'd do. "I'm sure you've got a hundred things to do."

"I've got a few minutes. And I happen to have a set of hands."

Kat was smiling more brightly than she had earlier. "How are you with a sharp knife?"

"I can be careful." Without having to be asked, Kat washed her hands in the sink before joining Wendy at the counter. Her fingers brushed against Wendy's when she took the knife. "I love it when sandwich bread is warm."

So Cory hadn't mentioned why they needed an extra set of hands. Maybe she wouldn't chew him out. She spread her jerk chicken mixture on the sliced loaf followed by the mango salsa. She caught Kat watching her. "Hungry?"

"That smells really spicy."

"It's spicy flavorful. It has a lot of different flavors, but it's not hot. Once I get the spinach on, we'll cut the individual sandwiches. We need at least twelve per loaf. Where is my spinach!" She checked the fridge for her tub of washed spinach. "Dammit. Where did Cory go?"

"Oh my god, oh my god!" Cory came running in straightening his tie. "All of The Absolites are here. I have to get a picture. Is my hair okay?"

"With all that gel? It's not going anywhere. But you will not go all paparazzi on them. I need you in here. Where's my spinach?"

"The spinach salad is already out. I threw the caramelized walnuts and raspberry vinaigrette on and tossed it."

"No, no, no!"

"What?"

"Some of the spinach was for the jerk chicken sandwiches!"

"Oops?" Cory said with nervous look on his face.

"And you dressed it all?"

"I was being helpful?"

Wendy scrambled around the kitchen trying to scare up something green. "The cucumbers! Go grab the veggie plate. I'm going to have to repurpose the cukes."

He turned to leave, his phone in his hand.

"No pictures! We have to fix this first!"

Cory looked longingly at his phone. "I can be discreet. Promise. They won't even know I'm there!"

"Cucumbers!"

"Got it." He pocketed the phone.

"I don't understand why they are already out of the service! I was supposed to have more time!"

"Maybe he wasn't that nice," Kat said. "If nobody has anything nice to say, everything wraps up quite quickly. From what I've heard, his heirs are more interested in his estate than remembering him."

"That's sad." Wendy paused in her sandwich prep to take the kabobs out of the oven.

"Pretty typical for families, isn't it?"

"I guess when there are siblings. Makes me glad to be an only. You're an only too, aren't you?"

* * *

Kat's ears were ringing, and the bread shook in her hand. So did the knife. Glad it was the last loaf on the tray, she carefully sliced it and handed both roll and knife to Wendy.

"Are you okay?" Wendy asked. She placed a hand on Kat's shoulder.

"Fine," Kat said. This wasn't the time, was it? She could distract herself. "Do you need any help with those skewers?"

"If you really don't mind, you could arrange them circling the edge of this tray working your way toward the inside. Then squeeze some fresh lime juice on them and a sprinkle of chopped parsley that should be in the fridge unless Cory swiped that, too."

Assembling more long sandwiches, Wendy went back to the topic. "Not that either of my parents is likely to leave me anything. They have no property. I always wished I'd grown up with more, a big house, more money, but it taught me about work ethic, you know?"

"That's something to be proud of. You take your work seriously. Not everyone does. Cory seems more interested in fame than the spinach."

"Speaking of that. It looks like I'm going to have to grab the cucumber myself. Be right back."

Kat had finished arranging the skewers and found the parsley garnish. Wendy swooped back in with the tray of vegetables. "Barely enough for the sandwiches! I feel like I'm improvising in the backcountry here!" She finely diced the cucumbers and completed the sandwiches.

"Backcountry?" Kat prompted to keep Wendy on the blessedly light topic.

"I was a camp cook near Yosemite one summer. There was this time I nearly screwed up a breakfast forgetting I needed my eggs for French toast. It's freezing in the morning before the sun comes up, so I always hated working with the eggs. The last of my five mornings cooking, I had to break a dozen eggs, and my hands were numb with the cold. I threw in the green pepper and was just about to shake in the garlic salt for my scrambled eggs when I realized my mistake."

"Oh, no! You didn't have other eggs?"

"Nope. I had to fish out all the green pepper. Thought I'd get frostbite that morning. I should be thankful this is an easier fix." Wendy had ten long sandwiches assembled with the cucumber, ready to be cut. "But my assistant should be in here to take these as I get them sliced and plated. Where is he!"

"I'll take them," Kat offered.

"I appreciate your help." Wendy expertly carved a dozen sandwiches out of each loaf and arranged them on the next tray.

"It looks like the band is thrilled to have a fan. They're all posing with Cory."

Wendy didn't look pleased. "I apologize for his lack of respect."

"You don't have to apologize to me."

"I'll save it for the dead guy."

"It's not like he's here."

"He's not? Doesn't a person have to be present for their funeral?"

"It's a memorial. You don't need a body."

Kat had delivered the last tray of sandwiches. Though she watched Wendy's precise movements appreciatively, her thoughts were far away listening to her parents argue about whether a funeral for a ten-year-old was appropriate, her mother insisting that people needed to see Ava to say goodbye, her father's certainty that it would be too disturbing.

In the end, they had compromised on a closed casket. Kat had wanted to see inside. But she hadn't wanted to, either. At the time, she'd stood in the church thinking maybe her sister wasn't in the small white box at all. Of course whether she was or wasn't didn't really matter. It didn't change the fact that Kat could not hold her hand or sing songs with her anymore. Not looking at her in the casket did, as her father had argued, force her to remember her sister's face alive.

Smiling.

That grin as she jumped from the diving board.

The memories threatened to crush her. Wendy looked up from the cookies she was arranging. "You okay?"

"Of course. I'm sorry. It's just that I have to make sure all the payments are squared away before the priest and organist get antsy." Without waiting for Wendy's reply, she slipped out of the kitchen and back to the safety of her office.

* * *

Wendy let the lie go. Something had upset Kat, but it wasn't like she could stop the production line and take her aside to insist she talk. Unfortunately, talking would have to wait.

Cory didn't leave until the church's kitchen was spotless. He had worked his tail off as a way to apologize for the spinach debacle. He was always a good worker, but that day, he outdid himself keeping the trays replenished, the dishes bussed and the workspace clear. It didn't hurt that he kept recognizing famous faces in the crowd. The pictures on his phone and his excited monologue kept her distracted for a good while. As their cleanup came to an end, Wendy grew more anxious and sent Cory on his way to help back at Fairbanks and the evening meal.

She grabbed a duffel with her casual clothes. Slipping into soft jeans and a long-sleeved tee, she felt eminently more comfortable and ready to help load the chairs and tables. She still had a couple hours' work dealing with the leftover food and dirty dishes piled in the bus tubs, but all that could wait until she'd had a chance to help Kat and maybe find out why she had left so abruptly.

She found Kat in her office behind her desk. Her gaze was wandering aimlessly.

"Your extra set of hands is here!"

Kat's head snapped up, and she covered her heart with her hand. "You scared me! Chair time?" She stood a little unsteadily.

"Are you sure you want to do this now? You seem a bit…"

"I'm fine! Just running through the to-do list to make sure I didn't miss anything important."

"You keep your to-do list in your head? I'd be sunk if I didn't put reminders in my phone."

Kat gathered her things. "I'll just pull my beast around, so we don't have to carry everything so far."

They headed outside to the patio. Wendy began to pull chairs back from the tables and lean them against each other. Without a word, Kat took them, two in each hand, to feed into the SUV. She remained all business as they passed each other, each time making Wendy feel more awkward. Unlike in the kitchen where they'd at least been able to have a conversation, the air felt charged.

"You really don't have to follow me over," Kat said when they had finished loading and locked up for the night. They stood in the yellow lamplight in the parking lot, tendrils of hair that had come loose from Kat's French braid shimmering in the gentle spring breeze. She combed the wisps with her fingers in an attempt to tame them, but they immediately fell loose again softening her profile.

Wendy was sorely tempted to twine one of the strands around her finger. "What if I said I'd like to have another look at the lights to make sure they look okay?"

"I'd call you a liar." The edges of Kat's lips tipped into a smile.

Wendy refrained from asking why Kat had really left the kitchen earlier.

"What are you thinking?" Kat asked softly.

"That I'd like to know if you really had to rush back to work. I was having fun talking to you, and all of a sudden you left."

Kat's gaze shifted inward, and a dozen emotions flitted across her face. "The best lies have some truth to them. I did have work to do."

"But something upset you. I've been spinning it around in my head trying to figure out what I said. First it seemed like we were having fun joking around about whether you need a body for a funeral, but then it was like you remembered something sad."

Kat's eyes glistened as if she were fighting tears. "I did," she paused. "I…I was thinking about my sister" Though she must have seen the surprise on Wendy's face, she placed a hand on her shoulder to silence the question poised on her lips. "Follow me?"

Wendy nodded. Anywhere, she thought. She jogged to her car for the longest twenty-minute drive of her life.

CHAPTER TWELVE

So much adrenaline pumped through Kat after she said *my sister* that her hands tingled on the steering wheel. The words meant no going back. Where did she start? How much was she prepared to say?

Twenty minutes was nowhere near long enough to work it out, but it wasn't like she could continue driving. She parked the SUV on the street and was glad to see Wendy follow suit.

"I want to put all this in the garage. I just need to grab my dad's keys to move his pickup. It's parked in there." They walked side by side up the drive, and Kat could see her mother sitting at the kitchen table. At the patio, she hesitated. She should invite Wendy inside, but her life would be so much easier if she checked on her mom and Travis alone.

"Take your time. I'll say hi to the tortoises." Wendy walked to the grapevines to pluck a few leaves, smiling and waving when she caught Kat watching her. Kat couldn't look away. Wendy behaved like she had always been a part of Kat's life, like she belonged.

Kat climbed the steps and let herself in the back door, praying that she could slip in and out quickly. The kitchen smelled of pizza, and she saw a takeout box on the range.

"Is that Wendy?" Her mom looked up from her phone, a plate scattered with crumbs in front of her.

"It is. She's helping me with the tables and chairs. I have to move Dad's truck to put them in the garage. Is that okay?"

Her mother lifted her hand and waved her off as if she were a fly buzzing around her head and then continued to scroll on her phone. Thankful her mother was not waiting to engage her in conversation, she hollered down the stairs. "Hey Travis! Come help your mom with some driving?"

He thundered up the stairs in response.

"Shoes?"

"Why?"

She'd given up trying to get him to wear anything other than shorts and tee-shirts but not shoes. "Because it's the law?"

"I don't think it is."

Millie inserted, "Why don't you get your license and find out?"

"And have to drive everywhere?" Travis rolled his eyes. "You just need it on the street, right?"

"There are palm-tree pits all over the front yard."

He ended the discussion with a shrug and extended his hand for the keys. After maneuvering the SUV around for easy unloading, Kat was surprised by Travis joining her at the garage.

"What's all this?" he said.

"Tables and chairs for the wedding."

"Need some help?" he asked.

"I've brought some, but thanks." He turned to look down the drive and then back to Kat, his eyebrows high on his forehead in question. "Wendy's feeding the tortoises."

"Oh! Cool. Are you two going out?"

Had she heard him correctly? She had been meaning to talk to him about the conversation her parents had started when Wendy brought dinner. Before she could respond, she saw Wendy locking the gate to the tortoise yard.

"For dinner," Travis continued. "Gramma and I already had pizza."

"I didn't know she'd fed you. Sorry I didn't call to say I had all this stuff to load after work."

"That's okay. You sure you don't need a hand?"

"You're turning away help?" Wendy asked, a wide smile on her face. "Hi again."

"Hey." Travis dug his hands into his pockets and flipped his hair back with a jerk of his head.

"You'll really help?" Kat asked. She rolled her eyes in response to his unenthusiastic shoulder shrug. "All right then, thank you! Let's get it over with."

They formed a chain with Travis pulling the chairs and tables from the car and handing them to Kat who passed them to Wendy to stack. Though Kat stood between them, Wendy and Travis chatted as they worked. Wendy complimented Travis on his performance and peppered him with questions, and Travis surprised her by telling Wendy how much he had enjoyed the dinner she had prepared for them.

"Too bad we didn't know you were coming tonight or we wouldn't have ordered pizza!" he said.

"Travis!" Kat exclaimed. "Wendy's been cooking all day. I'm sure the last thing she wants to do is make dinner."

"Stop," Wendy said. "He's fine. I'd be happy to cook for your family again."

"Gramma said we should hire you to cook for us."

"You make it sound like we never cook for ourselves."

"I don't think nuking beans and cheese in a tortilla is really cooking, Mom."

Kat closed her eyes to escape her embarrassment but opened them when she heard Wendy's laughter. "I'm always happy to cook for friends." Wendy caught her eye, and her expression held so much familiarity that Kat's stomach fluttered. Ever since the memorial, she had been flustered and anxious. Throughout the drive, her mind was a jumbled mess of emotions and memories that she had struggled unsuccessfully to sort out. Standing in the garage with Wendy and Travis, she felt it all settle, and she knew that whatever she ended up saying tonight, Wendy would hear her and understand.

* * *

They sat on a bench swing by the driveway, eating cold pizza and drinking wine.

"I feel embarrassed to serve you delivery pizza."

"Don't be," Wendy said.

"Of course, Travis says this is several steps up from my culinary skills."

"Delivery pizza takes me back to high school." Wendy set down her pizza and took Kat's hand. "It would be easy to slip into a fantasy about being at your party. I'd be sitting over here because, of course, I wouldn't know anyone, and then you'd come over to tell me not to stay on the sidelines."

"I never threw any parties."

"You're going to ruin my fantasy just like that?" Wendy snapped her fingers. She'd been aiming to lighten the mood, and it surprised her that Kat didn't respond. "I thought you were the party girl."

Kat set down her plate and picked up her wine. She didn't look at Wendy when she said, "Oh, I was definitely a party girl. I went to other people's parties because it helped me build a life away from home. I had cheer practice. Away from here, I could be the fun one. I could be the life of the party, not the child whose mother couldn't get out of bed, whose father spent his life at church. If I brought people here, I would have had to explain about my sister, and usually I do anything I can to avoid talking about it." Kat took several gulps of wine. "I don't even know where to start."

"How about with her name?" Wendy offered, setting her pizza aside.

"Ava," Kat said, finally looking Wendy in the eye. "Her name was Ava. She's the daughter who helped my dad build the stone cottage. He would tell her what kind of stone he needed, and she would bring ones she thought would work. She's the one who would have been happy to scamper up ladders and onto the roof to hang lights." She poured more wine and offered the bottle to Wendy.

She declined. Kat said her name *was* Ava and she had become upset at the memorial. "What happened?"

"She died," Kat said simply. Kat studied the wine in her glass, tipping it one way and then another before taking another deep sip.

"Oh Kat," Wendy whispered. She didn't know what to say. Kat nodded. Having known about Kat's divorce, Wendy understood how weddings were hard. What Kat just told her put a whole new perspective on the memorial. Remembering some of the things she'd said, she cringed. "I'm so sorry I assumed you were an only child when we were talking about inheritance."

"It's okay," Kat said. "You didn't know about Ava, and it's hard to know what to say. I don't know how much to tell you. I don't have a lot of experience with the whole honesty thing."

"Tell me as much or as little as you want." Wendy squeezed Kat's hand.

"I had a sister for ten years. I'd just turned thirteen. She was ten. There was an accident in the pool. That's what Jack and Travis know."

"Here? In this pool?"

Kat's frowned hard and her chin quivered as she struggled not to cry.

"I'm sorry. You don't have to answer that."

"No. It's just that Jack never asked. He knew she was doing flips into the pool. She hit her head." Her hazel eyes flitted to Wendy's. "It wasn't this pool. And I never told him we were at my dad's boyfriend's house."

Painful images of Kat and her father by a pool trying to save her sister flashed though Wendy's mind. Had her sister died in the pool or at the hospital? Who had called for help? How long had it taken for them to arrive? She saw how tightly Kat gripped her wine glass and held her questions. She was obviously wrestling with far more, and Wendy did not want to intrude.

"He didn't know my dad had boyfriends," Kat said. "He didn't know a lot of things."

Wendy gently rocked the swing. She had told Kat to share as much or as little as she wanted and she was content to sit without talking if that was what Kat needed.

* * *

Kat waited for Wendy to say something. Secrets were lined up behind dams, and the smallest crack would release a flood. Jack hadn't known she had been alone in the pool with Ava. Hadn't known that her father had never dated after Ava died. Didn't know why her mother wore only long-sleeved shirts, even in the hottest summer months. He had never to Kat's knowledge even noticed that Miranda had slipped out of her life after their wedding day. She worried that if one dam broke, it would trigger the others and there would be no end to what she ended up saying.

Instead, they rocked on the swing. The swaying helped to calm Kat, and eventually, she leaned her head on Wendy's shoulder. That felt so good, she pulled her feet up beside her on the bench, leaning fully against Wendy. "Is this okay?"

"It doesn't look at all comfortable," Wendy said. "Let me move my arm." She shifted her body and lifted her arm. Kat leaned again, this time nestling her head against Wendy's chest.

"Better?"

"Yes, better," Kat said. "I am thinking of what I can say. You must have a lot of questions."

"Don't worry about me. I'm happy listening to the music and thinking about how everybody is talking about us."

Kat laughed at Wendy's continued fantasy of attending a party at her house. She watched Wendy catch the cement with her toes and push off just firmly enough to keep the gentle back and forth of the swing. "They think we're a thing, don't they?"

"After I took a girl to prom? Of course they're thinking you're gay, or that I'm trying to recruit you. I'm kind of surprised you'd risk the rumors."

"Back then, I wouldn't have."

"But you'll risk it now?"

"Absolutely. And if I could put us in one of those seventeen-again movies, I'd swing with you in front of all the cheerleaders because I would have gained the wisdom to know that I was just using them to avoid the hard stuff in my life."

"When did you figure that out?"

"About two minutes ago." Kat reached across her body and put her hand over Wendy's, pressing it closer. It felt nice to be held. She couldn't remember when she'd felt as content as she did in that moment. "You would have liked Ava."

"Tell me what she was like."

"She was always completely herself," Kat said. She closed her eyes to see her sister better. "She looked like a little Laura Ingalls with two long brown braids hanging over her shoulders. She didn't care that they were never in style. They kept her hair out of her face, and that's all that mattered."

"You wore your hair that way when we hung the lights."

"I've been thinking about her a lot these days. The cottage was her space. I haven't been back there in years. She was always the one pulling me away from the books I loved to read telling me I couldn't stay inside all day like our mom."

"Was your mom staying in because of the boyfriend?"

"It's hard to say which one caused the other. Did my dad have boyfriends because my mom couldn't cope, or did my mom have trouble coping because my dad had boyfriends? All I know is that the three of us often spent the weekend with my dad's boyfriend to give my mom space." The night Ava died slammed down on Kat, and she refused to spiral into that memory. She bit down hard on the tip of her thumb to redirect her thoughts back to the present. "Her smile was a lot like my dad's. Her eyetooth was just starting to twist like his. They said she was going to need braces. I miss her smile."

"What made her smile?" Wendy asked.

"Being outside. Climbing." She stopped when she heard Wendy's phone chime in her pocket. When she didn't reach for it, Kat continued, "My parents used to walk us to a park about a half-mile away. The rocks have caves and are perfect for climbing. She never stopped. I'd climb one and wait for the trains to come by. She never sat still. If my parents wouldn't walk to the park, she'd run around the house. Literally. I'd be sitting inside reading, and she'd do laps around the house. Or she'd swing. She used to stand on that swing in the back and pump so high it looked like she'd go all the way around. She loved camping. She would have loved that backcountry cooking job you told me about. Right before the accident, we went camping at Big Sur. I remember how cold the water was, but she didn't care. There's a picture of her standing right in the middle of the freezing river skipping stones."

"She sounds like a lot of fun."

"She was." Wendy's arm tightened around Kat, and she felt contentment settle over her. Wendy made her feel like she could say anything, but what would she think if she knew what that night had done to Kat? From the bench swing, she could see Ava's window. Remembering how adventurous she'd been, Kat had an image of her little sister crawling out her window and down off the balcony. She would not have let their parents' bedroom stand between her and what she wanted. "I bet you would have liked her better."

"There you go inventing competitions that are impossible to score fairly." Wendy's phone chimed again, and this time she reached to pull it from her pocket. "Sorry about this. I didn't expect to be away from the kitchen so long, so I should make sure nobody needs me."

Kat swung her feet down and sat up to give Wendy room to read her phone.

"That's weird. Erin says she's at my restaurant. Why would she be there?"

"Did you have plans tonight?"

"No. We were supposed to do lunch yesterday, but it didn't work out, but she said she was in the neighborhood."

"You should go." Kat stood, self-conscious about how long she had kept Wendy.

Wendy read the message again and looked at Kat. "I don't have to."

Kat wanted to ask her to stay, but she couldn't justify keeping Wendy from seeing Erin, not when she had introduced them. "Sounds like she wants to make up for cancelling on you yesterday. Go. Thank you so much for your help." She bent to pick up the plates and wineglasses hoping to hide her disappointment. "I sound like a broken record saying that!"

Wendy squeezed Kat's shoulder and placed a light kiss on her cheek. "Thank you for telling me about Ava. I guess I'll see you here for the rehearsal tomorrow?

"Yes! I'm sure I'll see you." With difficulty, Kat turned and walked to the front door. As she climbed the steps, she raised her wrist to touch her cheek where Wendy had kissed her. It was such a simple gesture, yet it felt deeply significant.

* * *

Wendy started to text Erin as she walked down the drive but quickly decided it was too complicated. She hit the phone icon instead and waited to see if Erin would answer.

"You're alive!" Erin said. Wendy recognized the noise of Fairbanks in the background.

"I am. I'm sorry I missed your first text."

"Don't worry about it! I took a gamble hoping you'd be back."

"It'll only take me about twenty minutes to make it there from Kat's."

"You're at Kat's?"

Wendy noted the surprise in her voice. "Kat needed some help with the chairs and tables for the wedding that's happening at her house."

"What wedding?"

"Long story."

"Maybe you'll share when you get back?"

Wendy rolled her neck feeling the pops release the pressure of the day. "Unfortunately I'll still have some breakdown when I get back to the restaurant."

"Luckily, I'm not on the clock. Maybe I'll be able to convince the management to let me stick around past closing."

"I suppose I could give you an exciting peek behind the curtain of catering."

"Ooh! I'd love to see the chef in action."

The timbre of her voice suggested she was interested in seeing more than Wendy in cleanup mode. The last thing Wendy expected to feel at such a tone was reluctance, yet after building sandwiches with Kat, it felt oddly like betrayal to turn around and invite Erin to see her work. "I'll be there in about twenty," she said, seeing no way around it.

"I look forward to it!"

Wendy buckled up and turned over her engine. She looked past the hedge at Kat's house. The porch was illuminated, and she could see light from the kitchen beyond the oval glass door, but she could not see Kat. Had she expected her to be standing on the porch? Without knowing why and before she turned back to the road, she looked up. There in the smaller of the second-story windows, Wendy could see Kat standing with her arms wrapped around herself looking out at the bench swing.

Wendy was exhausted just thinking of the chit-chat she would have to sustain with Erin. She would have jumped at the chance to extend her conversation with Kat.

CHAPTER THIRTEEN

Kat could feel her mother thinking. Her eyes were on her phone, and she hadn't said anything, but Kat could feel the question coming as she dried and stacked the china and crystal her father had washed for the rehearsal dinner.

"You and Wendy talked a long time last night."

Kat hmmed noncommittally.

"You're spending a lot of time with her lately."

"She's been a huge help with the wedding. Thanks for letting them have the rehearsal here."

"That's your father's doing. He was fawning over the good serving dishes I offered for the couple's favors. It's been so long since we've used them."

Kat turned away from her mother. Her parents had often entertained, but since Ava's death a thick layer of dust had covered all the china and crystal. Now it shone on the counter, ready for tonight's dinner. Through the window above the sink, she saw Wendy pull up all the way in the driveway.

"Wendy's here. I'm going to help her unload." She tossed the rag on the corner, her lips tight with frustration at her mother who was still staring out at Wendy. Why couldn't she go upstairs and hide in her room as she usually did?

"What's up with the Jeremy and Evan?" Wendy asked, hugging Kat hello.

"What do you mean?"

"They look like they're facing off on the porch."

"That's where they're running through the ceremony."

"I hope they look happier when the guests are here!"

Kat took a box from Wendy to carry to the kitchen. "Do you think I should check on them?"

"You could offer them dueling pistols. Your dad seems like the kind of guy who would have a nice set in a velvet-lined box."

"You're terrible." Kat motioned Wendy into the kitchen in front of her and pushed the door closed with her foot. "Do you need more help?"

"Cory is here. He's got to earn his keep. You can go check on them."

"Okay. Let me know if you need anything."

"I'm sure your mom can help me if I figure out I've forgotten anything. Hi, Millie."

Kat's mother grinned without showing her teeth and returned her attention to her phone. Her outfit, black cotton pants and a long-sleeved purple shirt were identical to what she'd worn the day Wendy met her.

Wendy's eyebrows asked what was up, and Kat shook her head. From behind her mother, she imitated shaking her, bringing a smile to Wendy's face. Kat carried a similar smile out to the porch. "How's everything out here?" she asked.

"We'll ask Kat. She's seen a gazillion weddings," Jeremy said. Kat could hear the challenge in his voice.

"Ask me what?"

"Does the couple walk in separately or together?"

Kat frowned. "It depends. In the traditional wedding, the groom waits at the altar because the bride's entrance is a big deal. Are you guys going to see each other decked out in your tuxes before you meet here?"

"That's the thing," Jeremy said. "We're both down here anyway. If we've already seen each other, we might as well walk in hand in hand. It's not like either of us has someone giving us away."

"I pictured us walking in separately," Evan said. His voice was tight with emotion. "I want to be able to see Jeremy's eyes when I walk in."

"So I'm the groom and you're the bride?"

"I didn't say that. I don't need to walk down the aisle through our guests."

Jeremy smirked at Evan. "Are you sure?"

"We walk in from either side and then walk out together." Evan pointed down the sidewalk that separated the chairs.

"And then where do we go? Out to the street? Grab a bottle of champagne from the car? We should both walk in from the side of the porch with the aviary and then we walk out right here toward the swing. People come shake our hands and go down the drive to the party."

"That would work," Kat said.

"That doesn't feel momentous enough. We'll be married, and we just step off to the side?"

Jeremy tossed up his arms. "I thought you didn't want to come in from the street!"

"I need to see it! I need to see what it's going to look like. Kat, can you help us?"

"Sure."

Evan settled himself in one of the seats. He waved at them to proceed. Reverend Munson stepped forward, regal in her stature. Wearing a cream-colored blazer that resembled the robes she wore on Sundays, she brought the formality of the church with her. She removed her reading glasses from their perch on her curled silver hair, settled them on her thin nose, glanced above the rim and smiled kindly. "Ready?" Regardless of the space, her reedy voice was always set high to project far.

Jeremy nodded.

The priest said, "I'll pronounce you husbands, invite you to kiss, and then your music will start, and you'll proceed out. I'll follow."

"Okay," Kat said, reaching for Jeremy's hands. She was worried her smile looked more like a grimace.

"No! I can't watch! You can't practice with Jeremy. Is Wendy here? Could she stand in, too? Then we can both see."

With relief, Kat poked her head in the door. "Wendy! Can you help us out for a minute?"

Drying her hands, Wendy strode through the house. She looked comfortable, even after spending time alone with her mother. Kat was impressed with her composure. At the door, Kat explained the conundrum.

"Tell me what to do, and I'll do it," Wendy said.

Her response did not surprise Kat, and she squeezed Wendy's arm in appreciation. She hadn't expected her muscle to feel so firm, and she lifted her eyebrows in surprise.

"What?" Wendy looked at Kat's hand. She snatched it away.

"Nothing. Just…who knew chefs were so buff?"

Wendy flexed her arm, making Kat laugh. Kat hollered out the front door. "Which do you want to see first, walking in together, or walking in separately?"

"Together first!" Evan called.

"Okay! Watch for us." She pointed Wendy through the house. "We'll use the back door and walk around."

"Everything okay?" Millie asked as they passed through the kitchen.

"They're working out their jitters by stressing on the small details," Kat explained.

"Stressing on small details is your specialty," her mother said drolly.

"Ignore her, please," Kat said as they walked out the back porch.

"I think she's fun."

"Please tell me she wasn't talking to you in there or asking all sorts of embarrassing things."

"Nothing embarrassing. Course I'm pretty hard to embarrass."

"Oh no. What did she ask you?"

"When I knew I was a dyke."

"She did not!"

"No. She asked when I knew I liked girls."

"I'm so sorry!"

"Why? She initiated a conversation. She's nice."

"And slightly inappropriate."

"Why? It was just getting interesting! We were just getting into why most open relationships don't work out."

"Thank goodness I came in when I did." Kat tugged Wendy down the driveway toward the porch. She did not need her mother opening up the topic of open marriages with Wendy. When she had talked to her mother about Jack and Ember, Kat heard more than she'd ever wanted about how she was carrying on a tradition established by her grandparents. She had yet to recover fully from the details of her paternal grandparents' participation in Dr. Kinsey's studies.

"But now I'm curious!"

"I can tell you from experience that curiosity nearly killed this Kat, so count yourself saved." They walked up the stairs unceremoniously, though still holding hands, and turned to Jeremy and Evan.

"What in the devil are you two running from? Could you at least pretend that you're about to be married?" Evan said.

"We're doing you a favor, remember? Quit complaining!" Kat tossed back. She glanced at Wendy and had trouble reading her expression.

Wendy leaned over and whispered, "I'm cooking all evening here. If your mother's still in the kitchen, I'm going to find out."

Kat smacked her shoulder. "You wouldn't dare."

"Wouldn't I?"

"Blah blah blah blah. You're married forever and ever. Kiss and walk down the sidewalk," Jeremy said.

Kat saw the surprise she felt mirrored in Wendy's expression. They stood staring at each other, paralyzed. For Kat, Miranda's request for a kiss burned in her mind. What kept Wendy looking so serious?

"Don't listen to him," Evan said. "All we need to see is you exiting down the sidewalk and coming around the driveway."

Evan smacked Jeremy and leaned over to whisper something in his ear, and Kat blushed remembering how she had not corrected his assumption the last time they had spoken. He would be thinking that Kat was uncomfortable with all of this, and she was, but not for the reason he thought.

Wendy gently squeezed Kat's hands. "Come on."

With more reverence, they took the three steps and walked hand in hand down the sidewalk. Once they passed the seats on the grass and the hedge at the edge of the property, Kat said, "I'm sorry I froze." She led Wendy out through the small gate and back around to the driveway.

"What?" Wendy said. Kat could tell she was pretending she hadn't noticed.

"On the porch just now. When Jeremy said to kiss. It's…"

"It's okay."

"No. I don't want you to think I'm uncomfortable. I'm not. Two girls…you know…together? It doesn't make me uncomfortable." She bit her lip and started walking back up the drive to where they had sat swinging together only a few days before. The evening breeze lifted the leaves on the hedge behind the swing and sent a shiver up her spine. She remembered the warmth of Wendy's body when she had leaned against her. She hadn't been tempted to kiss her that night. Why would she be thinking about it now? Her gaze drifted down to Wendy's lips. How had she never noticed how invitingly full they were?

"It's not like I've never kissed a girl before," Kat said.

"I know."

"You do?"

"Erin told me."

"How would Erin…?" The words slipped out of her mouth before Kat remembered the drunken kiss she'd fumbled with Erin.

Wendy looked understandably confused.

"Yoo hoo! Ladies! Is someone going to the other side, so we can see what that looks like?" Evan yodeled.

* * *

Wendy couldn't tell if Kat was upset to learn that Erin had told her about their kiss. But if she was embarrassed about it, why did she get the feeling Kat was staring at her mouth? Evan's voice startled her into action. "I'll go around."

"Let me," Kat said, staying her with a brief touch to the shoulder. She was touching her more, Wendy noticed. Probably just in the straight girl your-sexuality-doesn't-intimidate-me sort of way, but still, Wendy felt her blood surge.

Wendy watched Kat walk across the porch thinking that her day could not get any weirder. Kat kept walking until she was standing by the large aviary under the balcony steps. She turned around and looked at Wendy with a new intensity.

"You can't stand there staring at each other. Remember it's supposed to be a surprise when we see each other. Go further back!" Evan said.

Wendy complied, walking along a brick path along the other side of the house. She stopped when directed.

"Okay. Now you can both walk toward the porch."

On the other side of the house, Kat was walking parallel to her. Imagining Kat's progress pulled her emotions like strings of a balloon bouquet. The joy she felt when Kat's ID lit up her phone a bright yellow balloon bobbing brightly. A green balloon the envy she had once felt for her growing up in this house. Blue, the memories of her sister Kat had shared. Red, how much she cared for her.

Wendy reached the porch, and the sight of Kat took her breath away. It wasn't what she wore. The old jeans and loose tee were more suited to doing chores than standing in for a groom, but even across the length of the house, she felt as if Kat was pulling her like iron to a magnet.

She cared for her.

When had that happened?

With only the sound of the parakeets chirping, she climbed the steps watching as Kat did the same. Kat's tentative smile made her look like a nervous bride. Had she been nervous when she walked down the aisle eighteen years ago? No doubt she was a lovely bride. She smiled herself, wondering whether her dress had been fancy or simple. Had she worn her hair up? What was she doing picturing Kat as a bride?

They stopped in the center of the porch and took each other's hands as the minister stepped forward. Kat's loose top brought out the green in her eyes, and Wendy did not want to look away. Physically and emotionally, Wendy had never been in this position before. Her heart began to race as if she was about to recite vows. Before she could explore what that meant, Jeremy and Evan were with them on the porch.

"That was so much better! We are definitely walking in that way, right honey?" Evan said.

"It is much better," Jeremy agreed.

"You don't need me anymore?" Wendy asked.

"We'll let you get back to preparing our scrumptious dinner," Evan answered.

Wendy excused herself, wishing that she had a reason to ask Kat to return to the kitchen with her. What had that been on the porch? She felt silly for getting swept up in the wedding mood, and she very much wanted to ask Kat what had been going through her mind. Not that they would have been able to talk.

Wendy found Kat's mom still seated at the kitchen table, reading the newspaper, a donut in one hand and Diet Coke within reach of the other. Suppressing the urge to ask what effect her diet had on her blood sugar, Wendy got to work on the taco bar for the rehearsal dinner.

She could feel that Millie spent as much time watching her as reading the paper. Was she thinking of a way to reengage the conversation about open marriages? While Wendy was curious, she didn't want to make Kat uncomfortable by prompting her mother to share stories that would embarrass Kat.

Wendy smacked a head of iceberg lettuce against the counter to core it and looked up to find Millie studying her intently.

"Someone as attractive as you are, who cooks like you do, it's a wonder you're still single."

Wendy smiled politely, not sure how to respond.

"Though Kat said that she introduced you to Erin?"

"We've been out a few times."

"I thought it would have been so nice if things had sparked between Kat and Erin."

"Why's that?"

"There was never any spark with her and her ex-husband. You can tell when people enjoy each other, and they didn't. At least Kat didn't enjoy being near him. I hoped that she'd find a partner to enjoy, man or woman."

Millie's frankness surprised Wendy. She was taken aback by the level of confidence she entrusted to Wendy and though she was curious to hear more, it felt disloyal to Kat to press.

Millie took another bite of her donut and sighed. "I worry that her dad and I ruined her by encouraging her to be sexual. I thought I was correcting my parents' mistakes by being different. Progressive, you know? When I was young my parents believed you only ever slept with your husband or wife. Of course they changed their minds later, after Clyde and I were married. Even before that, it never made sense to me why you wouldn't test sexual compatibility before making a lifetime commitment. So that's how I raised my daughter and look where it got her."

Wendy grabbed cheese from the refrigerator. "It seems like you did okay to me."

"The two of you seem close. I just wish she would allow that closeness to blossom into something else. She has always guarded herself. I'm sure that makes an intimate relationship difficult."

Wendy didn't know how to answer that. It certainly seemed like she was saying she wished Kat was interested in her. Through the window, Wendy could see the rest of the wedding party arriving to practice their parts. Millie followed her gaze, and the conversation ceased while they watched Jeremy and Evan's friends. It felt like glancing at a muted TV in the corner of a bar when you're not really sure what to say.

With the impeccable timing of a server, Kat swept into the kitchen through the back door. "How did it get this late!" She stopped suddenly and shut her eyes, taking a long, deep breath. "It smells fantastic in here." When she opened them, her hazel eyes landed on Wendy.

"I'm surprised you think so. It's full of green stuff."

"It smells good enough I might have tried it."

Wendy wrinkled her brow.

"If I didn't have bell rehearsal."

"Oh. I don't know why I thought you'd be here."

"Maybe because normal people come home from work and stay home. They don't go back out to their place of employ at the end of their day," Millie offered.

"Sorry. I really wish I could stay." Kat gave her a quick hug and whispered only for her to hear, "I can send my mom upstairs if she's in your way."

"We're good," Wendy whispered back.

"That worries me." Kat hugged her again, said goodbye to her mother and grabbed her purse, waving to them as she ducked out of the kitchen.

Wendy glanced up to see Kat get in her SUV. It sat with the back-up lights illuminated for longer than Wendy expected, then in a flash, roared in reverse down the drive. She smiled in surprise. Self-conscious, she glanced at Millie, chagrined to find her watching her.

"Interesting," she said, her gaze falling back to the paper in front of her.

Somehow, Wendy knew she was talking about her, not the article she was reading. Maybe because she, too, found what she was feeling "interesting." Why, when Kat had just set her up with someone beautiful and most certainly lesbian, did she find her thoughts lingering on Kat instead?

CHAPTER FOURTEEN

What was she thinking? She'd almost kissed Wendy. There in front of Jeremy and Evan, all Kat was thinking about was what Wendy's lips would feel like pressed to hers. She'd practiced standing at the altar with Jack. She remembered the minister prompting "and then you'll kiss." Her eyes were on the minister, not Jack. His repeated "and then you'll kiss" made her realize that he expected them to practice the kiss. The wedding party had laughed. Jack, always so good natured, leaned in for a chaste peck.

That wasn't what she was picturing with Wendy. She had wanted to lose herself in Wendy's lips. She wanted to press more than just her lips up against her. Her body thrummed at the imagined contact.

"Should we try it again?"

Kat couldn't place the voice. Her eyes were closed, and she could see Wendy standing in front of her, and she very much wanted a chance to try again.

"Kat?"

It was quiet. The music had stopped. Her players had stopped. She blinked back to the present. She was at rehearsal. "I'm so sorry. I completely spaced out there. Let's take a quick break. Get a drink, and we'll come back fresh. Start from the top..."

The group of three teen girls pulled off the gloves that protected the handbells from the oil on their hands and immediately pulled out their phones, eyes glued to the screens as they walked toward the drinking fountain and bathroom.

Kat pulled out her own phone, her thoughts still on Wendy and the way she had looked at her on the porch. She could have approached standing in for one of the grooms like her goofy, carefree teenagers, who seemed never to take anything seriously, but she had been utterly serious. Of course, there was how she'd been thinking about kissing Miranda when she said she'd kissed a woman before. She felt like she needed to explain that she'd kissed more than one woman.

She had never called Wendy without a business-related question. Her thumb hovered over the green phone icon. She only had a minute before the girls returned. She hit call.

Wendy answered immediately. "Hi there, sunshine!"

Her voice was rich and warm in Kat's ear, and her body reverberated in response like a struck handbell. "I'm sorry I had to leave this evening, especially since my mom was downstairs with you."

"I told you not to worry about it, remember?"

Kat heard the clatter of dishes in the background. "Am I totally interrupting you?"

"Everyone is eating. I'm plating my amazing brownies. You're keeping me company."

"Oh, good. My mom finally left you alone?"

"Jeremy and Evan insisted they join the wedding party for dinner. Even though they said to set it up as a buffet, Travis offered to help. They were so charmed, they invited him and your parents to join the party."

"I wish you hadn't told me that. I was already terribly distracted tonight, and that's not going to help."

"What's on your mind?"

Kat held her breath for a moment. Could she really say what was on her mind? "I can't stop thinking about the whole awkward 'then you'll kiss' thing that happened during the rehearsal."

"Oh."

The girls came back from their break. Their loud banter came to an abrupt halt when they saw that Kat was on the phone. She waved them in. "Do you think you'll still be there in an hour?" Kat asked.

"I could be."

"I don't want to hold you up if you were wrapping up. I'm sure you've got a lot to do before the wedding tomorrow."

"I'm in good shape on my prep. And...I'd like to see you again."

"Good." Kat turned away from the girls. "Then we're agreed. Save me a brownie?"

"I can't make any promises on that, but I'll try."

Kat tucked her phone in her purse and turned back to the group.

"Was that your boyfriend?" sixteen-year-old Kristelle asked.

"My caterer friend. Let's start back at the beginning and take it at a slower tempo."

"But you wish he was your boyfriend," Kristelle's little sister, Jasmine said. "You're blushing."

"I'm not blushing."

"You really are," Kristelle agreed.

"A boyfriend is exactly what you need!" Sunni said. "Then you wouldn't have to live with your parents!"

"I'm not living with my parents because I don't have a boyfriend. Besides, my caterer friend is a girl, not a boy."

"Then you can live with your girlfriend," Sunni said.

How easily Sunni switched from boyfriend to girlfriend showed Kat how this generation differed from hers, but though she wanted to move on from the subject, she could not let the dependent jibe slide. "My parents have a huge house. I'm helping them out by living there since they're getting older, and getting Travis set up for school. I don't need a boyfriend or a girlfriend. Can we please get back to practice now? I'd like to get out of here before my kid graduates from high school."

When she glanced at the music, she could have sworn she heard one of them whisper that she'd be less crabby if she was getting laid. She bit back the urge to tell them that she didn't need sex to make her happy and was surprised to feel her body suggesting that she might revisit that long-held position.

* * *

"Sit down, lady! Have a drink!" Evan hollered after Wendy had delivered the brownies.

The wedding party was already raving about her triple-chocolate recipe and complaining about how they were not going to fit into their wedding attire the next day if they didn't stop at one.

"I know there's still that beer you left in my daughter's Frigidaire," Millie said. "Clyde, grab it for her."

He rose and bowed slightly before he walked to the back door.

"You didn't have to send him," Wendy said.

"That's what husbands are for," she said. "Isn't that why you're getting married?"

The group laughed. "Plus, you needed a place to sit." Millie angled the chair next to her.

"I don't want to take Clyde's spot."

"Why not? We're not new lovebirds. We're happiest when we're not right on top of each other."

Jeremy coughed on a bite of brownie, and Evan patted him on the back. "We've been together for fifty years, and he's still happiest when I am on top of him."

"Stop!" Jeremy said, temporarily silencing Evan with a kiss.

The look that they shared brought back the image of Kat standing on the porch. She blinked in surprise at the way her stomach fluttered from the memory. She was happy to step away for a moment to grab a chair from the garage as she composed herself.

"How long have you two been married?" Evan was asking when she returned. Clyde returned at the same time. He handed an opened beer to Wendy and a Diet Coke to Millie.

"This September, it will be forty…" he looked at Millie.

"Forty-three," she supplied.

"What's your secret?"

Clearly enjoying the attention focused on them, Clyde took Millie's hand and raised it to his lips before he expounded on the things that had kept their marriage strong.

Wendy was intrigued at the drastic difference she saw between the couple bickering in the kitchen and the one smiling peacefully at each other. Likening them to the public persona Kat wore, she never would have suspected that their life was anything but picture-perfect.

Millie chimed in with the fact that neither of their families had given the marriage more than a year, yet all this time later, they had proved them all wrong.

Jeremy and Evan stood and took the opportunity to thank their friends and family for their genuine support. Wendy stepped away, giving them privacy for their goodbyes. To her surprise many sought her out to thank her for dinner, saying that they looked forward to the wedding meal.

"Don't tell me I missed the party!" Kat said striding onto the patio.

"We old men have got to get some sleep before our big day!" Evan said. They embraced, and Evan quickly introduced her to his guests making sure they all knew that she was responsible for their having the perfect place to get married.

Wendy stepped away to grab a bus bin to clear the dessert dishes. She was happy to have a task as Kat chatted briefly about the music. She stacked the dishes quietly, enjoying the melody of Kat's voice as she tried to deflect their compliments on her brilliance in helping them pull everything together at the last minute.

"You say that, but Wendy has done way more of the heavy lifting on this one," Kat said. Wendy looked up and found herself caught in Kat's gaze.

"You two are both so amazing," Evan agreed.

Jeremy pulled at Evan's elbow, leading the party toward their cars. Kat walked with them, and Wendy gathered the last of the plates. Wendy was agitated, anxious to be alone with her. She glanced up, impatient for everyone to leave and give her a chance to discuss what Kat had meant when she had begun to ask how Erin had known she'd kissed a woman before.

"Allow me to assist," Clyde said.

"Oh!" Wendy's hand flew to her chest. "You startled me."

He carefully placed some plates in her bin. "I do apologize. Millie sent me out to help."

"There's not much to do at all."

His smile revealed the crooked eyetooth that Kat said her sister had been proud to inherit. "Perhaps she thought if I offered aid, you could be persuaded to leave some of those brownies here."

Wendy laughed. "I'd be happy to. I was going to leave some for Kat, too. I wondered if she'd eaten."

"I imagine not. She gets lost in the tasks of the day, much like I do. When I met Millie, I insisted that I did not need her. She did not listen, and she would not take no for an answer. I did not think I would ever have a life mate, but she showed me how much sweeter life is when your heart has a companion. I fear that my daughter is much like me, and I don't know that there is anyone as patient or persistent as Millie to convince Kat to open her heart."

Kat gave her final hugs and crossed the patio to Wendy and Clyde. "Sounds like everything went smoothly and that everything is set for tomorrow."

"Indeed." Clyde picked up Wendy's bus bin. "Shall I take this to the kitchen?"

"That would be great. And I'll get you more brownies for Millie."

"Brownies! There are more brownies? Everyone was talking about how great they were."

"I have more of everything if you'd like some dinner first."

"Trying to take care of me? Hello, by the way." She hugged Wendy and whispered into her neck, "Thank you for staying."

Unsure of how to respond, Wendy headed for the kitchen, Clyde's comments about Kat mixing with what it felt like to have Kat's arms around her.

"Do you trust me to put together a few tacos for you before you get into the brownies? I can do something pretty close to your bean and cheese wrap."

Kat scrunched up her face. "I guess I should eat something nutritious since I had a bag of chips for lunch."

Wendy placed several brownies on a clean plate. "A bag of chips? Maybe Travis is right about you needing me around to cook for you." She handed the brownies to Clyde.

He tipped his head toward her in a slight bow as he accepted the plate. "Thank you. Unless you require my assistance, I believe I shall retire."

"We're good," Kat said without looking at him.

He appeared to accept the dismissal. He raised his eyebrows to Wendy and bowed again before he took his leave.

"I'm guessing chicken, not beef, for your taco."

"How'd you know?"

"The reunion. You had the rubbery chicken, not the petrified beef."

That brought a slight smile to Kat's lips. Wendy could practically see the thoughts spinning in Kat's head and would have loved for her simply to say everything she thought instead of playing the game of saying only what she thought was appropriate. But remembering Clyde's words, she focused her attention on making two chicken tacos wondering if she could sneak in more than meat and cheese. She could wait for Kat. She had the feeling it would be worth it.

* * *

"So I have a question." Kat swallowed a bite of Wendy's amazing taco. Kat eyed what looked like roasted pepper and reluctantly left it in place. She put on a ton of grated cheese and a healthy dollop of sour cream, and took a bite. She had to agree with Travis that Wendy's food was more flavorful than her bean and cheese burritos.

"Oh, good. Because I do too."

They sat across from each other at the kitchen table. "I figured, but I asked first."

"You haven't asked yet."

Because Wendy was teasing her, Kat took an enormous bite of taco and made Wendy wait while she chewed. "This is delicious."

"Glad you like it."

"I saw what you put in, by the way."

"I know, and I'm very impressed that you didn't pick it off."

Kat smirked at her. "What was the answer to my mom's question about how you knew you liked girls?"

Wendy blushed a little and took a sip of water. "Actually, your mom asked me when I knew."

"I know you knew in high school. Did you know earlier than that?"

"No. Junior year, I had a huge crush on the French teacher. I wanted to see her naked."

"Oh!" Kat couldn't mask her surprise.

"What?" Wendy laughed at her exclamation.

"Nothing. I had crushes on a few teachers, but I didn't want to see any of them naked."

"What about now if you crush on someone?"

Kat pressed some of the fallen cheese between her thumb and forefinger and popped it in her mouth. She couldn't look at Wendy. Even looking down at her plate, she was having a difficult time not picturing Wendy out of her crisp white blouse and pressed dark slacks. The top three buttons were undone tonight exposing her delicate collar bones. "Well, now that you've put that idea in my head!" She glanced up at a beaming Wendy and blushed hard.

"You're crushing on someone?"

"That's for me to know and you to find out."

"Every time I'm around you, I feel like I'm back in high school."

"Welcome to my life. Living with my parents, being teased by teenaged girls about whether I'm getting laid, I feel like I'm back in high school too."

Wendy had taken another sip of water and sprayed it into her hands. While she coughed, Kat jumped up and got her a paper towel. "When did that happen?"

"Tonight I grouched at my bell ringers, and they blamed my mood on not having a sex life. I didn't tell them I was just as grouchy when I was having sex."

"I'll be honest. I'm with them. I think sex fixes all sorts of things."

"Hmmm. I'll take your word for it." Kat remembered how hearing her parents having sex used to comfort her and make her feel like they would be fine and that her father wouldn't spend the next weekend sleeping over at his boyfriend's house. Sex hadn't fixed everything back then, and sex certainly never patched the holes in her marriage.

"Not everyone has the same sex drive. Ready for a brownie?"

"That's it?"

Wendy cleared Kat's plate and returned with the brownies. "What?"

"You're not going to try to convince me that I should like sex more?"

"Should I?"

Their eyes held across the table just as they had earlier when they'd stood on the porch. Kat felt something. A crush? A curiosity? A reigniting, she realized, like a candle once blown out lit again. "I've always felt envious when my friends talk about how much they enjoy it or miss it." She took a bite of brownie and put her free hand over her heart. "That's scrummy," she said, quoting *The Great British Baking Show*. She savored another bite of the chocolate wonderfulness. "Your ganache is nice and glossy."

"I love that you love that show!"

Kat finished the brownie. "That, I couldn't live without. I love chocolate like other people love sex."

"You want another as soon as you swallow the last bite?"

"Absolutely."

"A lot of people crave sex like that."

"I know, and I never have." *Tell me that you are not burning with desire from that kiss, and I won't say another word about it.*

She heard Miranda's words again and gasped. "Maybe not never. Just once a long time ago."

"The girl you kissed?"

Kat nodded. "It was a long time ago. I didn't realize I was in love with her, or maybe I did. I was scared of what I felt for her, and by the time she told me…" She ran her left thumb slowly along the palm of her right hand. "I was pregnant and about to marry Jack. Everyone was there. All the guests. My parents. His. All that money already spent. I had to marry Jack."

"And you never told Erin?"

"Are you kidding? There are three people who know I kissed Miranda, and you are one of them. I never even told my therapist."

"That's not why you were going?"

"I started going because when Travis turned ten, it brought back everything that happened with Ava."

"It's good that you could talk to someone about that."

Kat nodded. "It's all intertwined, really. Losing Ava, feeling trapped with Jack, but feeling like I had to stick it out because my parents did."

"But not about kissing Miranda."

"No. I couldn't tell him that. And I couldn't tell him the part about my dad's boyfriend either."

"Why not?"

"Because I still thought it was wrong for my dad to be gay. He was supposed to be with my mom. If he'd only been with my mom, then everything would have been fine. I didn't want to be like my dad, so I convinced myself I could be married to Jack and be happy. But that wasn't fair to him because it wasn't who I was. I thought I could choose."

"Your childhood…" Wendy began but stopped. Kat waited for her to finish the thought about her childhood, but she changed the subject instead. "Do you want any more brownies?"

"No. I can't. They're delicious, and you really are going to have to be careful. Bring more food like that around here, and my mom will want to keep you!"

Wendy placed the cover on the container. "I can leave the rest."

"I know my mom would be thrilled, and Travis would love them, too."

"And you?"

Wendy looked hesitant as she asked the question, and Kat's heart caught. She was the one who equated brownies with sex. And now she was mentally undressing Wendy. She wet her bottom lip with her tongue and caught Wendy's gaze. An unfamiliar fire rushed up her legs. "Yes, I think I would."

"I could leave the food too if you'd like. There's not enough to repurpose back at the restaurant."

"I'm sure my family would love it."

Wendy glanced at her watch. "I should get my gear back to the kitchen and get ready for tomorrow. It's a big day."

Kat stood on the opposite side of the island and appreciated the efficient way Wendy moved in the space. She recognized that Wendy was puttering as a diversion, and she wanted to know what she wasn't saying. "What were you going to say about my childhood?"

Wendy paused in gathering her gear. "It wasn't nice."

"But you have to say it now. Otherwise I won't sleep wondering."

Wendy held whatever it was in her head and then took a deep breath. "Your childhood was really fucked up."

Kat laughed. "Yes, well luckily it's all in the past!"

"I know, but I feel like a shit for feeling jealous of you living in this nice house with both your parents."

"Don't. That's what my family wants people to think." She joined Wendy on the other side of the island. "What can I carry?"

"If I'm leaving the food, I don't have much." Wendy handed her one of the bus bins and shouldered two insulated bags. "I'm parked out on the street."

Kat walked her out, her mind spinning. She'd perched the bin on her hip to open the door, but seeing Wendy paused on the porch waiting for her, she bent and set it down.

Wendy tilted her head in question when Kat stepped to her and lowered the bags to rest next to the bin. Her hands were trembling as she stepped closer to Wendy and reached for her hands. "When we were standing here before, I felt something I haven't felt in forever. I wanted to kiss you so badly, and it's all I've thought about today."

"I thought it was my imagination," Wendy whispered.

"I don't know what I'm doing." Kat leaned closer. Only inches away from Wendy, an image flashed through her mind. "Shit!" she said under her breath as she pulled away.

"What?" Wendy said, startled.

"Erin! What was I thinking?" She released Wendy's hands.

Wendy took her hand to stop her retreat. What had she been thinking when she told her that she'd wanted to kiss her? How had she forgotten Erin? Wendy was dating her. How had she forgotten how dangerous it was to listen to desire instead of reason? Just as her thoughts threatened to overwhelm her, Kat felt Wendy's fingers trace some of her hair back behind her ear.

Wendy's hand stayed there. "If I remember correctly, you're the one who said you can't help who you fall for."

Her lips found Kat's, tentative and oh, so soft. Kat's breath caught, and she felt the pressure of Wendy's lips leaving her too soon. Sweeping her hands into Wendy's hair, she pulled her closer, reclaiming the kiss. She tried to remember when the simple brush of lips against her own had ignited anything within her like this simple kiss. Wendy's lips cupped her lower lip and gently pulled. Her hands rested on Kat's hips, coaxing her close enough that their breasts brushed. A moan that Kat did not recognize escaped.

She broke away but kept her face close. "What are you doing to me?"

"What are *you* doing to *me*?" Wendy countered.

Kat could feel her smile before Wendy peppered her chin and neck with kisses. She brushed Kat's hair back and traced her ear with her tongue. Kat shivered and clutched Wendy closer, feeling weak in the knees. "Oh, you make me want you."

"How come that sounds like a bad thing?"

"Because this isn't who I am."

"No?"

"I'm straight, remember?"

"Mmmm hmm?" Wendy asked. "I think it's just taken you a very long time to figure out who you are."

Kat pulled Wendy's mouth to hers again and touched her tongue to Wendy's bottom lip, inviting her to deepen the kiss. She could lose herself in Wendy's kisses, and hadn't she spent her whole life being afraid of just that? Passion led to irrational choices and people getting hurt. She had never allowed herself the level of intimacy that crackled between her and Wendy, even with this first kiss. Perhaps she had to lose herself in order to be found.

CHAPTER FIFTEEN

Fingers snapped in front of Wendy's face. "Yoo hoo! Where are you today?" Cory asked.

Wendy was still on Kat's front porch, her stomach somersaulting at the memory of Kat's lips on hers. Her body still tingled from the silken invitation Kat had tentatively offered. For someone who argued she wasn't all that good at kissing, she had practically dropped Wendy to her knees. "What?"

"Take a break, Lover girl. Go get it out of your system so you can get your focus back on this wedding dinner."

"Get what out of my system?"

"Go suck face with your girl. Like I said, she's asking for you at the bar."

"Kat?" Wendy asked, stunned.

"Erin," Cory said, perplexed. "Wait, you kissed Kat? When?"

What was Erin doing at the restaurant again? Wendy could not deal with her when she was lost in the memory of kissing Kat. "You have to tell Erin I'm not here."

"No deal. I am not getting in the middle of this twisted triangle."

"Some friend you are!"

"Go. Do whatever you're going to do, so we stay on schedule."

"Should I be worried that you sound like the boss?"

"You're stalling." Cory returned to chopping mushrooms.

Wendy hung her head, defeated. Cory was absolutely right. She did not know what to say to Erin. She was ashamed to admit that until Cory had said her name, she hadn't thought of her all day. Kat had consumed her. After a restless night of lying in bed reliving their kisses, Wendy had spent the early morning worrying that Kat would wake full of regret, but at five, her phone had chimed.

Can you sleep? Can't stop thinking about your beautiful mouth.

Just lying here thinking about you, Wendy texted back.

You were thinking about what a piggy I was with those brownies, weren't you?

I was thinking that I could get addicted to your style of chocolate kisses.

Wendy had sat up in bed and pulled the pillow up to rest her back against the headboard, buoyed by Kat's text and nervously waiting for her reply. It didn't come. Where had she gone? Her screen went dark, and she swiped back in, rereading the message to make sure she hadn't said anything off-putting. On the edge of feeling anxious, her phone finally pinged.

I could get addicted to those brownies.

Brownies, not kisses. Wendy had wanted to talk more about kissing and whether it was likely to happen again. Instead, their texts had moved to the plan for the day, whether Kat was spending any time in the office and when Wendy would arrive to set up and serve dinner.

She knew Kat's itinerary didn't put her anywhere near the restaurant and still she was the one Wendy longed to see. She washed her hands and dried them with more care than was necessary.

Erin's face lit up when she walked up on the opposite side of the bar. "Hey, gorgeous!" She lifted herself up on the counter and leaned across to plant a kiss on Wendy. She had no time to react, and besides, she couldn't ditch the kiss. Erin had no context. She had no reason to think that Wendy might be kissing someone else. And yet she was. Or she had. Even though she and Erin had only begun seeing each other, it still felt like two-timing to Wendy. "Everything okay?"

She'd noticed. "Of course," she said, not quite truthfully. If she was certain about what had happened with Kat yesterday, she would lay it out for Erin as simply and kindly as possible. But she wasn't certain about anything. The way Kat had so quickly abandoned the topic of kissing made her reluctant to say anything to Erin.

"How late does the wedding go tonight?"

"Dinner service is at seven. I'm hoping they'll do the cake half past eight, nine at the latest. Wrapped up at ten?"

"You do the cake?"

"Once they've done the whole cutting and feeding each other, we plate it."

"Got it. Here's the thing. A friend of mine told me about this salsa band that's playing. Do you dance?"

"I've moved at the same time that music was playing. I'm told it didn't look much like dancing."

"If we get there early enough, they do some instruction. Doesn't it sound like fun?"

What sounded like fun was pulling Kat away from the party and putting the question of whether she was still interested in kissing directly to her lips. "Umm."

"Not your thing. I get it. We could get drinks instead. I wasn't ready to call it a night the last time I saw you." She reached for Wendy's hand.

There was no uncertainty in her action, no apology or sense that she was doing something wrong to touch Wendy. Erin added a seductive smile to accentuate the very clear message that if they got together, there would be some naked horizontal dancing in store. It seemed foolish to say no when she didn't even know if Kat would want her to stick around after the wedding.

"As appealing as that sounds, I'm not really sure what time I'll get out of there. I don't want to make a promise and not be able to keep it. It can be tough to get away from Kat's parents' place."

Erin's hand stilled. "Is it as crazy as Jack says it is?"

"What does he mean by crazy? The historical stuff is really neat, and the way they have it decorated makes you feel like you've stepped into a different century."

"He says it's unreal. Maybe it's the decor. I don't know. Kat's never invited anyone over now that she's living back there. Except these guys getting married. She doesn't invite her friends, but she'll let strangers get married there. Doesn't make sense to me."

"They're members of her church."

"The church where she works."

Her correction irritated Wendy. She stepped away and filled a glass with ice and then water from the soda hose. "It seems pretty typical for Kat to go out of her way to help someone. No?"

"That's true." Erin reached for her hand again. "She did introduce me to you. So when *do* I get to see you again?"

Wendy's stomach clenched uncomfortably. She was about to tell Erin that she was on dinner service in the restaurant on Saturday and that she'd be slammed, but she heard it from Erin's perspective and worried it would sound like she was blowing her off. "Let me give you a call when I'm finished up tonight, okay?"

Erin brightened, making Wendy feel like a real shit. She should have told Erin that she was suddenly unsure of her availability. Instead, she walked around the bar to give Erin a hug, begging off that she had to make sure her crew was ready to head over to the wedding. Her mind free to anticipate seeing Kat at the wedding, Wendy promptly forgot her promise.

* * *

Jeremy and Evan had chosen well to meet on the porch, and the piece Kat's harpsichordist friend played was perfect as she'd promised. When they joined hands in front of the priest Kat heard the appreciative hum from their gathered family and friends. Both looked handsome in their matching black tuxes, and Kat wondered what lesbians wore when they got married. Her father leaned over to whisper, "I'm so pleased that one of them did not feel compelled to wear a dress."

"Don't," she whispered. Her mother was up in her room and had told Clyde that he had no business attending the wedding, but he insisted that he would do as he pleased in his own home. He stood off to the side with Kat and her ringers, poised for the peal that would direct the guests to the backyard after the ceremony.

As usual, Kat held her own wedding up in comparison to this one, tallying the things she would have liked to have done with those she and Jack had done better. She held back a laugh hearing what she was sure Wendy would have said if she could hear her thoughts. She could turn anything into a competition.

Wendy.

She was back on the porch with Wendy rediscovering the wonder of kissing, promising that she could send Wendy on her way after the next one. The next one leading to one more. She craved another and had reacted the moment she saw Wendy arrive to set up her on-site grills. She had wanted to throw her arms around her neck and reclaim her lips. Kat deduced that she was now in the kitchen. Had she been alone, or even if she'd just been with Cory, Kat might have had the courage to coax Wendy away for a moment.

Though she'd been friendly, hugging Kat on arrival, the extra staff had elevated her level of professionalism. Kat would have to wait. She had waited decades to feel this way. Surely she could wait until the wedding was over to be with Wendy alone.

Clyde poked her with his elbow. "One wonders about forevers at a wedding. No one gave your mother and me more than a year."

Kat shushed him. "I know the story."

He was quiet for a moment. "Wendy looks like she sees forever."

"What?" Clyde's comment confused Kat. He redirected her attention from the porch past all the chairs to the aviary. Kat's breath caught at the sight of Wendy, arms crossed against her chest. She wasn't watching the wedding, and when their eyes met, she smiled and something began to coil deep inside Kat.

Fighting a smile, Kat returned her attention to the homily, happy she caught Reverend Munson's gentle reprimand of the clergy slow to recognize the beauty of all committed relationships. The couple exchanged vows they had clearly written themselves. Their friends started to pull out tissues as they talked about how they had found each other and stayed together despite all the obstacles thrown in their way. Kat misted up, remembering that they were standing on her front lawn because of the obstacle thrown by Reverend Thorn.

She didn't know their other obstacles and true to her competitive nature wondered if they were in any way close to what life had thrown at her. She glanced back at Wendy and caught her staring again.

"What?" she mouthed.

Wendy tipped her head toward the porch and then raised her eyebrows in a way that made Kat wish she could clear the yard. Reverend Munson closed the wedding.

"Inasmuch as Jeremy and Evan have exchanged vows of love and fidelity in the presence of God and Church, I now pronounce that they are bound together legally as husbands in holy covenant as long as they both shall live. Amen."

All gathered yelled "amen" as the couple kissed, setting off an eruption of cheers, applause, and the peal of bells.

Holding three in each hand, Kat alternated which played with a twist of her wrist, her arms in constant motion to create a steady stream of joyous notes. She rang for the celebration of all those gathered, but she also rang for her own elation. She wanted Wendy to hear how happy she felt. When she finally dampened the bells, Wendy put two fingers to her lips and blew Kat a kiss before disappearing down the path on the far side of the house.

She wished the moment had been private, especially when her father said that he thought Wendy was a lovely young woman. Though she agreed, she vowed to keep her distance during the reception, not trusting that she would have any restraint if she got too close.

With the ceremony over, Kat slipped easily into her role of administrator, directing the guests to the hors d'oeuvres and the candle station. She instructed them to write a note of celebration or advice on one of the cards attached to a rose-shaped candle. The cards they could put in a basket or hand to the grooms during the dancing. The candles were lit and set adrift on the water in the pool.

Cory waved to her when he began to run plates out with the other servers. When everyone was settled and raving about the food, Kat slipped into the kitchen.

"You're looking sharp," she said as he lifted the tray above her head.

"Boss said we all had to look and do our best tonight," Cory said. "She might be trying to impress someone."

"How does it seem out there?" Wendy interrupted.

"You're getting a lot of compliments on the beef," Kat said.

"Do you want to take a plate to your mother?"

"Are you allowed to give food away?"

"I'm the boss," she answered sassily. "I can do whatever I want!"

"That's not fair."

"Isn't it?"

"Not when I can't do whatever I want." She stepped close to Wendy. "All I want to do is kiss you," she whispered.

"What's stopping you?" Wendy didn't turn her head toward Kat and Kat could see a sly smile on her lips.

"Your staff, for one," Kat said as Cory joined them.

"I am in love with this house, Kat! Wendy said that you grew up here! It's so amazing! Have you seen the pool with that bridge and the candles? Your place and Wendy's catering… you're a dream team!"

Kat's eyes found Wendy's, and she looked for whether they were a dream team in other ways as well. The answer she found there made her look away.

"Your mom would go for the beef over the chicken, I'm guessing."

Kat loved that Wendy knew these things, and she admired the artistry with which Wendy arranged an assortment of greens that Kat had to admit looked delicious. She grabbed a cold soda from the fridge.

"Do you want me to make you a plate of chicken, no greens?"

"Fix me a plate you'd send outside."

"You sure?" Wendy's eyes sparkled.

"I'm feeling daring tonight."

Wendy didn't vocalize anything in front of Cory, but the way her gaze dipped to Kat's lips made her shudder inside. Could one kiss really form such a strong connection?

Kat tapped on her mother's door at the top of the stairs. "Delivery."

"Oh, goodness!" Millie said when Kat handed the plate to her. "I get all this?"

"Wendy thought you'd be hungry."

"She was right. That looks delicious! Thank her for me."

"I will."

"Was it a nice ceremony?"

"It was. And now that the guests are finishing their dinner, they're starting to float the candles. You might want to walk down the hall and take a look out the window. It's absolutely stunning."

Her mother did not acknowledge her as she cut a bite of the steak. "Is your father out there?"

"I think he's still out in the stone cottage. He wasn't impressed with the candy display, so he was rearranging it."

"Of course it wasn't to his liking. I'll look at the pool after I finish this. Tell Wendy it tastes even better than it looks."

"I will."

* * *

Wendy was caught in a flurry of activity plating the cake and supervising the Candy Cottage favors. She appreciated that

Jeremy and Evan had a precise plan for the reception and kept very close to the schedule, with the guests lingering only fifteen minutes or so past their nine o'clock departure. She blamed this on the charmingly lighted cottage and the candles still bobbing on the pool. She understood how difficult it was to leave the magic.

She'd let the waitstaff leave after the dinner service, and after they plated the wedding cake Cory took everything back to the restaurant. Technically, she was also off the clock, so she went to search for Kat. The lights illuminated the path to the cottage, and Wendy remembered the way she and Jeremy had joked about how the little cottage would have made parenting difficult. She could easily imagine taking advantage of the romantic space and was hopeful she would have the chance someday.

The shape of someone sitting poolside caught her eye, and she stopped. Wendy would have missed her but for the flickering candle she held in her lap. Wendy retraced her steps and circled around to the gate.

"I was wondering where you'd disappeared to."

Kat took a deep breath and smiled at her. "Hey."

Wendy sat down next to her on the diving board and put her hand on Kat's knee. "Happy with how it all went?"

"Yes, it turned out really well."

"It did. What's with this candle? You swipe it?"

"I did one for Jeremy and Evan earlier but..." She pressed her lips together. "I was helping clean up, and there was one unlit candle by the guestbook. This yellow one. Ava's favorite color was yellow."

Wendy hummed sympathetically. "She's reminding you that she's with you."

"I like that. I've sure been thinking about her a lot lately. I was scared to for so long because it was crushing. But thinking about how she would have loved this makes me happy."

"That's really good."

"Will you come with me? I want to release it in the middle."

"From the bridge?" Wendy was surprised. She remembered how Kat had kept her distance during its construction. She took Kat's hand. "I'd love to."

Kat kept a hold of Wendy's hand as she slowly walked to the middle. She let go and knelt to float the candle out onto the surface of the pool. Hands on her knees, she stayed kneeling long enough that Wendy wondered if she should sit. Finally, Kat stood. She wrapped her arms around Wendy and whispered into her neck, "All day I've been thinking about being alone with you. Now I am, and I'm so nervous."

"If you knew how much I've been thinking about our last kiss, I don't think you'd be."

"Or maybe I'd more nervous."

"What am I going to do with you?"

"Kiss me, I hope." Kat loosened her hold, her hands now resting on Wendy's biceps.

Wendy nuzzled Kat's neck, slowly tracing the collarbone Kat's dress revealed. She exhaled a hot breath as she reached for Kat's earlobe with her teeth, nipping her gently. She raised her hands to cup Kat's chin before she touched her lips to Kat's.

Desire flared in her like a wick touched to a flame and she pressed closer to Kat inviting her to deepen the kiss. Kat's lips remained soft and supple, but she didn't part them. Instead, she pulled away, her gaze everywhere but on Wendy. Wendy placed her hand on Kat's chin. "What?"

"I don't want to scare you."

"I'm not scared. You can tell me."

"All these feelings inside…I'm just not used to it."

"You don't think it's overwhelming to me?"

"It is?"

"This is different. Usually kissing is a way to figure out whether I'm going to sleep with someone."

"That's not what we're doing?" Kat took a step back, but Wendy did not let her get far.

She grasped Kat's hands and pulled her close again. "I didn't have to kiss you to know that I wanted to be with you."

Kat flinched at her words.

"Why does that upset you?"

Did she dare tell Wendy how sex made her panic? How could she explain that she had spent her life avoiding what so many eagerly sought? "I'm not good at intimacy."

"I want to spend time with you," Wendy clarified. "There are a lot of ways to be intimate that don't involve sex."

"Normal people want sex."

"My dad always said 'normal is a setting on a washing machine.'" She had hoped Kat would laugh, but she didn't respond. Something occurred to Wendy. "Can I ask you something?"

"Of course."

"Did you get to date very much before you got pregnant?"

After some hesitation, Kat said, "Jack and I went out for a while."

"That's a no?"

Kat laughed. "I guess that's a no."

"You're setting your sense of normal on one dude who was more interested in the destination than the journey?"

"I talk to people. I know I'm different."

"May I make a suggestion?"

"You think I need to date."

"Bingo. And I happen to know someone who does a super good date. She's got to work tomorrow evening, but she could come up with something really good in the morning if you're game."

"I'm worried that you'll get frustrated with me." Kat took Wendy's hand.

"I'm worried you won't give me a chance. Come on a date with me."

"Erin would be a lot easier to date."

It was Wendy's turn to flinch. She grimaced when she pulled out her phone and looked at the time and the number of missed calls. "Shit, shit, shit!"

"You had plans?" Kat asked quietly.

"She dropped by the restaurant. It wasn't the right time to talk about things. I said I'd call."

"What are you going to tell her?" Kat's thumb was moving across her palm the way it did when she was worried.

"I don't know. I thought something would come to me today, but weirdly, my mind has been preoccupied." Wendy took Kat's hand, and they walked off the bridge together.

"Inconceivable," Kat said.

Wendy's jaw dropped. "'I do not think you know what that word means.'"

Kat beamed. "If I ever get married again, I want the minister to say 'Mawage. Mawage is wot bwings us togeder tooday.'"

Wendy easily recalled the scene Kat was quoting and added the impatient Prince Humperdinck's line. "'Skip to the end!'"

"Will we be watching *The Princess Bride* for our date?" Kat clapped her hands together.

"It's not what I had in mind, but I could be persuaded."

"I'd love to watch it with you, but movies in the morning just don't work for me. That will have to wait for when you have an evening free."

"But you're free tomorrow morning?"

Kat studied her.

"What?"

"I want to say yes."

"Then do." She adopted the clergyman's voice from *The Princess Bride*. "I wasn't planning on getting mawied or anything." She had meant it as a joke, just an extension of their riffing with the movie lines, but the memory of standing in for Jeremy and Evan nudged her, flipping her stomach like a pancake. The more time she spent with Kat, the more she wanted, despite Kat's warnings about not being suited to relationships. "Where's your irresponsible teenager?"

"With his dad."

Wendy laughed. "I meant you. Go with what you want to do without worrying about what it will become."

"You make it sound so easy."

"It can be," Wendy said, though she wasn't so sure she believed herself.

"Okay. It's a date."

Wendy hugged her, taking a deep breath of the soft citrusy sweetness that was Kat. "I can't wait," she said. She forced herself to walk toward her car, and Kat escorted her. "Until tomorrow, Princess," she said. As she drove home, her thoughts turned to how best to court the hesitant recipient of her affection.

CHAPTER SIXTEEN

The next morning, Wendy smiled at Kat through the round oval of the front door.

"This is perfect," Wendy motioned to Kat's pink lightweight hoodie and jeans rolled above the ankle.

"'Whatever you want' is not a very helpful response for what to wear today." Kat hollered goodbye to her family and joined Wendy on the porch.

"I didn't want you to worry about what to wear. I wanted you to feel comfortable."

"Now will you tell me where we're going?"

"Is the Santa Monica Pier okay?"

"I haven't been there in ages!" Kat said. How many years had it been? More than ten because Travis had been big enough to try some of the rides but had been too scared. That had spoiled the day so badly for Jack that even years later, he had always torpedoed the idea if she suggested it.

"But is it a good destination?"

"Yes! My dad used to give my mom a break on the weekend by taking me and Ava on an adventure, and the pier was one of our favorite places." It was always their first choice. He had often taken the sisters out on his own. Why had she never ventured out on her own with Travis?

"You never took Travis?"

"I was just thinking about how the one time Jack and I did, it turned into a nightmare of tantrums."

"Did Travis throw a lot of tantrums?"

"Travis, no. Jack, all the time."

"Jack!"

"He was such a baby when he didn't get his way. I was so proud of Travis for saying he didn't want to go on the rides. It didn't matter to me, but Jack kept pushing and pushing. He couldn't let go of the version of the day he had pictured."

"Did Jack give you weekend breaks, too?"

"He tried to. But they have such different tastes that one of them was always disappointed."

"Why didn't you take Travis back to the pier?"

"I was just asking myself the same thing. Partly it never occurred to me. Travis and I were together all the time, so why would he want an outing with me. But mostly…" Kat had been watching Wendy expertly navigating the 405 traffic. She hadn't even commented on the drivers making hair-raising last-minute dives across her lane to catch the exit for the 101 or the slow drivers bogging down the left-hand lanes.

Wendy glanced over at her. "Mostly what?"

"I hate parking and driving to the pier requires parking somewhere."

"They have parking lots."

Kat grunted. "I'm already praying to the parking gods that there will be spots available."

"Have some faith! You might have to walk a little farther or pay a little more, but there will be something."

"You're not tense at all."

"That's your competition brain. If you don't get a good spot, you think you've lost."

"How did you know I was thinking that?"

Wendy rolled her eyes. "I turn the dial in my head to 'winning is everything' and it's not that hard."

"What else is on the dial?"

"Mine is set to 'do your best with what you've got.'"

"Has it always been, or is that something you taught yourself?"

"Always. I watched my dad do the best on his one income. We didn't live in a great place, but he made sure we were safe. He made sure we had enough to eat, and I did my best to make it taste okay."

"Is that why you became a chef?"

"Absolutely. It's a great challenge to look at the ingredients in your kitchen and figure out the most creative way to use it all."

"My parents were the opposite. If they didn't have what they needed, they went shopping or ordered in."

"I didn't have that luxury."

"I'm sorry."

"I'm not. It made me who I am. I feel rich now because I can buy what I want, not just what I need. I worked for that, and it feels good."

Kat had never experienced having to work for the basics. Her parents had covered their needs with enough frugality that growing up she typically got what she wanted. Jack had made enough that he had never set any limits for her. It didn't make her feel especially proud of herself. When they separated, she had chosen to live with her parents rather than look for a job that would have paid her enough to sustain her own home. "I've never lived by myself," she said softly.

"What about when you went to college?"

"The university was three miles away."

"Have you thought about living on your own?"

"It never seemed important." Kat studied Wendy's expression, but she was checking over her shoulder to merge onto the 10. "You think it's important."

Wendy glanced at her. "Maybe not for everyone."

"You think it would be good for me to live on my own. I can tell by your face." Wendy's guilty expression told her she was right.

"Your parents are nice, and I think it's great that they have room for you and Travis. But they seem very…present in your life."

"Kind of a red flag." Kat looked out the window, the blue of the Pacific now within view.

"I don't know. I guess it depends on whether you see yourself living there forever."

"I don't think about it," Kat said honestly. "Travis talks about going away to college. He's already warning me that he's considering out-of-state schools."

"I think that's great. You learn just as much living on your own as you do in the classroom."

"I don't know if I'll stay at my mom and dad's after he graduates."

"You don't have to decide now."

"Whew!" Kat smiled, thankful that Wendy was giving her an out.

"What you do have to decide now is what our focus is here. Rides? Food? Games?"

"Food first." When Wendy pulled off the freeway, Kat rolled down the window and filled her lungs with sea air. "I think I can already smell the churros!"

"We'll be first in line!"

* * *

An ocean breeze swirled the sounds of the pier around them—the roar of the metal coaster, the screams of the riders and music clashing from various carnival rides as they walked under an octopus sculpture into the throng. Kat watched as the crowd of tourists and locals shuffled together like a deck in the hands of a magician, taking in the colorful souvenir shops and restaurants that lined the arcade side of the pier. Blue surrounded them, not a cloud in the sky, the ocean stretching to the horizon, the salty breeze competing with the sweet aroma of the food stands.

Cinnamon and sugar from a churro dusted Kat's lips and sorely tempted Wendy though she didn't dare kiss Kat with an audience. She settled for holding her hand. Each step seemed to take years off Kat, and when they reached a ride that had spinning shark heads, she jumped up and down like a pre-teen. "Can we ride this one?"

"You stand in line. I'll get us some tickets. Should I get the wristbands, so we can hit a bunch of rides, or are we just going to do a few?"

"Someone has to work later. I don't think we'd get our money's worth."

"Good point." Not for the first time, Wendy wished there was someone else to take over the dinner service. José only asked her to take a few days each month, and he deserved the time off. She knew his family always made plans. Still, she felt just as she had when her dad had taken her to Disneyland. From the minute they stepped into the park, she wanted to slow down time to take in every tiny detail. "Do you want to take a look at the other rides first?"

"You said to tap into my irresponsible teenager," Kat reminded her. "That means instant gratification, doesn't it?"

"As you wish," Wendy said.

They stepped forward into the gaping mouth of a great white shark and pulled the bar down on their laps. "The Dread Pirate Roberts could have been a woman."

"Absolutely," Wendy said. "In fact, when Inigo was ready to retire, he asked me to take over. I must be back on the ship before it leaves the harbor."

"Is it docked nearby?"

The ride started to spin them around, making conversation more difficult as Wendy clung to the lap bar. "We may be able to spot it if we ride the Ferris wheel." Head thrown back in laughter, Kat radiated carefree happiness that Wendy wanted to bottle. Wendy tried to tell her how beautiful she looked, but the centrifugal force got the better of her grip, and she squished Kat against the outer edge of the shark's mouth.

Kat squealed with delight and let go of the bar to hold onto Wendy.

Too soon, the ride was over, and they stumbled back onto the pier. "That was so fun, and I don't need to do anything like it ever again."

"You didn't look like you were feeling your age in there. You were glowing like a teenager."

"I'm not that hearty anymore. It's a good thing you didn't get the wristbands. Can we really see your ship from the Ferris wheel?"

Wendy bumped her playfully with her shoulder. "You're a lot of fun, you know that?"

"If I recall, this was your idea. That makes you the fun one."

"I still argue it's the company."

They people-watched while they waited at the Ferris wheel. They held hands as it rotated to the top, and when they crested, Kat squeezed Wendy's hand, but it squeezed Wendy's heart, and she knew that her stomach bottoming out was from more than gravity. When Kat had opened up and shared her past and her fears, Wendy got a taste of intimacy she had never known. Spinning around and around, she discovered that she wanted to be by Kat's side for both the highs and the lows.

She was certain that other couples had their eyes closed and were lost in romantic kisses. In their cart, they scanned the horizon for Wendy's imagined ship, but Wendy was far from lost. She was exactly where she wanted to be.

"The Ferris wheel was always my favorite! Thank you for bringing me here," Kat said when the ride ended.

"Did you ride it every time?"

"Too expensive. We alternated between the Ferris wheel and the carousel. That was Ava's favorite."

"Did you play the carnival games?"

"Every once in a while, we could cajole my dad into trying to win us a bear. None of us were any good at them, though."

"We'll have to give it a try, then!" Wendy steered Kat toward the games. "What prize do you have your eye on?"

Kat walked slowly past the offerings. "My dad always said if we wanted a toy, it was smarter to save our money than waste it on trying for toys that were cheap anyway."

"I guess I see his point, but what shop ever has a giant purple bear like that?"

"You think you could win it?"

Wendy watched a trio of boys try their hand at the beanbag toss. They threw them as if the milk bottles were empty, and Wendy guessed that they were weighted at the bottom to make them more difficult to topple. It seemed likely that strikes at the narrower tops were more successful in knocking them over. "You need that bear."

"It's a pretty awesome bear!"

"It's as good as ours." Wendy paid for three throws. Two of her bean bags didn't even hit the bottles. The last toppled only one of the six.

"You can walk away. There are other bears in the world."

"I am not giving up. I can hear that bear, and he wants you as much as you want him."

Two of the next beanbags found their target, but not the third. Kat looked worried. "This isn't fun for you, is it?" Wendy asked.

"I don't want you to waste your money."

"Stop worrying. I'm not paying for a bear. I'm paying to have fun, and I'm having fun figuring out how to beat this." Kat relaxed, and Wendy shook out her arms in preparation for the next throw. She rolled her neck from one side to the other, and Kat massaged her shoulders. "That's the ticket!"

* * *

Both arms clasped around the huge purple bear, Kat beamed like a five-year-old. She had always wanted to be the kid holding the toy everyone wanted, and though she knew some of the grown-ups' smiles were mocking, the kids' awestruck looks were so worth the wait.

"Do you want me to carry that to the car?" Wendy asked.

"I'm sorry I'm so slow. It's not the bear, it's the food coma. I didn't need that ice cream after the pizza."

"But it was good!"

"If I just lay my head down, I could fall right asleep." Kat made the mistake of shutting her eyes. It felt much too nice with the sun warming her back.

"One more block and you can snooze in the car."

"I'm sure that would make me the worst date ever." She yawned and then laughed. "I'm already a terrible date. I swear it's not the company."

"I didn't take it personally. If I didn't have to get to work, I'd take a nap with you."

"So you *are* trying to get me into bed."

Wendy blushed hard.

"Now who's worried?" Kat said to rescue her. She bumped against her shoulder playfully.

Traffic was kind to them on the way home, and though Kat thought she would take Wendy's suggestion to close her eyes, she found she couldn't take her eyes off her. She could get used to looking at Wendy's profile, the way she always looked on the verge of smiling, her ringlet curls. Kat wanted to nuzzle past those curls and inhale the spiciness that was all Wendy.

"You're staring."

When Wendy glanced at her, Kat's whole body fluttered. "I was."

"Next time, you're driving, so I can stare."

Though it felt forward, Kat reached across the console and rested her hand on Wendy's thigh. Wendy's surprise thrilled her. She dropped her hand down to the seam at her inner thigh, watching Wendy try to control her reaction. Even though Wendy kept her eyes on the traffic, Kat knew she was completely tuned into her. And turned on? Was that her intent? Did she really have that kind of power? She knew she did, had always known that she had the ability to turn Jack on. She just hadn't wanted to.

Kat closed her eyes to explore her feelings about following through on what she was starting here. Today she had the safety net of Wendy having to work, but what about another day? Wendy said that that there was more to intimacy than sex, but did she believe it? There had to be a point at which she, too, would grow frustrated with Kat's vacillation.

"What are you smiling about?" Wendy asked.

"Was I smiling?" She opened her eyes. Wendy held hers for a moment before looking back to the road.

"You were, and it looks good on you."

"I was maybe thinking about whether, if you didn't have work, and we did take a nap…" It was difficult to vocalize what she'd been imagining, and she waited for Wendy to help her. When she didn't, Kat cleared her throat and tried to keep her voice level. "If there would actually be very much sleeping going on."

"You're making it extremely difficult to go to work, you know." Wendy shot her a mock glare.

They passed the miniature golf course, and Kat put it on the list of places she'd like to go with Wendy. She could see Wendy shaking her tush as she leaned over for a putt. "You make me want to do all sorts of things I've never done before," she said, her gaze still focused on the trees and rooftops visible from the freeway.

"What kinds of things?" Wendy's voice seemed to vibrate across Kat's skin.

"Miniature golf, for one," Kat admitted.

Wendy burst into laughter. "I did not see that coming!"

Too soon, Wendy slowed for Kat's exit and navigated the few blocks to her house. She was not ready for their date to end. The clock warned her that she didn't have very much time to say goodbye, and she wanted to make it a good goodbye. But when Wendy pulled into the drive, they saw the back-up lights of a familiar sports car.

"Jack's here to take Travis to rehearsal."

Wendy nodded and put her car in reverse. She backed into the street far enough to let Jack out of the drive, but instead of pulling away, Jack kept the car in reverse and pulled up next to Wendy, the passenger-side window lowered.

"Hi!" Travis said, waving like a much-younger child.

Jack ducked forward across the console. "Have fun at the pier?"

The tone in Jack's question hinted that he would just as easily believe that they had spent the last few hours at a hotel together. "We had such a good time!" She tapped Wendy and said just for her to hear, "Roll down the back window." When she did, Kat projected her voice again. "Look what Wendy won for me!"

Jack backed his car up adjacent to theirs, so they could look in the back seat.

"Sweet!" Travis said.

Jack pulled back up parallel to the driver's window. "We need to talk when you have some time." He looked uncomfortable, but she couldn't tell if it had to do with Wendy being there or something else.

"Sure," Kat said.

Travis waved adorably again as the window went back up and Jack sped away.

Wendy pulled back into the drive. "I have never been less motivated to go into work."

"If I remember correctly, we both have Mondays off. I could be convinced to keep my calendar clear." She gathered her things and Wendy got out to retrieve the bear from the back seat. Kat took it from her. "Thank you for this, for such a wonderful morning." She kissed Wendy like she wished she had on the Ferris wheel, her stomach still spinning and spinning.

CHAPTER SEVENTEEN

"If you found this on your desk, would you think sweet or she's trying too hard?" Wendy held her phone out, so Cory could see the picture of the arrangement of a dozen red roses. She'd been thinking of something to do since their date a few days earlier.

"Who are they for?"

"Kat. Remember the whole kissing thing?"

"You could still be dating Erin."

"Um. No! I am not dating two people at once."

"How'd Erin take it when you told her you were going to date Kat?"

"You're hilarious."

"You haven't told her yet?"

"Not about Kat. Just that I was sorry it wasn't going to work for us."

"She looked like she was willing to put in the work for two. She let you off that easy?"

"I didn't say it was easy. I was as honest as I could be."

"Are you going to sign the card 'I love you'?"

"No! I can't write that in a card until I've said it. I haven't said it yet."

"Then you can't send a dozen red roses."

"This one has red and yellow." Yellow was Ava's favorite color. If she sent those, she risked reminding Kat of her loss. That was far from the intended message.

"You don't want to send a mixed-message bouquet. Red and yellow says 'I'm not sure if we should be friends or lovers.' Wait. On second thought, that's exactly what you should send."

"Couldn't it represent the shift from friends to lovers or how lovers can be friends?"

"Let me see again." He held out his hand for the phone. He looked closely at the screen and yelped. "Have you seen how much these are!"

"I wasn't asking if you thought I was getting a good deal. I'm asking what's appropriate."

"What's the card going to say?"

"Something that says I want to be serious. I want her to know I'm courting her."

"What does that even mean?"

"You know, sending flowers and sweet nothings to let her know that I'm thinking about her. Cards and poems and such."

"Going on a buggy ride."

"A drive will suffice. I don't think I need to rustle up a pony and wagon."

"Are you sure? Cars go pretty fast."

"You think I'm a dork?" Was it just Kat's house that made her think of an old-fashioned approach to dating?

"I don't know. To me, courting means marriage."

"Asking for someone's hand means marriage. Courting means I'm interested in something serious." Wendy scrolled through the bouquets trying to find something right.

"Marriage is serious."

"The timer for the zucchini just went off."

"She has a child," Cory tossed over his shoulder.

"You say that like she's got a nursing infant who is up all night. She has a teenager who seems super cool." A bouquet of roses and stargazer lilies caught her eye, and she clicked on the link for more choices with the latter.

"What do you think of stargazers?"

"What are those?"

"Those big pink lilies that smell really good."

Cory removed the sautéed vegetables from the heat. "Let me see." Wendy gave him her phone. "Hmmm."

"What?"

"It looks like a funeral flower."

Wendy quickly tabbed his observation into a search bar. "It says here that white is associated with sympathy. Pink ones are romantic. And look. They symbolize opportunity and optimism. That's perfect." Aware that Cory was looking over her shoulder she ordered a bouquet of lilies and irises.

He whistled softly. "You're spending more on flowers than I spend on a dinner date!"

"Maybe you should take your date to a place without a drive-through window."

"Maybe someone needs to give me a raise."

"Earn it," Wendy teased.

"As far as I can tell, I'm the only one working here."

"I'm almost through. But I have to put something pithy on the card."

"Roses are red, violets are blue," Cory prompted.

Wendy grabbed that and ran with it. *Roses are red*, she typed. *Violets are blue. But only a stargazer can sparkle like you.*

She hit submit and pocketed her phone. When she looked up, Cory was staring at her. "This seems serious," he said.

"I know."

"Do you know what you're doing?"

"Not really," Wendy admitted. What was building with Kat was unlike anything she had experienced before. In the past, her libido had pulled her into fiery encounters that quickly burned out when there was nothing to talk about. With Kat, her desire to know more was pulling her closer. What was building was not a fast fire, but a blaze started with kindling on hot coals. "But I think I get Kat and what she needs."

"I can see that," Cory said. He paused as if he didn't want to say what he was thinking. "Does she get what you need?"

Wendy started to say of course, but was that so?

* * *

Kat pulled chicken strips, eggrolls and sauces from one of the take-out bags and put them on a plate to carry upstairs to her mother. "Dinner," she said, already turning toward the door.

"I had to talk to Jack today."

"Weren't you hiding up here when he dropped Travis off?"

"I don't have a car. He knows I'm here."

"He came up here?"

"Like I said. I had to talk to Jack today."

Kat crossed her arms. "About what?"

"He seemed surprised that you weren't here, and he waited for a while."

"Up here?" Kat asked getting worried. "He knows I have bell rehearsal."

"You're usually home a half hour ago."

"Oh. Is it that late? I had a phone call on the way out of the office," she lied. It was a simple alteration from what had actually happened. In the parking lot, she'd found a note Wendy had tucked beneath her windshield wiper sometime during the day. She had enjoyed similar gestures ever since Wendy had sent the gorgeous bouquet and she delighted in hearing Wendy's voice as much as she delighted in the gestures themselves. The thank-you call had felt like just a few minutes, but there seemed to be so much to say once she had Wendy on the line.

"It is. I've said it before and I'll say it again, you put in full-time hours at the church. They should give you a full-time salary."

"I don't want to be there nine to five. I like my schedule." Her mother had complained about her hours before, and Kat knew that there was no changing either one of their minds. She changed the subject instead. "Did Jack tell you what he wanted?"

"He was quite amiable today, full of questions about the wedding that was here. Sounds like he and Ember are pretty stressed out about their upcoming nuptials."

Kat wasn't sure why Jack would have come up to talk to her mom about that, but the last thing she wanted was a rundown of their wedding plans from her mom. She turned to go.

"He wanted to know about you and Wendy, too."

"What?" Kat had to sit down. "What did he want to know about us?"

"Whether you're seeing each other."

"Why would he think that?"

"Maybe someone told him about the flowers?"

"What did you tell him?"

"That if she wasn't so young, I'd throw myself at her."

"Please tell me you didn't really say that."

"I said you went on a picnic and that you seem happy."

"Why'd you tell him that!"

"Because you seem happy. Aren't you happy?"

"Yes, but he doesn't have to know that."

"I don't see what's wrong with him knowing that."

Kat worried her palm with her thumb. She wasn't even sure Wendy had talked to Erin. Why hadn't she made sure Wendy had let Erin down before they'd gone out? "I can't talk to you about this. I have to feed Travis."

"I'm sure he can feed himself."

"Well I haven't eaten." She didn't wait for her mother to say anything else. As Millie had predicted, Travis had come up to the kitchen for his food and was probably eating in front of his tablet downstairs. Her father, too, was already well through his dinner, his plate balanced on his knees and his favorite show playing on his laptop.

She carried her bag downstairs to Travis's room. "Mind if I join you?"

"No."

"How was your day?"

"Good."

"Practice?"

"Good."

"How about some broccoli with your burger?"

"What? Gross."

"I didn't know if you were really listening." He nodded, so she continued. "How's your dad?"

Travis didn't look away from the tablet. "Good. Fine. Why?"

"Gramma said he was waiting for me."

"Oh…yeah." Travis took another bite.

Her burger was still passably warm, but the fries were cold and soggy. She leaned over and swiped some ketchup from Travis's plate. "What does he want to talk to me about?"

"I don't know." His eyes flitted from the screen. He knew something that he wasn't saying.

"'Don't know or can't say?'" Kat asked, quoting *Dave*, another of her favorite movies.

"Mom!" he complained. He hated it when she quoted movies.

She waited, but he wasn't talking. "You know something."

"I know you need to talk to Dad."

"That's weak."

"No it's not. It's the truth."

"What do I need to talk to him about?"

Still distracted by the show, he said, "The wed—" He snapped his mouth shut, but it was too late.

"Is the marriage off?" Kat made sure to keep her face neutral.

"You really need to talk to Dad."

"Oh." Kat ate some more burger and pretended to watch Travis's show. She made herself sit until she'd finished the burger. Then she ate more soggy fries. Travis glanced at her a few times, but she kept her eyes on the screen. "You want the rest of my fries?"

"Sure." He reached for them. "You calling Dad?"

"I'll call. I'll call. Need anything else?"

"No thanks. You want to call him now?"

"Fine. I'm sure I can be grown up about it."

"Really?"

"Of course."

Kat climbed the stairs. At the landing, she heard his voice again. "Love you, Mom."

"Love you too, kiddo," she called back.

After puttering around the kitchen, she poured a glass of water, said goodnight to her father and climbed the stairs. She pulled up her phone and then closed it out again, still trying to figure out what he'd want to talk about. Enough! She scolded herself. Just dial.

"Kat!" Jack sounded happy.

"Sorry I was running late."

"I know how hard it is for you to get away during Easter season."

Kat laughed silently. He'd never understood that when they were together. "What's up?"

"Travis was telling us about the ceremony, and it sounded amazing."

She waited for him to continue, but silence stretched between them on the line. "Yes, it was lovely."

"And your mom and dad. They were okay with them using the house?"

"Why? Because they're gay? Jack..."

"No! I'm sorry. I didn't mean that. I just wondered how your mom coped with all the guests there."

Kat could not imagine why he would care. "You know my mom. It was stressful, but it went okay."

"And the bridge Travis told us about. Is it still over the pool?"

"What's going on, Jack?"

"Remember how the venue Ember picked had some pretty bad water damage?"

"I remember you saying that everything was going to be fine."

"The repairs went according to schedule, but they didn't pass inspection. They've had to cancel our booking."

"Please tell me you're not asking what I think you're asking."

"I know it's unconventional..."

"To ask your ex if you can use her house for your second wedding? You couldn't have at least asked me to check the church schedule?"

"Ember doesn't want a church wedding."

"Can't you postpone?"

"You have no idea how stressed out Ember is, first with the planning and now with this hiccough. I just want to get it over with."

"Do you hear yourself?"

"I didn't mean that."

"Jack…" As she searched for a reason to say no, he adopted his lawyer's voice and pitched his best case, and in the end, it was easier to say yes than it was to argue with him.

By the time she hung up, she needed chocolate. A lot of chocolate. So much she was tempted to call Wendy and say that she was having a chocolate emergency and required an entire pan of her brownies. Phone in hand, she heard how much like her mother she sounded. There had to be something downstairs.

She said a silent prayer that she would find the kitchen empty. Some See's candy would help bring her world back into balance. The box she found on the mantle in the dining room was mostly empty papers. A lone cherry as if Ava was still with them. She loved the chocolate-covered cherries the best, and Kat had never understood why she wouldn't eat them first. *Duh! Nobody else likes them, so I know they'll still be there after I've had the ones everyone likes.* Kat could still hear her laughter.

In the china cupboard, she found a stash of Hershey's Kisses. The orange and black foil gave away that they'd been there since Halloween, but she unwrapped one and popped it in her mouth anyway. Travis arrived at the top of the stairs just as she spat the stale chocolate in the trash. "I need chocolate. If you're not here to help, then you're not welcome."

"You talked to Dad?"

Kat rolled her eyes and. "Uh, yep."

"Gramma was talking about making chocolate chip cookies. Would that help?"

In the baking cupboard, there was, indeed, a fresh bag of chocolate chips. Kat pulled open the bag and sat down at the kitchen table. She poured a handful of chips into her palm and tossed them back.

"Aren't you going to make cookies?"

"Since when do you think I bake? You must be smoking something down there. Come here and let me smell you."

He stepped forward with his hand extended, and she shook some chocolate chips into his palm. More restrained, he popped them into his mouth one at a time. "Are you mad at me?"

"You? Why would I be mad at you?"

"For telling them about the dudes who got married here."

"No. I'm not mad about that. You didn't make your dad call and ask me if he could get married here."

"But they wouldn't have known if I hadn't said." Travis extended his hand for more chocolate chips. "I wanted them to stop fighting about it."

"Oh. I didn't know they fought." Kat remembered how she had struggled not to fight with Jack in front of Travis.

Travis shrugged.

When they all dined out together, everything seemed perfect between Jack and Ember. She'd forgotten the public persona she'd worn for years, so well that their friends were shocked to learn that there was any strife at home. She'd continued to believe that their marriage ended because of her lack of interest in sex. Jack and Ember seemed so affectionate with each other that she felt sure they were happy.

"He wanted to know what's up with you and Wendy," Travis said without looking at Kat.

"What did you tell him?"

"That he should talk to you."

"Good answer. You want some milk?"

"If you put chocolate in it."

This brought a smile to her face, the juxtaposition of his boy self still present in the man he was maturing to be. She prepared the chocolate milk as she had so many times before and delivered it to the table. He sat across from her now, sporting a milk mustache after his first sip. "Do you want to know what's up with me and Wendy?"

"Only if you want to say."

"I like her. And her taking me to the pier was a real date. I'd like to keep dating her. Would that be weird for you?"

Another shrug. He gulped the rest of his milk. "She seems cool, but it's not like it matters if I like her or not."

"It matters to me."

"Everything she's cooked has been super good."

"So as long as she keeps feeding you, she's in?"

"And if she makes you happy."

His words warmed Kat's heart. "She does."

He got up to rinse his glass and put it in the dishwasher. He stood there long enough that Kat finished her plain milk and joined him by the sink.

"Do you think you'll get married again?"

Kat exhaled in surprise and crossed her arms over her chest. She leaned against the counter. "That's really hard for me to say. I haven't really thought about it."

"Did you marry Dad because of me?" He kept his eyes on the floor.

"He told you that?"

"No. But if you're dating Wendy now…I just wondered why you married Dad."

Kat thought about how afraid she had been to feel anything for Miranda and how safe it felt to get married and have a family. "You were only part of why."

"If you hadn't gotten pregnant, do you think you'd have married a girl?" He looked at her now, and it struck Kat how grown up he was.

"I don't think I would have been brave enough. Things were a lot different eighteen years ago. Bottom line, I wouldn't change any of it."

"Okay."

"One hug, one kiss?" she asked.

He complied.

"Love you," Kat said.

"Love you too, Mom."

Listening to him trot down the stairs, she appreciated how lucky she was to have a kid who would talk to her. She knew that Wendy considered her childhood to be messed up and hoped that her adult self wouldn't scar her own kid.

CHAPTER EIGHTEEN

Wendy cleaned when she was angry, and she was really angry. Her phone hit the counter with a clatter, and she pulled a spray bottle out from under the sink and squirted the front of the stove. She was still trying to wrap her head around the fact that Kat's ex-husband had called her to ask her to cater his wedding. At first, she had thought it was an elaborate April Fool's joke. That he was entirely serious made her all the more pissed.

She wanted to know why Kat would have passed on her private number, but she needed to calm down before she spoke with her. Maybe she hadn't done it willingly. Jack sounded like the kind of person who usually got what he wanted. Maybe it was his idea to have Wendy cater, not Kat's. That made her feel better. But if Kat knew it was a bad idea, why wouldn't she have given Jack her business number? Maybe she had but Jack had called back to badger for Wendy's personal number when he got the message that played before the restaurant opened. Why were they talking on the phone anyway?

They had sat at the same table when Travis played at the bar, but Wendy had thought that was for Travis's benefit. She got that Travis forever tied Kat to Jack, but his getting married again had nothing to do with their son. His call made Wendy worry about how involved they still seemed to be. Divorce was supposed to mean Kat was free. Maybe she should be on board to help Jack get married. That was sure to put more distance between them, wasn't it?

Talking to herself wasn't making her any less agitated.

Wishing she didn't feel so nervous she called Kat.

"Hey!" she chirped. "I'm so bummed that it's not going to work out for Jack's wedding."

Wendy was so taken aback that she couldn't immediately reply.

Kat continued without prompting. "I was just thinking about calling you. I was remembering how Cory said we made such a good team, me with the setting and you with the food. If you're all booked up, what would you think of doing only the food prep, and I could manage the setup here? If we did something like Jeremy and Evan's rehearsal dinner, I could pull it off, don't you think?"

Wendy found her voice. "Why would you do all that for Jack?"

"What do you mean?"

"He's your ex, and he's marrying someone else. At your house. You don't think that's weird?"

"But everything is still set up, and it's perfect."

"What did your parents say about it?" Wendy asked, trying to ascertain whether she was the one being unreasonable.

"My mom said as long as I can keep people downstairs, it's fine with her."

Wendy squirted the front of her fridge with cleaner and scrubbed.

"What about your dad and Travis?"

"They're fine. But you don't seem fine. What's wrong?"

The number of times Kat had said "we" was a starting point, but Wendy bit her tongue. For a second. "Why do you keep saying 'we'? Isn't it his wedding that he's planning with someone else? I'm having a tough time with the energy you're investing in this."

Kat took a moment to reply, and Wendy wondered if she was moving somewhere more private. "I don't understand why you're upset. You helped before."

If Kat couldn't sense Wendy's discomfort, how was she supposed to explain it? And if she had to explain it, was there any point? "Why didn't you call me?" she asked.

"What?"

"To ask about catering. You called for Jeremy and Evan."

"I offered to call, but Jack said he didn't want you to feel like you had to say yes."

"And he got what he wanted," Wendy mumbled feeling like what she wanted didn't matter to Kat at all.

"But you can't do it, and it doesn't sound like my idea will work, either. I was just trying to help."

"Why isn't his wife-to-be helping?"

"She's…not feeling well," Kat stammered. "She's got really bad morning sickness."

What a train wreck, Wendy thought, glad that she already had a legitimate booking. "I hope they have a lovely day," she managed.

"Wendy?" Kat said, keeping her on the line.

Wendy found her throat had tightened up. "Yeah?"

"You never said why you called. We got sidetracked with the wedding."

"Jack's wedding? The food?"

"Right. Um. Did you want to try to get together before you go into work on Saturday?"

Hearing Kat search for a way to make her happy made Wendy's heart hurt. "I'm guessing you'll be busy with Jack's wedding, and I can't help with that."

"Oh."

Kat sounded so puzzled that Wendy wanted to scream. *How can you possibly think it's okay to plan all the details for your ex to marry someone else in your childhood home instead of pointing out that it's the new bride's job? You remember, that friend of yours who agreed to the couple swap? How does that not seem fucked up to you?*

Her inner monologue reminded her that she had told Kat out loud that her childhood was fucked up. Was that why it felt perfectly fine to help Jack? It had been so easy to let her feelings for Kat snowball, but recalling Cory's question about whether Kat got what Wendy needed sucker-punched her. Kat didn't get what she needed at all. She was still the straight girl caught up in her ex's straight world planning another straight wedding. She wasn't part of Wendy's world at all. And it didn't seem like she ever would be. "I'm so sorry Kat," she said, her throat even tighter.

"For what? Wendy? What's wrong?"

The fear in Kat's voice made Wendy want to say it was nothing, that they'd get together after the wedding, go to the observatory at Griffith Park or watch the sunrise at Vasquez Rocks. But that would happen only if something with Jack or her parents didn't come up because if they needed her, surely they'd come first. She felt like when Kat carved up her time, Wendy would always get the last serving.

She wanted someone who was free to hang out after work, not someone who had errands to run for her mother, or father, or ex-husband. She saw Kat's mother not as someone waiting to be served but someone who took heaping spoonful after spoonful of Kat's time before the bowl even got passed around. She did not begrudge Travis his portion of Kat's attention, but it was a whole lot easier for her to understand that Kat was always going to be his mom than it was to understand why she felt obligated to help Jack. "I don't know if I can do this," Wendy finally said.

"The wedding? I know. You already said that."

Silence extended between them as Wendy tried to put into words how she felt. "I am having trouble seeing where I fit into your life."

"What are you talking about? I want to spend every extra minute I have with you."

"Except when Jack needs help with his wedding."

"That's not fair," Kat said sharply. "I didn't expect him to drop this on me, and it's not like he's going to ask me to plan another wedding for him after this one."

"What else will it be? Did it occur to you that you could say no?" More silence. Wendy's heart sank. "No. You want to do the wedding. That makes it seem like you're still part of his life."

"I want to help him with this one day. It's not that big of a deal, is it?"

Wendy refused to get sucked into the drama of Kat's former life. "Sure. No big deal."

"Wendy, it will be fine. Right?" Kat sounded worried.

"I don't know, Kat. I really don't know."

By the time she hung up, every item in her refrigerator was on the counter. She rinsed her rag in the hot soapy tub she had next to her on the floor and attacked the sticky calcified spot at the very back of the lowest shelf.

* * *

She'd been wrong about letting Jack and Ember get married at the house. Kat could see that now, and how she wished she'd realized it two weeks ago. When she'd hung up, she'd been momentarily crushed, but what she felt for Wendy was so new that she quickly shoved it aside and leaned into feeling angry with Wendy for refusing to help. She tracked down a taco caterer and shopped for the goodies for the cottage treats and gift bags and the candles to float in the pool.

Despite her mother's adamant stance about the upstairs being off-limits, Kat insisted that her room was the logical place for Ember to get dressed. Somewhere between the cold click of her mother's door shutting just as Kat and Ember reached the top of the stairs and Ember descending in her white dress, a stone of regret settled in Kat's belly. It had brought her no pleasure to hear Ember complain about the impact a second child would have on her body and the months she would have to suffer without alcohol.

Kat had helped Jack coordinate a minister, photographer and guests. Now she found herself retreating like her mother. She texted her father. *Does everything seem under control?*

Organized chaos. Will you be joining the gathering?

Think I'll stay up here if that's okay.

Shall I deliver that message to Jack?

If he asks.

As you wish.

His text transported her back to the pier with Wendy, and she wished that she could exit the wedding on a pirate ship and sail away from it all. She tried to think of an apology quote from *The Princess Bride* but came up empty. Then an idea popped into her head. Pretty certain that Wendy would have seen *When Harry Met Sally*, she texted Wendy *You're right, you're right. I know you're right.*

Her heart lightened when her phone chimed, but the message to Wendy was still the only one on the screen. She went back to her inbox and found a message from Travis. *They're starting!*

Ok, she thumbed back.

Aren't you coming?

It's too weird.

Couldn't you have thought of that before?

Sorry?

You are so busted for this.

Not as busted as you're going to be for texting in the front row.

How do you know where I am? From the patio, he looked up to her window and saw her. She could tell he was growling at her. She pointed to his father and soon-to-be stepmother, hoping he would intuit his need to be respectful.

She watched from the window, her mind filled not with the memory of exchanging vows with Jack but rather with the desire to kiss Wendy as she'd stood with her on the porch. And how it had felt kissing her. Why wasn't she checking her messages? Or had she seen it and decided not to answer?

After Wendy had said she shouldn't host Jack and Ember's wedding, Kat ever so briefly considered calling Jack to cancel, but having already said yes, it would have been so much harder to call and tell him no. Her stomach knotted with worry that Wendy would not forgive her the weakness of catering to her family's needs. But of course, Jack wasn't her family any longer. She realized that now.

Her phone chimed, and she found a text from her mother, right on cue. *Is it over? I'm hungry. I hope they at least got a decent caterer.*

Kat pocketed her phone. She didn't have the energy to deal with her. She groaned when she heard the door down the hall open. Millie entered the room without knocking and joined her at the window. "Back up," Kat whispered. "People could see you if you stand there."

"Like I care. It's my house."

"And some of the people out there are still my friends."

Her mother sighed her disagreement. "Well Travis looks sharp. Can't believe that woman would wear white. Must've lost its meaning since I got married."

"You weren't a…" Kat tipped her head back. "You know, I don't want to talk about it."

Millie moved Kat's purple bear from her corner chair, propped her cane and sat. Kat remained tucked behind the curtain. "You didn't answer my text."

"I'm watching the wedding."

"Who have you been texting with?"

"Dad. Travis."

"I was hoping you'd been texting with Wendy."

"She's working." Kat didn't want to admit that she wished she'd been texting with Wendy too.

"Too bad she's not catering here."

"Did you need something, Mom?"

"I told you. I'm hungry."

"I'm not going back down there." Kat hadn't known she was staying upstairs until she said it out loud, but with the decision came instant relief.

"But what will we eat?"

"Text Dad. Maybe he'll bring you something."

"You said yourself your friends are here. Why won't you go down?"

"I'm not feeling up to it. This is Jack's day, not mine. Everyone's going to want to know how I feel, and I don't feel like saying I'm fine right now."

"But that's what you always do."

Kat couldn't argue that point, but she also didn't have to continue to do what didn't feel right. She was tired of lying. She would have loved to share her small step of progress with Wendy, but seeing as she hadn't answered Kat's last message, Kat would have to hold that thought. She had so much to say to Wendy. Maybe if she called, Wendy would talk to her. Her mother waited for her to say something, but Kat didn't have the energy. She was finished. "I'm sorry I didn't tell Jack to find another venue. Sorry that we're stuck up here until it's over."

"Everyone is going to notice that you disappeared."

"I'm aware."

"And they're going to talk about it."

"Yep."

"You're okay with that?"

Kat remembered talking to Wendy about what her friends would have said if she'd befriended her in high school. Now she knew it would have been better to have told Wendy how good she looked at prom. What had she gained by being a part of the inner circle? Then or now. "It's time to be honest and live my own life."

"Whose life are you living now?"

She'd been talking to herself, not to her mom. Millie was still talking, trying to decipher what Kat meant when the meaning was just coming to Kat herself. She wanted to be alone, she concluded. Every word her mom said crowded her more until she started to feel like the room was so full of words that she couldn't breathe.

"Mom," she finally interrupted. "I need you to do something for me."

Her mom leaned forward. "What? You need me to get Travis? You look overwhelmed."

"I need you to leave."

Her words gave her more room to think.

"Please. I want to be alone."

Millie's mouth opened, and Kat dared her mother with her fiercest look to say a word. To her amazement, Millie got up and walked to the door. She hesitated for a moment, but blessedly left, shutting it quietly behind her.

Kat leaned back against the wall. The party had started, and Kat felt the reverberating thump, thump, thump of the bass. As the crowd celebrated the beginning of Jack and Ember's commitment, Kat started to imagine what her life could be like on her own.

CHAPTER NINETEEN

"Hi there, sweetness," Wendy's dad said, kissing her cheek.

Wendy closed her door and hugged her stepmother, Marie, who had stayed back in contrast to her dad who had continued inside. The yellow two-bedroom house sat back from the street. Light and shadow rippled from a slight breeze blowing through the majestic magnolia in her front yard. White trim accented the cream-colored walls of her living room.

As was Drew's habit, he checked on his creations, two walnut chairs facing the large front room to separate the living room from her dining area. He raised the leaves of a tea-service table he had crafted from cherry wood. With fewer than eight-hundred square feet, Wendy usually left the leaves down, but each month when her dad visited, the first thing he did was pull them up to admire the full wingspan.

"What smells so good today?" Marie asked.

"I'm trying a recipe for spicy cauliflower curry," Wendy said.

"Let's get the wine breathing," Marie said carrying her things to the kitchen.

Wendy followed her into the kitchen that had been the major selling point of the home. Though the structure itself was small, the kitchen was roomy and came with an industrial stove and generous counter space. "I was thinking about making tomato chutney to go with the curry."

"You're the expert. Is this something you and José are going to put on the menu at Fairbanks?"

The question led them into an easy and familiar conversation about what was new at the restaurant and how her catering was going. When Marie had first started dating her father, Wendy hadn't taken them seriously. She was still a teenager, and in her mind, they simply didn't match. Marie had a good six inches on Drew, even without the heels she always wore with her tailored suits. Wendy had been polite to her because she couldn't see someone as poised and stylish staying with her father who wore the same jeans and T-shirts until they were full of holes. And yet they were still together almost twenty-five years later. Her dad's jeans were newer, and his shirts intact, but he still wore his long hair pulled back in a ponytail and his beard bushy.

The curry ready to serve over couscous, Wendy pulled out four of her favorite pottery wine goblets from leaded-glass cupboards.

"Expecting someone?" Drew asked

"What?" Wendy asked. He pointed to the glasses and, realizing her mistake, she blushed. All weekend she'd been curious about how the wedding had gone, yet she had not texted. For two days, she had been crafting and rejecting responses. Now that she had waited so long, it was even more difficult to find the right words. "I don't know what I was thinking," she said, placing the extra goblet back on the shelf and pouring wine into the other three.

Now that Wendy's subconscious had imagined having Kat join her family dinner, she couldn't stop thinking about it. She'd told them about past girlfriends but had never felt compelled to introduce them. Like she'd told Erin, social expectations had never prompted her to take a date to a holiday event. Unless she was serious about someone, she was not going to suggest such a thing, and she'd never been that serious before.

So why had she pulled out four goblets?

What would Kat make of her dad and Marie? She wagered that Kat would match Principal Marie's stories of angry parents and troubled kids with observations about the church congregation. Would Kat and her dad have anything to talk about? Wendy tried to find something they had in common. Failed first marriages?

The text Kat had sent a week ago refreshed in her mind. *You're right, you're right. I know you're right.* She'd immediately recognized Carrie Fisher's line in *When Harry Met Sally.* With a smile, she had started to text back to ask what made her finally realize her mistake, but then it occurred to her that Kat had said this as her ex-husband got married in her backyard and Carrie Fisher's other line came to mind. *He's never going to leave her.* Because of Travis, how could Jack really ever leave Kat? The parallel of the single parent with a teenaged child dating for the first time socked her squarely in the solar plexus.

"When you started dating my dad…" Wendy began, but her mouth was ahead of her brain. Marie motioned with her fork for Wendy to continue. But now Wendy was too embarrassed. She fumbled around and found a suitable substitute. "Did you worry about whether I'd like you?"

"Never."

Drew laughed and kissed Marie on the cheek.

Wendy's brows knitted together. "Really? Never?"

"I'm a principal. I'm used to kids not liking me. But that wasn't your question."

"How do you know?" Wendy asked.

"I can tell when kids are lying, even grown-up ones. What's on your mind?" She flicked her always-perfect shoulder-length dark hair back from her face and waited, poised yet genuine.

Wendy took a bite of curry and chewed it slowly, pleased with the flavors and textures. She rolled words around in her mind, trying to pin down her own worry about Kat. "Did you ever worry about my mom?"

"Judy? God no. Why would I have worried about her?"

"Having an ex-wife didn't make him seem less available?"

Marie considered Wendy's question carefully, and Wendy could see her principal persona thinking not only about her own answer but what was behind Wendy's question.

"When I met your dad, it was clear that the package was you and him, together. He rarely talked about Judy, but when he did, it was like he was talking about a different lifetime. By the time I met him, he was a totally different person."

"But it helped that my mom wasn't local."

"Why would that make a difference?" her dad asked.

"If she wanted you to do something for her, wouldn't it have been harder to say no if she still lived nearby?"

Drew easily dismissed the idea. "Nope. You, I couldn't say no to, and Marie knew that. But Judy? She'd had her chance."

"Is something going on with Judy?" Marie asked.

"I don't know," Wendy said. "I haven't talked to her in a long time."

"Why the sudden interest?" she asked.

"I've met someone I really like. I'd like to think it could go somewhere, but she's already got so much going on in her life."

"As in she's busy or as in she's unavailable?" Marie asked. She rested her fork on her plate, her expression full of concern.

"Part of it is how busy she is. She works at a church where I do quite a bit of catering, and she has a teenage son."

"Isn't that the friend you ran into at the reunion?" Marie asked.

"Yes."

"Was she with her husband then?" Drew asked.

"Separated and since divorced."

"And no longer living together?" Marie asked.

"Who lives together after they're divorced?"

"Financial struggle sometimes makes it necessary," Marie explained.

"She and her son live with her parents."

"How many high school friends of yours are living with their parents?" Drew asked.

"Only Kat."

"Wait, this is the same girl you knew in high school?"

"Woman," Marie inserted.

Drew let the correction stand, though Wendy could see that in his mind it was okay to call a high-school-aged female a girl. "Kat and I both went to Garfield. But she was part of the popular crowd. We never ran in the same circle, and I thought she was too hoity-toity to be friends. But after the reunion a couple years ago, I found out that wasn't who she was at all, so since then we've been friends."

"So the person you knew in high school became the married woman you liked and began to work with, but that too is a past identity. Now she is single," Marie summed up.

"Those all sound like completely different lives to me," Drew said.

Marie chuckled. "Her name, then is apropos. Cats are said to have many lives."

Her father laughed. "Just hope she's not on her last one."

"I can see where some lives would end. She's not the same as she was in high school. And she's not married anymore, but she's always going to be a mom. That's a permanent identity, isn't it?" Wendy asked.

"It's not as literal as the end of a marriage, but there comes a point when the relationship dynamic changes. You and your father are good examples of that," Marie said. "You were already autonomous when I met you, and now look, you're your own person who hosts us once a month. It's nice to be here with you, but we don't depend on you. One day we will, but that will be yet another phase of your life."

"I see what you mean," Wendy said. "I can see where her son is now in a place where he doesn't need her so much, but she still lives with her parents. That seems like a red flag when I think about pursuing something more than friendship."

"Has she ever lived by herself?" Marie asked.

"No," Wendy said, remembering her conversation with Kat at the pier.

"I've always said that everyone should live by themselves for at least a year in order to know who they are and what they want," Marie said.

"You've never said that," Drew laughed.

"Just because you didn't hear it doesn't mean I've never said it," Marie said. "Neither of you ever needed to hear it, for which I am very grateful, by the way." She wrapped her arm around Wendy's shoulder. "Is there anything we can do?"

"Dessert might help."

"How can you think of putting another thing in your stomach?" Drew asked.

"It's not going in my stomach. It's going in my dessert pocket," Wendy said.

"Now your chocolate request makes sense," Marie said. "Chocolate makes everything better."

Except that chocolate made her think of Kat and how much she had liked her brownies. She knew the no-lying-about-the-artichoke-dip, chocolate-loving Kat, not the white-lies high-school Kat. The sexy drummer that she'd like to see more of. Those, together with the wife, mother and daughter brought her up to six distinct lives. But Kat had also been a sister, as well as a survivor of her sister's death. Eight lives. What would she do with her ninth?

* * *

"How do you get this fucking screwy thing in the turny thing?" Kat looked for some kind of release on the drill but didn't see anything. She went back to the garage and looked for a regular screwdriver and found a drawer with at least a dozen. She carried the whole drawer to the pool yard.

Jeremy and Evan had scheduled Dave to take the bridge apart the weekend following their wedding. They agreed to leave it up for the second wedding but didn't know when Dave would be available to come out to disassemble it. At the time, that had seemed fine, but all week, she saw Jack and Ember illuminated by the candles in the pool and hated herself a little more for acquiescing to Jack and not listening to Wendy.

Had she said no, she would have been able to picture herself and Wendy on the bridge. She would have felt the exhilaration of anticipated kisses instead of the disappointment of Wendy's excuses for her tardy reply.

So here she was, screwdriver in hand, determined to take apart the bridge. The screws had an x in the middle, so she selected a pointy screwdriver. Hoping that *righty tighty, lefty loosie* held for more than just mayonnaise lids, she poked the point in and cranked. It didn't budge. With two hands, she twisted, but the tool started to move without the screw loosening.

"The wrong tool will strip the head." Kat jumped at the sound of her father's voice. "May I recommend the electric drill for the number of screws involved?"

"It wouldn't hold the screwdriver part."

Clyde entered the pool yard and in less than a minute assembled the necessary pieces and deftly removed the damaged screw.

"It is not my intention to intrude if your desire was to disassemble this on your own."

Why couldn't he just ask if she wanted his help or to be left alone? "I appreciate your help."

"You could look in the recycling for a yogurt container, something to hold the screws."

Kat returned with a small shipping box thinking she would tell her mother how her habitual online ordering had come in handy. She should have been prepared at least mentally if not emotionally when she returned. Her father. Poolside. Crouched.

Only not over a bridge and screws.

Over her sister.

Push, push, pushing on her ribs.

Breathe.

Breathe, dammit.

When had the ambulance arrived? She did not want to remember the lights and sirens. She didn't want to remember.

She was so cold. It was so cold sitting in the hospital in her wet swimsuit. Even with a blanket wrapped around her, she was so cold. She heard her mother's roar when she arrived. Her throat burned raw, and she fought against hands that held her. She opened her eyes to see her father, startled, his hands on her shoulders.

"Kat?"

The sound was coming from her.

"Don't touch me! Don't touch me!" Her body suddenly burned fire hot.

He backed away. "What is this?"

"Why was he more important? You chose him when you should have been by the pool." The panic she had felt as a child collided with her adult anger.

"It was an accident. What do you want me to do? Say I'm sorry?"

"Are you? Or were you more upset to lose Antòn?"

"You are not the only one who grieved."

"And you still won't say you're sorry."

"Would it help?" Clyde's voice was eerily calm. Only the rise and fall of his chest betrayed how upset he was.

"Never mind."

"Still you cannot forgive."

"No. I can't. Because of your choice, I have to carry that night. You were the parent but that didn't matter. All that mattered was getting laid."

"Ava did not die because Antòn and I were lovers."

"You were distracted."

"Parenthood is full of distractions."

"You should have been outside telling her not to mess around."

"In other words, it's your guilt that you did not tell her to be careful. Perhaps you should forgive yourself."

"No. You put your happiness first, and we all paid the price."

"Has your mother not put her happiness before others as well?"

"I can't do this." Kat threw her arms up in the air. "This is why I don't talk about Ava. The only thing that you care about is proving it wasn't your fault."

"It grieves me that you don't think I have paid for my mistake. I lost both my daughters that night."

Kat could not disagree. Without another word, she walked away from her father. He was absolutely correct that she never trusted him again, and when Millie attempted suicide, she'd lost her mother as well. She knew that her father saw the opposite, that he felt redeemed by preventing Millie's death with his quick action. It was true that she survived opening a vein at her elbow. But he could not erase the silence on the other side of the bathroom door when Kat had knocked. Could never erase the silence in the car as he drove them all to the emergency room, Kat alone in the back seat wondering which sister would get to have her mother.

She was no longer a sister, and she didn't feel like a daughter either. It wasn't such a surprise, really, that she'd gotten pregnant so early. Her childhood had been pulled out from under her. Being a wife and a parent gave her a clear sense of self and purpose.

She stormed to her room and grabbed a duffel bag, blindly tossing in clothes from her drawers. Abruptly she stopped and sat on her bed. There was nowhere to go. Maybe if it was just her, she could call Wendy. She threw the bag across the room and screamed into her pillow. Wendy was the only one who knew enough about her dad for her to unload, but how could she call when she knew Wendy was angry with her?

For a second, she considered calling Erin. She knew Erin had room in that huge house, but she could not ask her to take in Travis as well. She sat there in her old room stunned. All she had known was this bedroom and the one she had shared with Jack. She had never had a space she had created herself. Could she have her own apartment? She really didn't have the first clue how to go about it. Jack had set up the phone and the electricity and the… She grabbed a pen and started making a list of all the things she would need. But first she needed to find a place, and if she was thinking about a new place, maybe she should be looking for a new job. Taking a deep breath, she booted up her computer to see what she could do about her own life.

CHAPTER TWENTY

I have a favor, Kat's text read. Wendy hadn't even had time to formulate a response when another flash of messages came in.

I keep bothering you. Sorry.

Wendy started to type an apology for being less available. In the weeks following Jack and Ember's wedding, any time the happiness from their pier date urged her to get in touch with Kat, the anger she felt when Jack had called had stayed her hand.

So much happened after the wedding. Sometime maybe we could do lunch.

What had happened since the wedding? Was Kat embracing her lesbianism? Not that she ever used the label. Was that significant? She allowed herself to contemplate what it would be like to keep dating Kat and be a part of her self-discovery.

I miss talking to you, Kat texted again.

Marie's question about whether Kat had ever lived by herself resurfaced. Like Marie, Wendy thought that it was important. As hard as it was, she had to back away and give Kat space to discover who she was for herself. She wanted to be part of her life but not at the expense of Kat's independence.

So much has changed.

What had changed? Her connection to Jack? With his marriage to Ember, that tie didn't feel like a threat. The relationship Kat had with her parents was much more troubling. Though Wendy felt certain about Kat needing to live on her own, she also didn't feel like it was her business. Who was she to dictate what Kat should do with her life? If she really loved Kat, wouldn't she accept her as she was, despite the tangled connection to her parents?

Hence the favor.

Love? When had that happened? The one-way conversation had evolved to the point that her first message made no sense. She hit backspace on the phone wishing it was as easy to back up one's feelings and find a different trajectory as it was to delete words and begin a new idea. Love? How did she redirect that?

Can I list you as a reference?

Reference? Wendy couldn't say what she thought Kat was going to ask, but would not have guessed that in a million years. Instead of typing, she hit the phone icon.

"Hi!"

Even that one word sounded breathless with gratitude, and Wendy felt bad for sitting and letting her type as much as she had. "Hey. I've been trying to reply to you, but you're too fast for me."

"I'm sorry. I'm just so excited, it's hard to slow down."

"Don't apologize! Tell me what's exciting."

"I'm filling out an application for a place that does event planning in Pasadena. At the end, there's a box where I can say what I'd bring to the position that is unique to me. I've put in all my church ties, and how I have experience with weddings and funerals and concerts and…just lots of stuff! I'm sorry I'm rambling! I was wondering if it would be okay with you for me to say that we have worked together and that you could refer both me and the agency to your clients."

"Absolutely!" Wendy said without hesitation.

"Really? You would do that for me?" Kat's voice lost the confidence that had rung clear initially.

"Are you kidding? That sounds like a great job for you!"

"I know, but I was worried about you."

Wendy was confused. "Me? Why would you be worried about me?"

"I wouldn't be referring business from the church anymore."

"Don't give that idea any more of your brain space. You're allowed to make decisions based on what's best for you, you know."

Kat laughed. "Easy for you to say. That's probably how you've lived your whole life. I'm not used to thinking about me first."

"It's wonderful," Wendy said honestly.

"So I can put you as a reference and talk about how our jobs could complement each other?"

"I'd love to be a reference."

"Super! I'm going to finish it up."

"I'll think good thoughts for you!" Wendy said. Selfishly, she wanted to keep Kat on the phone a moment longer. She missed the sound of her voice, missed hanging out with her. Hearing Kat so focused on something other than Kindred Souls and her family was both wonderful and crushing. Part of her wanted to hear that Kat needed her and missed her.

"Thanks! Hey Wendy?"

"Yeah?"

"How are you? Are things good? I feel bad for…" Kat took a breath, and Wendy waited for her to finish her thought. "I don't want you to think that I've forgotten what was happening between us."

"I don't," Wendy said, even though that was precisely her worry.

"Right now, though…All of a sudden I feel like there's a bunch of stuff I need to do for myself."

Wendy smiled. "I totally get that."

"You're the best, you know that?"

"I didn't. Thanks for telling me."

Kat's wonderful laugh came through the line. "I'll try to tell you more often. We need to get together soon. There's so much I want to tell you. Stuff I'm still sorting out."

"There's time."

"I totally know what you mean! I think this is the first time in my life I've felt like that. I'll call you soon, okay?"

Wendy agreed. When she hung up, she tried to only feel happy about Kat's excitement, but it was hard to watch from the sidelines. Selfishly, she wanted Kat to suggest they get together to celebrate. But it had only been a few weeks since they had fallen out. This new Kat was all the harder for Wendy to resist, and though she missed spending time with her, she knew that giving Kat space was the right thing to do.

* * *

"Do you like it?" Travis asked.

Floating on the high of submitting her job application, Kat took Travis to see some of the apartments she had found. This two-bedroom apartment would be perfect. Travis could walk to school. The rent would eat up most of her new salary, and her commute to Pasadena would stink. She mustered up as much enthusiasm as she could. "I think it could work. What about you?"

He shrugged.

"What's wrong with it?"

"It's just so…small."

"Travis…"

"I know. It's fine. If it's what you want."

"Honey…"

Kat keenly felt the attention of the apartment manager. Long brown hair hung from beneath his greasy Yankees baseball cap. His thick glasses and scraggly beard gave him the appearance of a mole reluctantly extracted from its burrow. She did not want to have a private conversation in front of this unappealing stranger. "There are a few others we could look at," she offered.

"Two bedrooms?" Travis asked.

"Yes." Inside, she was pulling the same attitude Travis was. A two-bedroom apartment. Kat had moved back in with her parents to avoid Travis having to live in an apartment. She thought of Wendy on the other side of the freeway in a much sketchier neighborhood than this one. And Kat had started here because the rent was cheapest. The other apartments were in better neighborhoods and would seriously push her budget.

"Mom?" Travis pulled her from her thoughts.

"We'll give you a call," she said to the manager.

"Mom. I don't want to live in an apartment. How am I going to practice?"

The manager looked as uncomfortable as Kat felt. She thanked him for his time and walked to the car.

"Mom." Something in his voice made Kat stop. "I want to go home."

She heard the assertiveness in his voice that she was just now trying to emulate. She hadn't missed that he said "home." She spent so much time worrying about him feeling angry about living with his grandparents, yet he had said "home."

Travis was absorbed in his phone, and Kat left him alone. She had already uprooted him once, and here she was about to uproot him again. In a matter of minutes, she was pulling into the drive at her parents' house. "This doesn't seem like Gramma and Grandfather's house to you?"

"No. I like living here. There isn't a place you could afford that would give me this much room. But you need a place like this." He handed her his phone with a photo and description of a lovely mother-in-law unit in Glendale.

"This is a one-bedroom place. It's way too small for us, and I'd be fighting traffic to get you to school and then again to get to work."

"I just said I like living here. I want to stay here with Gramma and Grandfather. And you could live in Glendale."

Her stomach felt like it had bottomed out. "What? That doesn't make any sense."

"Why not?"

How could she trust her parents with her son? But she couldn't tell him that. "You're supposed to live with a parent."

"Says who?"

"Says everyone. What will people think?"

"You don't care what people think," he said.

"Yes, I do."

"Well you shouldn't."

Kat walked to the house. She heard Travis trotting behind her.

"Don't be mad."

"How am I supposed to feel after you say you don't want to live with me?"

"You should be psyched to have the chance to live on your own without your parents or your kid."

"What about your dad?" Travis started to open his mouth, and she waved at him to stop. "I know how uncomfortable you are there. I'm sorry. It just doesn't sit right with me to leave you here."

She left the front door open and climbed the stairs. He wouldn't follow her. He never came upstairs. Her room was her territory, and the basement was his. She needed to get away from that conversation and talk to someone else. But not her parents. Jack? She already knew that he would fully support Travis's idea to keep his life uncomplicated. She wanted to talk to Wendy, but she had the feeling that Wendy would be on Travis's side, too.

Travis followed her.

"What are you doing?" she asked at the top of the stairs. She glanced in her parents' room and saw the familiar mound of her mother and prayed she was fast asleep.

"Trying to talk to you!"

"Travis, I didn't even tell Gramma what we were doing today. There's no way I'm going to ask her about leaving you here with her and Grandfather."

"You don't trust me?" He sounded equal parts offended and hurt.

"My head is spinning right now. I have never had to think about so many things in my life, and you throw this new option on top of it all. I need time to process it all."

He confused her by waking up his phone. Within seconds, her phone buzzed with an incoming message, and details of the Glendale grandma unit. "It's the perfect place for you. And if you don't jump on it, someone else will." He stalked out of the room leaving Kat to perch on the edge of the rocking chair in Ava's room.

"Did I hear Travis's voice?" Millie stood in the doorway, pulling on her housecoat.

"Yes."

Millie dropped into the cushioned chair across the room. "Why was he up here?"

"Trying to talk me into renting this place." Kat passed her phone to her mother.

Millie took off her glasses and rested them on her chest to study the pictures. "There isn't room for both of you there."

"No."

"Hmm." Millie put her glasses back on and returned the phone to Kat.

"What do you think?"

"I think there's some vodka downstairs and we're going to need two glasses."

* * *

Kat picked up another piece of paper with the rental contact number on it. Travis must have made a whole sheet of them to place in Kat's path throughout the week. She'd found one balanced on her toothbrush, another on top of the sodas in the cupboard, one on the driver's seat of her car. When she discovered he had penned the number on the paper towels, she had to respond. *How are you going to get to school?* she typed.

His reply came lightning fast. *Grandfather.*

I can't ask him to drop everything and be your chauffeur.

I can Uber.

You'd have to get your license.

Jack had been complaining about Travis's lack of interest in driving for years. Though shuttling Travis was inconvenient, Kat insisted they let Travis decide for himself when he was ready to drive. She herself hadn't learned to drive until she was married. She was the only one of her friends who used a California state ID to get into clubs instead of a driver's license. Kat took the lengthy pause as a sign of surrender and set down her phone.

It pinged, and she opened it to find a screenshot of the DMV homepage, "New Driver's License" circled.

Then a picture of the mother-in-law unit popped up. *I call, you call.*

You call, I call, she fired back.

Calling…

Would he really?

* * *

Mixed feelings swirled through Wendy when Kat's number lit up her screen. Her body still tingled with the thrill of knowing that Kat was thinking of her, but then she reminded herself of how frustrating it had all been and was able to level herself out and answer as the supportive friend.

"Enjoying your day off?" Kat asked.

Wendy studied her voice finding that she still sounded excited but not the full-throttle excited she'd been on their last call. "I am," Wendy said. Did she add that she wished her plans involved Kat? No, Jack's wedding had shut that down. "I was throwing together a salad for lunch."

"Oh." Kat sounded disappointed. "I'm in Glendale and was going to ask if you'd eaten yet."

"You're right around the corner! Did you want to grab something together? I know a great deli."

Kat didn't respond immediately. "Could I maybe bring something out your way? I wanted to get your advice about something, but it's kind of hard to talk about."

"Kat, do you want to come here?" Wendy glanced around her house. It was presentable, but she hesitated. What would it mean to have Kat in her home?

"I didn't want to invite myself over."

"Should I make more salad, or is that too green for you? I could make sandwiches."

"Are there croutons involved?" Kat asked.

"I could arrange that."

"I can handle green in a salad."

Wendy gave Kat her address and gathered more salad fixings. It was just waiting to be dressed when she saw Kat's big SUV pull up in front of her house.

At the door Kat smiled broadly and gave Wendy a hug with warmth somewhere in between the professional welcome hugs she'd received at Kindred Souls and the passionate embrace they'd shared on the bridge. She told herself not to overanalyze whether it tipped more toward cool or hot and instead focused on how Kat looked like she had a lot on her mind.

"This is the cutest place I have ever seen. It's like walking into a magazine picture."

"Thanks. It was turnkey when I bought it, and my dad's wife helped me a lot with the decorating."

"She has good taste."

Wendy marveled at the way Kat traced her finger over the chairs and table much like her dad did. If they ever met, maybe they would talk about furniture design. They made light small talk as Wendy dressed the salads, and then they sat down to eat. Wendy took it as a personal victory that Kat did not reject the baby spinach she'd mixed with the red leaf lettuce.

"My son thinks I should live here." She pushed her phone toward Wendy.

Wendy looked at the address. "You were looking at it before you called?"

Kat nodded. "It's in my budget, and it does seem perfect."

"Did you say that he thought it would be perfect for you, not the two of you?"

"He wants to stay with my parents."

Wendy sat back, surprised. "I didn't see that coming. I guess it makes sense that he wouldn't want to be at his dad's right now. But he'd really stay with his grandparents? How do you feel about that?"

"Scared. Self-conscious. Sad. But mostly scared."

"What scares you?"

"Leaving him with them. I don't know if they can manage these days. My mom's so fragile, well at least mentally. And my dad... I told you we were at his boyfriend's when Ava..."

"Yes, I remember."

Kat pulled her hair over her shoulder and swiped a section of it across her lower lip, lost in thought. Finally, she took a deep breath and spoke. "My dad says it was the way she hit her head that killed her. It was instant. He has said over and over again that it wasn't anybody's fault. They told me it wasn't my fault." She noticed what she was doing with her hair and folded her hands in her lap. Wendy scooted her chair closer and placed her hand on top of Kat's. "I had to leave Ava unconscious in the pool so I could run inside. They couldn't hear me calling."

"They weren't with you?" Wendy asked.

"They were inside. They couldn't hear me from the pool. It was late. Ava wanted to swim with the lights. Antòn's pool had underwater lights, and she'd always wanted to swim there at night. Once I turned thirteen, we were allowed to swim together. The buddy system, you know? I didn't want to go. I…"

"It's okay," Wendy said when Kat couldn't seem to finish the thought. She put an arm around Kat's shoulder. "You don't have to say…That must have been…" She blew out a long breath. She couldn't find the words, either.

"I didn't want to tell you any of this. I never wanted to tell anyone."

"Why?"

"Because I thought it would make you like me less or make you reconsider wanting to be with me."

"Why would I think that?"

"Because I didn't stop her."

"You were thirteen and your dad left you alone in the pool with your little sister. He trusted you."

"He made a mistake."

"I'm looking at you and wondering how you managed to weather it all as well as you have. You are amazing and wonderful, and your parents' mistakes are theirs. They may have made some big ones, but they are their mistakes, not yours."

"I've tried really hard not to make any mistakes, and now Travis wants to live with them, and I won't be there to protect him."

Wendy had been wondering when Kat said she hadn't ever wanted to tell anyone, why she would have decided to tell her today. Now she understood that Kat was scared to leave her child with her father. "You don't trust your parents?"

"How can I?"

They sat in silence as Wendy weighed all that Kat had chosen to share with her. "You made it," she finally said. "He's almost eighteen, isn't he? And he'd only be responsible for himself. Don't you think he'll be fine?"

"You're saying I'm fine?"

Wendy wasn't sure whether she was supposed to say yes or no, and Kat's expression was utterly serious. "Fine is the wrong adjective. I think you're amazing. I think you're strong. I think you've got a whole hell of a lot to work through, and if I can help in any way, now you know where I live."

Kat laughed. "I don't know how much of that I agree with, but thanks for your offer. I appreciate that you listened."

"Anytime. I mean that. Anytime you need to talk, I'm here."

"Do you think it would be a mistake to leave him? I feel like it would be so selfish of me to abandon him there."

"Wasn't it his idea?"

"Yes."

"Then that's not abandoning him. It's treating him like the grown-up he's going to be one day."

"Some days I think he's going to make it there before I do." Kat looked like she was going to rest her head on Wendy's shoulder, but instead she stretched and stood. "Thank you for understanding. About this and about what was happening with us. I think about you all the time." Her gaze fell to Wendy's lips, and Wendy remembered how delicious Kat's body had felt pressed to hers. "Being with you was like being seventeen again, with no responsibilities. It was so tempting to give myself over to what I was feeling with you, but I didn't get it right back when I really was a teenager. I need to get it right this time."

"I meant what I said about how strong you are. You're so much stronger than I even knew. You deserve the do-over you want."

She hugged Wendy again, and then she was gone, trotting down Wendy's steps and pulling out into traffic. Of all the things Kat had shared, the one that resurfaced was how she thought about Wendy. *She thinks about me.* A small smile ticked up the edge of her mouth. When she was young, she had played the "he loves me; he loves me not" game pulling petals off daisies. She'd learned so much since those days, that it was a she and not a he that captured her interest and that far, far before love was the question of whether Kat's thoughts mirrored hers. Wendy had noticed the way Kat had looked at her lips, and she heard Kat's words again. *I think about you all the time.* That made two of them.

* * *

Kat sat at the top of the basement stairs listening to Travis practice his guitar. He couldn't hear her, and the way the chords came and went, she could tell he had his headphones on. She closed her eyes and waited for the pieces of the song to come together. She knew the number, and it didn't take long for it to surface. "It's been a hard day's night," she began to sing along softly, tapping out the percussion.

Hoping he wouldn't feel like she was invading his space, she descended and sat down at the drum kit. He may or may not have heard her footfall on the stairs, but when she synched to his rhythm with her kick drum, she heard his slight hesitation. He was reaching the end, but Kat hoped he would keep playing as she added in the snare and cymbals as best she could.

He stopped and pushed back the curtain that separated his room from the storage space at the bottom of the stairs. "You need to practice, Mom."

"If I'd known you were learning something I could actually keep up with, I would have been!"

He shrugged and sat down on the basement stairs. He started back at the beginning of the song, and Kat joined him, singing along easily.

His mouth pulled to the side the way it did when he was pleased but didn't want her to know. Once they had limped through the song, she asked if they could play another. He surprised her by laying his guitar flat on his knees. "Have you thought about it?"

"Only every single day. I worry, you know. What if something happened and I wasn't here?"

Travis practiced a finger-picking pattern on random chords. "You can't protect me every minute of every day. You never could. And I'm almost an adult. What's going to happen when I'm eighteen? Are you going to go to college with me to make sure I'm safe there?"

"There's an idea!" The cowlick she had fought with since day one spiked straight up from his forehead, and Kat resisted the urge to pat it down.

"I'm not asking to live by myself, Mom. I'm asking you to let me stay here so I can finish high school with my friends. I'll be living with two…at least one capable adult." Before Kat could decide which grandparent he meant, he added, "Between the two of them, I have what I need, and that isn't much. I can take care of myself."

"You can't cook."

"Neither can you!"

"I can at least go buy food."

"So you can come by once a week to stock us up on food. And Gramma has her phone. She won't let us starve."

"You make it all sound so reasonable, and it's a seriously cute place. I went to take a look."

"What? I thought we'd go together."

"This is my place, remember?"

"Oh." He looked down at the fret, but then his head snapped right back up. "Wait! Your place? Does that mean you rented it?"

"I said I'd call tonight to let them know."

Travis jumped up and high-fived her. She could not imagine how a child of hers could be so confident and self-assured.

"So I should call?"

"Right now! And then pizza to celebrate!"

"Let's run this idea by Gramma while I cook dinner."

"Wait. You're cooking?"

"Don't get too excited. I just picked up some spaghetti sauce and noodles."

"You know how to boil water?"

"If you're trying to make it easier to leave you here, it's working!"

She followed him up the stairs relishing the sound of his laughter.

CHAPTER TWENTY-ONE

May began with Kat signing the lease for her grandma unit. For the first time, she stood there alone. From the outside, it didn't look like much, a square tan box behind the main house. The gate opened to a small patch of dirt carpeted in the purple blossoms of a giant jacaranda in the neighbor's yard. Kat was relieved that the place would require no gardening expertise. The living room windows faced the street, and the door faced the front unit, though the houses were separated by a six-foot wooden fence. She pictured a bar table and stool she could use to enjoy an evening meal outside.

Inside, she was not in the least bothered by the stacks of boxes that surrounded her. She smiled remembering Travis's offer to help her get settled. He had been ready to reassemble her bed frame or put her dishes away, but she'd only allowed him to help her move the couch and the bamboo TV cabinet. He had wanted to connect the TV, but she assured him that it could wait. As excited as she was to have the move completed, her chest had hurt driving Travis back to her parents' house.

"It feels too far," she said as they crept back over the Sepulveda Pass.

"We talked about this, Mom. You don't want to fight traffic every day to get to Pasadena. It's going to be fine."

She had to laugh at the role reversal. Kat had only ever moved twice before, to the house with Jack and back home again. Jack had coordinated the first move, and Kat remembered consulting him at every step as they settled in. Moving back into her childhood room, she'd been so overwhelmed that her father had done most of the work fitting in the pieces of her married life. He had simply made it all happen as she stumbled through her days.

Now every choice was hers, including where to start. She tucked her scallop-edged round table by the couch and pulled out a lamp that had stayed packed since her move back home. She searched through her jewelry box for the tiny iron frog. When she found it, she settled onto the couch and balanced it on the tip of her pinky.

When she and Ava were young, they loved to listen to the Smothers Brothers tell Aesop's fables. Kat's favorite was the story of the two frogs, one impulsive and one who always looked before he leapt. Kat had always thought the older frog was so wise and identified with it. Having spent her life refusing to leap out on her own, Kat now saw the wisdom in taking a risk.

Her phone startled her out of her reminiscence.

"How's the move?" Wendy asked.

"Exhausting, but I'm home now, and I've started to unpack."

"Do you have food?"

Kat frowned in the direction of the kitchen. "My mom sent me with the staples."

"Dare I ask?"

"A case of Diet Coke, a loaf of white bread, butter, sugar."

Wendy's rich laugh filled the line. "Stop! Stop! That is insanity."

"It's her version of being supportive."

"Would you mind if I supplemented her staples?"

Though her stomach growled, Kat hesitated. She still very much wanted to set up her place without help. But it would be rude to turn down Wendy's offer. "That would be great," she said.

"Are you lying?"

"I stopped lying, remember?"

"Hmm. I'm going to have to test your ability to say no."

"How?"

"Yes or no, and you have to answer without thinking or dithering."

"I don't dither."

"Liar! Are you ready?"

"Yes," Kat fired back, having fun.

"Will you eat Brussels sprouts?"

"No!"

"Do you want a pet iguana?"

"No."

"Do you want to travel outside of the States?"

"No."

"Will you let me bring you something nutritious to eat?"

"Yes."

"You're sure?"

"I thought we already went over that."

"Okay. Give me a little less than half an hour."

Kat smiled. "You spoil me."

"If you'll let me."

* * *

The professional in Wendy wanted to wow Kat with dinner and show her how delicious green food could be, but she stopped herself. She had no idea what she'd find in Kat's kitchen, and more importantly, Kat was setting up her own space. The last thing Wendy needed to do was interfere. She ran by her market since she could quickly locate what she needed along with a few housewarming items: some hard cider, a jar of raspberry jam and some fresh strawberries.

She'd only seen Kat's new place once, when Kat picked up her keys. Before they grabbed lunch together Kat had given her a quick tour of the quaint unit tucked behind a tall hedge of Japanese honeysuckle. She was tempted to buy plants for the bare flower boxes that hung outside the living-room windows but held back.

Without making the stop for groceries, it took a third of the time it had to drive over the hill to the valley. While she had not mentioned it at lunch, Wendy hoped that Kat's choice had been influenced by her proximity. She knew that Kat's job and her son contributed as well, but she secretly hoped the closeness would lend itself to seeing more of Kat.

She parked on the street and pushed open the gate. Kat had heard her and had already stepped out to greet Wendy. Her feet were bare on the stone path, with the rolled-up-at-the-cuffs jeans she'd worn to the pier and a T-shirt featuring a dreadlocked musician she didn't recognize. Wendy shifted both grocery bags to one hand to give Kat a hug, but Kat frowned and took the bags from her, setting them on an iron bench next to the door.

"I get a better hug than that, don't I?"

Wendy happily obliged, wrapping both arms around Kat.

"I probably stink," Kat mumbled into Wendy's shoulder.

"You absolutely don't," Wendy said still trying to sort out the floral scents of Kat's perfume. "But you must be famished after all the moving."

"About that…" Kat led her inside and paused outside of her nook-like kitchen. "I don't really have a whole lot here."

"You have plates?" Wendy asked setting her bags on the counter.

"In the cupboard above the microwave."

"What about a can opener?"

"Drawer beneath the microwave."

"If the microwave works, we're set!" Hoping she had made the right decision, she pulled out tortillas, a can of beans and a bag of shredded cheddar cheese. "Do you trust me with your recipe or did you want to take over?"

Kat clapped her hands together and then pressed them to her lips. "I trust you," she whispered.

Wendy leaned over and kissed Kat's cheek. "Good. Then you can handle beverages. You said you had Diet Coke, but I brought some Angry Orchard, too."

"That sounds so good!" Kat squeezed Wendy's shoulders and leaned against her briefly before passing her to step into the kitchen. Everything was white, the cabinets, laminate counter and tiny fridge. Kat had placed a few trinkets along the windowsill above her sink including some glass angels and a heart-shaped rock.

Whether it was the tight space or the fact that she was no longer in her parent's home, Wendy felt a difference in Kat's touch. It wasn't sexual, but it wasn't cautious either, and Wendy's body reacted, warmth whooshing through her.

In a matter of minutes, they sank into the wine-colored velour couch enjoying their simple burritos. Kat pushed a number of accent pillows to the carpet, and Wendy took in the open boxes and stacks of unfinished projects. "Are you feeling more liberated or more swamped?"

"Liberated, for sure."

Wendy bumped her with her shoulder. "You sound like you're back in high school."

"I didn't say 'gag me with a spoon.'"

"It's just a matter of time," Wendy said with mock sorrow in her voice.

Kat pulled her laptop off the ottoman and did a quick search. "This is the eighties," she said hitting play on Modern English's "I Melt with You."

When the song ended, Wendy searched for The Icicle Works and played "Whisper to a Scream." "This is the eighties."

"The drums in this!" Kat said, leaning forward.

"You should learn to play it. Do you have your drum kit here?"

"I don't think that would endear me to my neighbors."

"Too bad. I'd love to hear you do this."

"I wonder if Travis would learn it with me."

"Did your dad help with the move, too, or just Travis?"

"My dad helped on that end, but Travis and I did all the unloading here. It was hard driving him back. It's not like it's the first time we haven't been together. He has slept over at Jack's before, but somehow this feels different."

"It is different. And it's totally impressive."

"Okay." With one word, Kat reflexively deflected the compliment.

Wendy set her plate on the ottoman. "I was being serious. I think you're really brave to embrace all these new things. Have you started the new job yet?"

"Next week! I have to say that packing up the office at Kindred Souls didn't come with any emotional ambiguity."

"Good to leave?"

"Jeremy and Evan's wedding wasn't the first thing that my boss and I disagreed over, but somehow that did it. It didn't feel right to keep working there." Kat scrolled through the choices that came up after Wendy's video. "Remember this one?"

Kat didn't move to clear the dishes or unpack anything more, and Wendy decided not to ask if she wanted help with either. Kat looked relaxed and happy. "Of course I remember that one." Wendy leaned back against the couch and squeezed Kat's shoulders.

Kat groaned and let her head fall forward. "Your hands are just like heaven."

Wendy scooted behind her to have better access to Kat's back. "You're the DJ now."

"You don't have somewhere else to be?"

"Nowhere better, but say the word, and I'll skedaddle and let you get back to settling in."

"You haven't said anything about my stacks of stuff."

"That's because they're your stacks. I'm guessing they're not going to stay scattered all over the place, but hey. It's your place. If you've always dreamed of piling things up all over, who am I to comment?"

"I like you," Kat said.

"Well that's a plus because I like you, too." She stopped rubbing when Kat leaned forward to type in another song. When she leaned back, Wendy didn't hear anything at first. A full minute passed with strange street sounds before she heard the opening chords. Still, she didn't recognize the song until it reached the chorus. At that point she sang along. "I might like you better if we slept together, but there's something in your eyes that says never. Never say never!" When the song ended she said, "You're not really worried that I'd like you better if we slept together, are you?"

"Maybe?"

"You can stop worrying about that."

"What if I can't stop worrying?"

"Then I guess we'd have to sleep together."

Kat leaned back to squish her. Wendy tried to extract herself, but Kat kept blocking her, even when Wendy tried tickling Kat. She found freedom by sliding from the couch and rose to her knees laughing. Kat reached for her and pulled her so close Wendy could feel her chest rise and fall beneath her. She wasn't sure who she was to Kat. They were certainly friends, friends who had been on a date, but it wasn't like they were girlfriends. But for some reason, she didn't feel like she could move forward and kiss Kat.

Despite the conundrum, when Kat's lips touched hers, there was no doubt that they were something. The kiss was still cautious, but at the same time assured, and Wendy felt as if Kat expressed through the kiss emotions for which she could not find words. She followed Kat's lead, maintaining her slow and sensual exploration, just the barest flutter of her tongue starting a new song in her head.

Kat must have felt Wendy's lips shift into a smile. "What?"

"That kiss changed the song, and I like it."

"Put it on."

Wendy turned to type in Madonna's "Crazy for You." Kat smiled and pulled Wendy back up to the couch and accompanied the song with a kiss so sultry it took Wendy's breath away.

Kat was also breathing heavily by the end of the song. She stroked Wendy's hair and said, "Kissing you, I think I finally get that song. So much makes sense."

She continued to run her fingers through Wendy's hair and then stroked her face. She stopped but did not lean forward to kiss Wendy again. Wendy's stomach fell. Kat's expression had shifted. "But..."

Kat broke eye contact. "It was really nice of you to come and make dinner tonight…"

"But…we won't be doing it again for awhile."

Kat's eyes found her again, and she looked both relieved and puzzled.

"That's why you paused," Wendy pulled back and sat next to Kat on the couch again, "When I asked if you wanted me to bring food, because you worried this would happen." She stood and gathered their plates to take them to the kitchen.

Kat was right behind her, her hand on Wendy's shoulder. "I'm not sorry you came over."

"But…" Wendy said a third time. Her heart felt like someone was squishing it. She knew what Kat was going to say and what hurt the most was that she knew Kat was absolutely right.

"I wish that I was in a place where I could say that everything makes sense. I know that I want to be with you, but I worry that if I give into how good it feels to kiss you, I might never figure out who I am."

"Knowing that is important."

"I'm not asking you to wait for me," Kat said. She wrapped her arms around herself.

Wendy unfolded her arms and hugged her gently. "Why wouldn't I?" she whispered into Kat's neck.

"Because I've never done this before, and I don't know how long it will take."

"You're allowed to take your time."

Kat pulled away and kissed Wendy's cheek. "I hope that's true because I like you a lot."

"I'm not saying it will be easy because I like you a lot, too. But people are always saying that the best things are worth waiting for."

CHAPTER TWENTY-TWO

A month later, Kat met Wendy at the burger joint they liked halfway between their places. She sat down on the bench across from Wendy and plopped over sideways.

"Your day was that good?"

"June brides are the worst. Remind me why I wanted to work full-time with brides."

"Because you're good at it?" Wendy ducked to the side and smiled at Kat under the table. "Do you want a cheeseburger? I ordered you a Diet Coke."

"Yes. Cheeseburger. Can we share fries?"

Wendy sat up and gave the waitress their order. After she'd left, Kat sat up and drank half her soda. "I needed that. How come you're so peppy? I feel like I want to crawl into hibernation."

"I didn't just move into my own place and have to figure out a new job."

Kat raised her drink to acknowledge the truth in Wendy's words.

"Bridezilla?"

"To say the least. She's not even my client, but she was yelling her head off and had Tasha in tears. The young girls I work with looked absolutely petrified. I walked over and sat down next to her and asked what was really bothering her. I said I'd been there and knew that getting stressed out about every detail was really about control. Or perhaps losing it. I got into some tiff with Miranda right before Jack and I went to pick out flowers, and I remember he had to take me out of the shop and talk to me about the tone I'd taken with the florist."

"Did the bride say what was really bothering her?"

"Turns out that her sister has been dating a woman for a few months. She's pregnant…"

"The sister?"

"No, the girlfriend was already pregnant when the sister met her, and now they're going to get married before the baby comes."

"And before this bride gets married."

"Bingo."

"Upstaged."

"Twice. First kid to get married and first grandchild."

"Ouch. Did you fix it?"

"I took her next door for some tea and listened to her. I think all she really needed was to get it off her chest that she was pissed at her little sister."

"Ouch again. Big sisters are supposed to go first."

"And she's only marrying a guy. Everyone is so excited that the sister's marrying a woman."

"Upstaged by the lesbian sister. That *is* tragic."

Their burgers came, and they dug in. "Did you want to slap her hetero-privileged face and tell her to be happy for her sister to have people be excited for her?"

Kat stopped chewing. The sister being lesbian had not seemed significant to her. She had wanted to slap her, but her anger had not come from identifying as a lesbian. She'd had to bite her tongue to keep from saying that she would give anything for her sister to be alive and in love with anyone. As she had done with the bride-to-be, Kat found a way to keep the conversation light. "I wish I had thought to say that."

"You handled it better than I would have, I'm sure. You have so much more patience than I do!"

Was it patience, Kat wondered, or was it how quickly Wendy had aligned herself with the sister? It seemed that she felt a kinship with her that Kat hadn't. Kat had connected with the competitive older sister and had managed to talk her out of her hysterics, nothing more. She had thought she was finished feeling angry with the woman, but talking about it with Wendy poked at the ambiguities of sexuality that haunted Kat.

* * *

"There you are!" Wendy said when she saw Kat stride into the kitchen.

"You need me?"

Kat's tone was utterly professional as always. In the two months since she'd moved and begun her new job, they had met as friends or had worked weddings together. Even so, her words and the slight brush of her shoulder made Wendy wish they were alone again as they had been that night at her new place. She could so easily let herself drift into the fantasy of giving herself completely to Kat and had to mentally slap herself to redirect her brain out of the bedroom and back to business.

"I was supposed to have three serving tables outside, and I only see one," Wendy said.

"The bride's sister-in-law was going to pull out her craft tables. She may not be back from the church. This couple must have a ton of friends, and they are all on their way somewhere."

"The roads are packed for Fourth of July weekend," Cory said, his brow wrinkled in confusion.

Wendy shared a secret smile with Kat remembering their trip to the pier when she had taught Kat to see the traffic as a gathering of friends traveling beside her instead of a hoard of enemies keeping her from getting to her destination.

"The holiday traffic has almost doubled the time it will take them to get here. Will that throw off your service?" Kat asked.

"It shouldn't. They'll get here hungry and thirsty, and we'll be ready for them."

"I'll see if I can track down the tables." Kat waved her phone and stepped into the backyard to make the call.

"She's cool as a cucumber," Cory said.

"This job is perfect for her. She has a real gift for helping a bride actually enjoy her wedding day. The other day, she told me that she started planning her wedding when she was a child. She dreamed out all the smallest details for a dozen years, and then when she got married, it was nothing like she'd imagined. She was so stressed about making everything perfect that she wasn't actually present."

"What's going on with you two?"

"Nothing."

"You two sure work together a lot for nothing to be going on."

"I've worked with you longer," Wendy countered, "and there's nothing going on between us."

"You know what I mean."

"If I remember correctly, you were the one who said that we made a great team."

Cory crossed his muscular arms, not buying her response for a minute. "You're both available, and you like each other. What are you waiting for?"

Wendy watched Kat on her call in the backyard. While she talked, she futzed with the flags in the centerpiece. One of the brides was Canadian, so each table had crisscrossed flags, Stars and Stripes and the red Maple Leaf.

Dawn and Sheryl had come to her first, and she'd suggested they work with Kat. They had kept it quite simple. They had been together for years, and Wendy had enjoyed hearing the pieces of their courtship when they had selected their menu. Dawn repeatedly teased Sheryl about how often they had traveled to Canada together. Each trip, Dawn had pointed out that they could get legally married in Sheryl's native country.

Every trip she had an excuse. We haven't been together that long. Won't your family be hurt that they couldn't attend? They only had a week to spend with her family, and she didn't want their vacation complicated by wedding plans. She didn't know where the office was or what the procedure was.

"What she was really saying was that she wasn't sure about me. But it was okay, I was always sure about her," Dawn had said.

"But once the States legalized it…" Sheryl rolled her eyes, but with a smile on her face.

"No more excuses," they had said in unison, humor in their voices.

Wendy wondered whether she was foolish to keep waiting for Kat when she had said she didn't have to. She didn't really know what they were waiting for. All Wendy knew was that it wasn't something concrete like a graduation or a divorce to go through. "I guess we're waiting for the right time," she finally answered.

"Whatever that means," Cory said.

Wendy could understand why he'd be puzzled. She could see where it didn't make sense. Waiting to marry Sheryl hadn't made sense to Dawn, yet Dawn hadn't pushed it. She said with or without the label of wife, she was meant to be with Sheryl. Wendy couldn't use the label of girlfriend, but she felt just as certain that she was meant to be with Kat.

* * *

Months later Kat entered through the back door of her parents' house. She heard the shower and checked her watch. She and Travis were leaving in ten minutes which wouldn't be enough time for her to get ready, but he wasn't typically late, so she continued into the kitchen.

"Hello!" her mother greeted her in a chipper, sing-song voice.

"Hi." Kat set her purse on the table and sat down to wait for her boy. "Everyone is adjusting to Travis being back in school?"

"Your dad misses his help in the yard, but I think Travis is glad to have an excuse at the ready."

Kat helped herself to a Madeleine cookie from the container on the table.

"How are all the brides?"

"I've got a new couple that I just don't understand. Sometimes I wish the shop offered premarital counseling."

"You'd be qualified. How many years did you work at the church?"

"Too many," Kat said.

"What bothers you about the couple?"

"They haven't been together that long, and the bride told me the only reason they're getting married is because her parents found out they're living together. The father said he'd only pay for the wedding if they took the first date their church had available. They're getting married on September thirteenth."

Her mom glanced at the large wall calendar on the bulletin board. "Friday?"

"Yep. Friday the thirteenth."

"Oh, that's a riot." Millie pushed back from the table, grasped her cane and walked to the fridge. "My dad would have done the same thing. Do you want a soda?"

"Sure."

Travis passed by with his towel wrapped around his lean tanned abdomen. "Give me four minutes. I'll be ready."

"Okay," Kat agreed, but he had already disappeared down the steps. Millie handed Kat a Diet Coke and returned to the fridge for her own. When she settled back in her chair again, she reached for a cookie.

"Your dad and I went to pre-marital counseling. The minister said that he never advised against weddings, but he said I shouldn't marry your dad because he was queer."

"You never told me that part! Why'd you still marry him if you knew he was gay?"

"I was young. I thought queer meant quirky."

Kat was speechless. Her parents had long told the story of the minister's warning, but neither had shared that detail with her. "And look at you now, still married after all these years."

"Yep. So you never can tell who's going to make it."

"Were you disappointed that Jack and I didn't make it?"

"Only because you always had such high expectations for yourself."

Kat cursed Travis's punctuality when, as promised, he emerged from the basement four minutes later. She would have liked to have continued the conversation with her mom.

"Let's go," he said.

"You don't want to say bye to Gramma?"

He looked in their direction, having already passed them. "I'm not five."

"That's no reason to be a troll."

"See you, Gramma," he called, walking to the door.

Millie waved, already focused on her phone.

"Bye Mom!" Kat kissed her mom on the cheek and followed Travis out to the car.

"Nice chatting with you!" her mother called after Kat, her thoughts obviously not spinning on their brief conversation.

Travis now saw more of his dad, so Kat had started taking Travis to band practice whenever she could. On the way, they usually chatted about how school was going which meant Kat asked questions, and Travis replied in as few words as possible. That evening, though, she ruminated on the conversation with Millie, comparing her failed marriage to her parents' successful one.

"Is something wrong?" Travis asked.

"No. Why?"

"Because there aren't any questions tonight. You always have questions."

"And you had already crafted your verbose responses?"

"You're thinking about Dad?"

"Not really. I was thinking about Gramma and Grandfather. They've been together such a long time." Who would she have been if her mother had left her father? His leaving her didn't even enter her mind as a possibility even though his affairs would have made that scenario more logical. Despite their having plenty of reasons to split, Kat could not picture one without the other and, truth be told, their being together had always comforted her. She actually took great pride in sharing that her parents were still married.

Because life's a competition? Kat knew Wendy would needle her if she could hear her thoughts. *They won because they stayed together?*

"You think you'll get married again?"

Kat weighed his question. As both a divorcée and a wedding planner, marriage looked a lot different to her. "That's kind of hard to answer considering I'm not even dating."

"Are you going to date again?"

"Probably."

"Wendy?"

"I hope so."

"Why aren't you dating now?"

"It's not time yet."

"For you or for her?"

"Me. I've still got a lot of stuff to figure out."

She waited for him to ask what kind of stuff, but he didn't. Alone in her apartment, she'd been listening to "Crazy for You" and other love songs from the eighties. She'd compiled them in a playlist and imagined what it would be like to slow dance with Wendy. Based on their few kisses, there was a lot she could imagine, but when she thought of giving herself to Wendy, fear always held her back.

Were the tables turned, she didn't know if she would have Wendy's patience. She kept waiting for Wendy to say "Enough!", but it never happened. They worked well together professionally, and socially they had much to talk about. Every once in a while, there would be a pocket of silence that made Kat hold her breath with worry that Wendy would bring up how long Kat had lived on her own. But then the moment would pass, and Wendy would kick the conversation back into motion. Kat would relax and remind herself to appreciate the moment. She was learning not only to forgive the past but also to embrace the new life in front of her.

* * *

Kat's eyes misted as she watched Penny and Bruce share their first dance as husband and wife. When she had first started working with them, she had thought a wedding so close to Christmas would seem weird, but instead the decorations in the fellowship hall contributed an extra air of magic to the reception.

The Disney touches didn't hurt. Sleeping Beauty's castle topped the cake, and she had heard Bruce's animator colleagues talking about how they were going to recreate the fireworks when they cut the cake after the first dance.

"Not the song I would have chosen, but I guess it's appropriate."

Wendy stood close enough to Kat that she half expected her to rest her chin on her shoulder. A shiver ran through her despite the heat from Wendy's proximity. Or maybe because of it. "Come on. I love *Beauty and the Beast*."

"The story is so much better, though. I don't like how the movie made it seem like she was taming him."

"Maybe they like the message of learning to see beauty beneath the surface," Kat suggested.

"What's good about the story is that the enchantment is her own creation. He's always kind, but she has to learn how to overcome her fear."

"But she's afraid of him because he's mean."

"She's afraid of him because he's different. You could just as easily say the beast is a woman, and the unexpected attraction scares her. That's what I think the story is about."

"Oh!" The epiphany struck her so unexpectedly that Kat could not contain the exclamation. Miranda's words echoed in her mind. *Tell me that you are not burning with desire from that kiss, and I won't say another word about it.* Miranda's kiss had awakened something she wasn't ready for, and Kat had fallen back asleep. For decades. Until Wendy.

"What?" Wendy asked.

How could she explain? The song faded and as if cued by Kat's memory of sleeping princesses "Once Upon a Dream" began. "Do you waltz?"

"What?"

On the dance floor older couples joined the bride and groom floating into the graceful waltz. Kat extended her hand to Wendy.

"You know how to dance like that?"

"You've met my father…" Kat took Wendy's hand. "Come on. I'll teach you, and we can talk about princesses that have been asleep too long."

It took a moment for Kat to rearrange the waltz in her mind, to take Wendy's right hand with her left, to lead with her left foot instead of follow with her right, but once they moved, her blood rushed through her veins, and she was awakened once more.

CHAPTER TWENTY-THREE

"Wendy Archer—so glad to meet you," Wendy said, shaking hands with both attractive women who had called to set up their menu. She'd spoken to Ngozi who introduced herself and her wife-to-be Dinandrea.

"We're so excited that you were free!" Ngozi said. "Kat said she's worked with you a lot and that the food is always amazing."

"How did you find Kat?" Wendy asked. With Kat coordinating weddings full-time, more and more of Wendy's referrals were matrimonial.

"Our minister suggested her. We go to the Unitarian church here in Pasadena," Dinandrea said. "Kat's like me," she continued. "It wasn't easy for me to come out of the closet. I was really struggling. And then this one…" She wove her arms through Ngozi's. "She held the door open for me. Our eyes met, and we connected."

"I didn't even know your name, but I knew you were important to me." Ngozi's broad smile revealed a gap between her front teeth.

"But we didn't meet then," Dinandrea said. "I was late to my meeting. I was so anal about being on time to everything back then."

"We got each other's numbers on one of those dating sites," Ngozi said. "Only I was having trouble with my personal phone and had to call her from work."

"And when I saw the clinic's name, I said oh, my god! It's the beautiful woman who opened the door for me!"

"But we had met even before that," Ngozi said.

"Stop! We didn't come to share our life story," Dinandrea said. "We came to see if you can make Caribbean food. Ngozi is Jamaican American, and I'm Cuban American, so we'd like to bring the flavor of the Caribbean to our reception."

"Something like Ackee'n sal'fish," Ngozi said.

Dinandrea pushed Ngozi's shoulder lightly. "You already got your black rum cake." Her food requests came fast and interspersed with Spanish. Wendy caught the lists of spices, garlic and onion and ropa vieja and plantains. "But no fish." She slowed down to deliver this idea, her delicate chin directed first to Ngozi and then to Wendy. "This is going to be vegan all the way."

"All right! All right! You win. We'll go vegan," Ngozi said. "Anything to make you happy."

"You're in luck! I have experience with Caribbean food. This is going to be fun," Wendy said.

When the couple was satisfied with their choices, they stood.

"Thank you for all of this. Hiring only lesbians was the best choice we've made," Dinandrea said.

"Yeah. You don't happen to know a lesbian baker, do you? So far, we've come up empty, and it's looking like my mom is going to have to make the cake," Ngozi said.

"You're only hiring lesbians?" Wendy wasn't sure she had heard Dinandrea correctly.

"That's… not a problem is it?" Dinandrea shot a questioning look at Ngozi. "I thought you would have mentioned that on the phone."

Ngozi looked from Dinandrea to Wendy. "Kat said you were family."

"Oh, I am." To this, both women looked relieved. "I'm sorry. You just caught me off guard."

After they left, Wendy sat back down at the table with her notes. She turned the pencil tip to eraser, tip to eraser, lost in thought. Kat was identifying as lesbian now and hadn't said anything to her? There had been no promises made between them, but now Wendy was even more uncertain about what she meant to Kat.

"Ready to order?" Cory stood at the table.

"Nothing you have."

"Ouch!" Cory put his hand over his heart and pulled out a chair. "Is that couple going to be difficult?"

"No. They are lovely, just like all the couples Kat sends our way. But they said something about Kat that keeps spinning around in my head."

Cory stretched out his legs, ready to listen. "Out with it."

"What if Kat's into women but not into me?"

"They said Kat's into women?"

"They said they will only work with lesbians."

"Ouch!" he said again. "What's wrong with me?"

"It's not about you! It's about not wanting anyone there who would see two women getting married as a curiosity. And stop making this about you when it's about me."

"I thought it was about Kat."

"Now you're just being difficult."

"You two kissed. You're a woman. I don't see how her liking women is news to you."

"Kissing women is not an identity. If she's told them she's a lesbian, that's different."

"But she hasn't asked you out."

"Right."

"Hmm." They sat in silence for a few minutes. "I can't help with that, but I can give you a job to do."

"You're my assistant. Shouldn't I be giving you a job?"

"You would be if you weren't sitting out here moping."

"Point taken," Wendy said following him back into the kitchen.

She would try her best to stop questioning whether the label Kat used changed anything between them, but it wouldn't be easy.

* * *

How was it, Kat wondered, that she still felt nervous calling Wendy? After more than a year of always having the excuse of their overlapping careers, she still experienced a little flutter when she pulled up Wendy's name on her screen.

Maybe because this was far from business. This was personal.

"Hey there, sunshine!" Wendy picked up, and Kat couldn't keep from smiling.

"Have time for a personal call?"

"I always have time for you," Wendy responded.

Kat hadn't thought her smile could get any bigger, but Wendy's words stretched it even wider. "I finally found the perfect thing to hang on the wall by my couch, but I need another set of hands."

"I've got a functional set you could borrow. Do you want me to swing by after work?"

"That would be fantastic." Kat's stomach tightened as the words she wanted to say next skittered around.

"Do you need any tools?"

"I borrowed what I need from my dad, so all I need now is you." The last words sent another anticipatory shiver through her. She felt like a teenager figuring everything out for the first time.

"Sounds good," Wendy said.

"Wendy?" Kat said, so she didn't lose her.

"Yeah?"

"Do you want to stay for dinner?" There. It was out there. She'd said it. Since her first night in her little house, they had spent no time there together, alone. If Wendy picked her up, she didn't even stay long enough to set down her keys. Kat had been by Wendy's but only when she had other friends over, guaranteeing their interactions would remain social instead of drifting to something romantic. She had been so tempted to give herself over to what she felt when she kissed Wendy, but as much as she had wanted that, she knew that she'd moved into her own place for a reason.

"I'd like that," Wendy said. A pause extended between them, convincing Kat that Wendy had picked up on the importance of the invitation. "Do I need to bring anything?"

"Just yourself," Kat replied.

Immediately after their goodbyes, Kat tipped her head back and closed her eyes. The Cure's "Close to Me" started to play in her mind and continued on loop until she heard the scrape of the gate announce Wendy's arrival.

* * *

Wendy couldn't go empty-handed, so on her way out of the restaurant, she cut a generous slice of the restaurant's chocolate cake.

"You think you earned that cake?" José asked as she passed him at the bar. His thick black hair was styled off his face with gel. His outfit was a direct contrast to his grooming: baggy black cargo pants and scuffed rubber clogs.

"No, I know I did. I worked my tail off today."

"Not so hard that you're too tired to play?" He motioned to her outfit. Instead of leaving in work clothes, she'd changed into form-fitting jeans and a soft jade-green three-quarter-sleeved tee.

"I'm helping a friend out."

"I'm sure you are. Have a good one."

January had yet to bring any rain, and Wendy was not surprised to find Kat's door open to let in the afternoon warmth.

"Knock knock," she called at the door, inhaling the aroma of cooked onions.

Kat emerged from the bedroom in a blue cotton top with a deliciously low-cut neckline. "Oh, you brought chocolate!" She took the plate and set it on the counter before she wrapped her arms around Wendy.

The hug came from a different Kat, one seemingly unafraid of contact. Wendy tried and failed to ignore the press of Kat's breasts on hers. She wrapped her arms around Kat and took a long, deep breath.

Kat's hands swept across her shoulders and down her back, pressing at her hips before she released Wendy. "I'm so glad you're here! It took almost a year, but my stacks are finally gone! What do you think?" She gestured toward the small living room.

Like Wendy's house, Kat's had one space for her living room and dining room. In addition, since she had only one bedroom, Kat housed a small writing desk off to the side of her small dining table as well. Unlike Wendy's house, Kat had covered nearly every surface with pictures. One wall chronicled Travis from infant to teen. Wendy stepped closer to study the images admiring both the snapshots and school portraits.

"I love this one." Wendy pointed to a toddler Travis blowing a dandelion puff.

"For months, I've been sorting through pictures deciding which ones to put into albums and which ones to hang."

On top of a wooden cabinet, she'd collected family pictures. "This is Ava?" Wendy picked up a stained-glass frame. She recognized the garden swing. Kat and her sister leaned against each other with matching smiles, though Ava held a red flower between her teeth.

"Yes," Kat said.

"Everything looks so great! And once you have this up, you're officially all moved in?" She pointed to the huge mirror leaning against the couch.

"Yep. I've already got the hooks in, but it's too awkward to get into place by myself."

"It looks super heavy. Are these hooks going to hold?" Wendy tugged on the hook closest to the cabinet.

"Trust me. I've been to the hardware store a dozen times with pictures of my wall and the mirror. I learned all about drywall and toggle bolts and finding studs to make sure the bolts aren't going to pull right out."

"In other words, you did all the hard work and I'm here for the glory."

They stood on either side and hoisted the frame constructed from what looked like a weathered window. Half the space held a mirror, the other half three horizontal boards with the words *Live. Love. Laugh.* printed on them. They guided the eyebolts onto the hooks and took a tentative step back.

"It looks good!" Kat beamed. "What do you think?"

"The mirror makes the room look bigger, and the words suit you perfectly."

"I thought so, too." Their eyes met in the mirror, and Kat stepped closer, wrapping her arm around Wendy's waist. "How does that look?" she asked as they looked at themselves in the mirror.

Wendy tipped her head, so that her temple rested against Kat's. "Really, really nice."

* * *

Kat wished that the image in the mirror was a picture she could frame. She also wanted very badly to turn her lips to Wendy's. If she did, they might never get to dinner, and she wasn't sure how long she could leave it in the oven. Reluctantly, she stepped away from Wendy. "I promised to feed you, and I hear that chefs are picky about their food."

"Can I do something to help?"

"No. It'll just take a second. Sit. I'm in charge of the kitchen tonight."

"Sounds good. I've been on my feet all day."

Kat brought a beer and a hard cider to the table. "I hope I remembered the kind you like."

Wendy accepted the Lost Coast Tangerine Wheat. "This is great."

Kat left her with the bottle opener and pulled dinner from the oven. She plated it quickly and took it to the table.

"That was fast," Wendy said when Kat was settled in across from her. They clinked bottles and sipped their drinks.

Kat waited for Wendy to take the first bite of the baked burrito, hoping she'd chosen well. Wendy nodded. "I love the chayote in this!"

Kat wasn't sure what Wendy was talking about. "Chayote?"

"The Mexican squash?"

"Oh, the green stuff. The guy at the grocery store suggested it. He said I'd hardly notice it steamed. And he said to put in fresh corn. What do you think?"

"It's delicious, and plated nicely with the rice and beans."

"I kind of cheated on the Spanish rice. I stirred salsa in after I steamed it."

"It's like a grown-up version of your original burrito. I'm impressed at how you've branched out this year."

"So much of that is thanks to you. You've been so amazing, and I was so worried that you would get tired of waiting around and not knowing whether I was ever going to figure myself out. When we danced at Bruce and Penny's wedding, I didn't want to let go."

She extended her hand across the table, and Wendy took it. "I didn't want you to."

Kat scooted her chair closer, so she could lean over and kiss Wendy. Her body stirred. "I'm crazy for you, you know."

Wendy threaded her fingers through Kat's hair. "That's good because I've been thinking about that kiss and where I would have liked for it to have gone for a long time."

They kissed again, and Kat could feel exactly what she meant. By the time she pulled away, she was out of breath. "Just so we're clear, I invited you over to talk about being your girlfriend, but I'm not sleeping with you tonight. I don't want you to get the impression that I'm easy."

Wendy laughed again. "Oh, I know very well that you're not easy."

Kat's face flushed and she took a bite of her burrito to hide her embarrassment. Wendy touched her chin lightly, and she looked up.

"And still, I couldn't help but fall for you."

"You," she said because it's all she could say. So many feelings swirled around inside her, all of them wonderful and new. "Finish your dinner. I want some of that cake, and I have a surprise for you."

After dessert, Kat called up a playlist of love songs she had been assembling. She settled down into Wendy's arms to "Hold Me Now."

"We Close Our Eyes."

"Take My Breath Away."

"Why Can't This Be Love?"

They slowly kissed their way through the eighties.

CHAPTER TWENTY-FOUR

"I think we kissed our way to the end of your playlist," Wendy whispered as the last song ended and the only sounds were those they were making together.

"I underestimated..." Kat tried to find words to finish her sentence, but Wendy had moved from her lips to her neck which made thinking difficult.

Feeling on the other hand...

She had never felt such a burning desire to be closer to someone. She surprised herself when her hands began to wander, tracing the edge of Wendy's breast. Wendy shuddered at her touch, at such a small touch, and Kat felt her own nipples tighten. Wendy's hand ducked under the hem of Kat's shirt and curled around her hip, and she wanted to feel that warmth everywhere.

"You underestimated...?" Wendy's whispered low and breathy behind Kat's ear.

"Your repertoire of kisses."

Wendy's thumb traced along the hem of Kat's jeans. "Oh, I haven't even pulled out the good ones yet."

Kat sucked in her breath and pulled her legs up on Wendy's lap, so that both of her hands could explore. Wendy leaned into her touch, tipping Kat so they were stretched sideways on the couch. "I think I underestimated how hard it was going to be to keep my hands to myself."

"You think?" Wendy kept her arms extended, and Kat swept her hands up Wendy's belly and around her back and pulled her close enough to kiss again. "Everything about you is so soft."

"Is that what you like best, soft?" Wendy asked placing featherlight kisses along Kat's collarbone.

"I don't know what I like," Kat said.

Wendy gently nipped along Kat's neck, and Kat's breath caught. "You like?"

"Yes."

"What about hickeys?" Wendy asked as she lowered Kat's V-neck, her tongue lightly tracing along the line of Kat's black lace bra.

"You wouldn't do a hickey!"

"No?" Wendy's mouth was hot against Kat's skin as she began to suck harder.

Kat wove her hands into Wendy's hair and pulled her closer to let her know how much she was enjoying the pressure of her mouth. She throbbed against her jeans and moved her leg to put Wendy between hers. She had to have Wendy's mouth back on her own. There was so much to tell her, and the only way she knew how was to wrap both arms around Wendy, shutting out the entire world until it was only their two mouths.

Wendy broke away, her breath ragged. "You are making it really hard to go home."

"Who said anything about you leaving?" As Wendy pulled away, Kat raised her body to keep their contact. Then her mouth was on Wendy's neck, and she was using her teeth more roughly than Wendy had used hers.

Wendy angled her head to the side, and Kat pushed the curls aside to broaden the canvas for her kisses. "You said you didn't want me to think you were easy."

"About that…" Kat said. "I underestimated how much kissing you would make me want you."

"We could do something about that."

"You want to?"

"Oh, I have wanted you for a very, very long time."

Kat heard the desire in Wendy's words and remembered how much she had wanted Wendy after their first kiss. Why had it scared her so much? Why had she again insisted on throwing down a boundary by telling Wendy that they wouldn't be sleeping together? What was she scared of? She sat up, took Wendy's hand and led her the few steps to her bedroom.

* * *

Wendy had imagined taking Kat to bed more times than she could count, but in none of those scenarios was it Kat leading the way. She had imagined Kat being shy about her body. Her clothes would be coaxed off slowly and seductively. But Kat had her shirt off already and was unhooking her bra.

"Your hands, my skin." Kat grasped Wendy's shirt and hiked it up over Wendy's head. "Please," she added as she made quick work of Wendy's bra.

With one hand, she was pulling back the covers of her bed, but her eyes remained on Wendy's body. Everything inside Wendy tightened like a wound rubber band as she waited to see what Kat wanted.

Kat's hands returned to Wendy's hips which she guided to the turned-down bed. Wendy sat and swept her own hands up Kat's belly until her hands cupped her perfect breasts. She swept her thumbs over Kat's pale pink nipples before pulling Kat to her mouth. Kat tipped her head back as her tongue worked each nipple into a harder peak. She leaned back and let Kat unbutton her jeans and shuck them down her hips. She stripped off her jeans and the two quickly became a tangle of limbs on the cool sheets.

Legs intertwined, Wendy shuddered at the press of Kat's center against her own.

"Oh, that feels so good," Kat said grinding against her. Her hair fell forward tickling against Wendy's breasts. If she didn't stop, Wendy was going to finish, and she hadn't had a chance to touch Kat at all.

She scooched down so she could take Kat's breast back in her mouth.

"No fair," Kat said breathily.

Wendy took advantage of her distraction and tipped Kat onto her back. "I have a whole set of kisses to show you, remember? You've got to be patient."

Kat grabbed her ass and pulled Wendy back against her, her legs spread wide enough to feel how wet she was. Helpless, Wendy rocked against Kat even though it brought her closer to climaxing. For a moment, their bodies were in perfect sync, and she thought they might both tip over the edge together, but something changed. Kat's hands? Her breath? Wendy tried to regain the power to think.

"What is it?" Wendy said out loud.

"Come back," Kat said. "Don't stop."

Wendy swept her hair back from her head. Kat's eyes were locked shut. "Hey." She leaned forward and kissed Kat. Her lips had lost the suppleness that they had had on the couch and when they'd first come to her bedroom.

Kat attempted to roll Wendy over. "You were so close. Tell me what to do."

Wendy stilled her hand and stayed on her side, so she and Kat were face to face. "Where did you go?"

"I'm right here." Kat kissed her again, her eyes shut again.

"Kat. Slow down. I want you to enjoy this. Can you look at me?"

Kat opened her eyes and Wendy saw what she had felt, that Kat was scared.

"We don't have to do this," Wendy said.

"I want to."

"That's not what your body is saying."

Kat wouldn't look at her.

"What changed? When we came in here, you seemed like you were enjoying what I was doing."

"I was. I am." Kat ran her hand along Wendy's naked torso. "I want to touch you."

Wendy stilled her hand. "Should I not have flipped you onto your back? I'm trying to understand."

* * *

Kat blew out a frustrated breath. If she'd been with Jack, they would have been done by now. He would have been satisfied and dropped off to sleep, leaving Kat to sort through her feelings. Feelings that Wendy wanted to pull out and explore right now. Wendy was asking to understand something that Kat had never been able to figure out herself, but it didn't look like anything else was going to happen until she talked.

What had Wendy asked? She wanted to know what had changed when they came into the bedroom. Putting her thoughts into words made her feel even more naked. She reached down and pulled the blanket halfway up her body.

"Out there, I was only feeling. In here, I start thinking, and when I think too much, then I don't feel anymore."

"What are you thinking about?" Wendy didn't sound angry with her. She pulled the blanket up to her hip as well and stroked Kat's arm softly.

"Things I shouldn't be. Things I can't change."

Wendy's hand stopped. "Oh."

"Not sexy, I know. I should have warned you, but I was feeling so much that I thought maybe it would be different with you. Maybe my brain wouldn't think about how much can be lost when you listen to desire."

"You think that if your dad hadn't had a boyfriend, you wouldn't have lost Ava?"

"I know it sounds ridiculous."

"You can't protect those you love by denying your desires." Wendy's words were soft, and she ran her fingers through Kat's hair.

"I know that up here." Kat pointed to her head. "But somehow, the message doesn't travel."

"So you go into it thinking maybe this is the time your brain will stay quiet, and you don't want to think too hard because once you ask if your brain is going to say something, it says 'Now that you mention it…' and you're stuck."

"Exactly." Kat whooshed out a relieved sigh.

"Tonight your strategy was to race to stay ahead of your brain?"

"Everything felt so good." Kat said sadly.

"What did you like best?"

Kat couldn't stop the smile that crept to her lips. "It was so sexy when you were using your teeth. Like you were reminding me to stay in my body."

Wendy pulled Kat's hand up to her mouth. Kat felt the warm lips touch her palm. Then her tongue traced each of the lines on her palm. Her teeth followed, a gentle nip on her wrist, her palm, the tip of each finger. Each nip stoked the fire that Kat thought her thinker had chased away. Wendy wrapped her lips around Kat's index finger.

Kat sucked in a breath. "You are so sexy."

"You are," Wendy whispered. "When your body was on mine, I could feel how wet you were. I so wanted to be inside you."

Wendy's words entered her, and Kat's body responded.

"I am in no hurry." Wendy kissed Kat's inner arm, alternating between tongue and teeth. "As long as this feels good, that's what matters."

"I love your mouth on me, but you don't have to…"

"Stop thinking. Keep feeling. How about if I kiss you here?" She kissed Kat just above the hip.

"Yes."

"And here?" She kissed the base of Kat's breast.

"Yes," Kat whispered.

"It's okay to let yourself feel."

Palms spread wide, Wendy's warm hands were everywhere at once, calling all of Kat's nerve endings to attention. Her blood pounded between her legs. "Will you touch me?" Kat whispered.

Wendy propped herself up next to Kat. She kissed her ear and pulled on the lobe with her teeth. "Touch you here?" She gently pinched Kat's nipple.

"Lower."

Wendy's hand brushed from her hip down to her knee. She dragged her nails gently up Kat's inner thigh. "Here?"

Kat gasped when Wendy's hand nestled between her legs. "There."

"More?"

Wendy's kisses made Kat shiver, and her hand felt so good. She felt her body start to tighten and worried that… Before the thought took form, Wendy slipped inside her. All thought ended, and she only felt Wendy's stroking.

"Wendy!" Kat called.

"I'm here."

"That feels…"

"Okay?"

"So good. That feels…Don't stop!"

Wendy's voice, warm in her ear, urged her to stay in her body, and she didn't know her body could feel the way it did under Wendy's caress. Kat clung to Wendy as she coaxed her to the edge where she usually froze. Kat hovered, and Wendy held her tight. Slowly, surely, she drew her closer and closer until an orgasm ripped through her body pulling sounds from her that she had never made before. She felt herself fracture into a million pieces as waves kept crashing through her. As they ebbed away, she came back to herself.

She opened her eyes, and Wendy was there. She stroked Kat's face. "Oh, Wendy…" She had so much to say and no words to express herself. She turned back to kisses, and now Wendy was hers. When she languidly rolled Wendy to her back and began her own exploration, Wendy lay still and let Kat take her time. She tasted Wendy's breasts, rolling her tongue across the surface. They tasted different than Wendy's skin, but still no words shaped in her head.

Kat worked her way around by taste, by feel, by the sounds Wendy made when she touched her, and oh how she loved feeling Wendy respond to her touch, to her kiss. She marveled at how wet Wendy was. She had made her that wet. Her touch elicited that desire. She growled herself when she entered Wendy, feeling herself grow excited again as Wendy's breathing changed. Wendy grabbed her arm as she shuddered inside, and Kat lay in wonder at how powerful she felt as Wendy gave herself to Kat completely.

Hearts pounding and out of breath, they were silent but still communicating in caresses. Wendy's fingers found a nerve that seemed to still be turned on. Each time her fingers passed over it, a shudder ran through Kat's body again. And again. And again until she had to put her own hand over Wendy's.

"I'm going to need more of that." Kat licked her lips. But right now, she needed water and more chocolate cake for strength.

"That wasn't enough?" Wendy teased.

"Nowhere near."

CHAPTER TWENTY-FIVE

Kat's body felt different the next morning when she rolled over and bumped Wendy. She had never understood the appeal of morning sex, yet that morning, her desire for Wendy spoke louder than her hunger.

"Good morning."

Kat could hear the smile in Wendy's voice as she pressed her whole body against her and wrapped her arm tightly around Wendy's hip, pulling her closer. She could not stop her body from moving.

Wendy folded her arm back, stroking Kat's thigh, pulling her legs closer.

Kat explored Wendy's body marveling again at Wendy's presence in her bed. She felt no apology in Wendy's nakedness, but she also felt no pressure. She understood that they were building something together and that Wendy was listening to Kat as much as she was communicating with her hands.

When Wendy turned in her arms, bringing her breasts to Kat's breasts, her lips to Kat's lips, breakfast and all the day's demands slipped away, and Kat gave herself completely to Wendy once more.

* * *

"It should have been enough." Kat's voice came softly over the line.

Kat's words caught Wendy so much by surprise that she had to take the call into the walk-in refrigerator. "What was that?"

"You heard me."

"I did, but I'd love to hear it again."

"This isn't normal," Kat whimpered.

"What isn't?"

"To be so distracted by my body. My clothes are touching me everywhere. I can't turn off the high beams, and it's painfully obvious and inappropriate. I had to put on a sweater because the groom-to-be kept glancing at my chest. I don't blame him, but I don't want to start a fight with the future bride."

Wendy chuckled.

"Sure, you laugh, lady. I'm sure everyone thinks I've got a bladder infection because I have to keep running to the bathroom. It's entirely your fault my panties are soaked."

Now Wendy groaned. "You could always take them off."

"Oh…"

Was the pause because she had said too much or…

Kat's voice came back lower. Sexier. "Would you like that?"

Wendy bit her lip, battling to keep her attention at work and failing spectacularly. All she could think about was Kat's perfect body. "I wish I was standing next to you. I'd love to test out how bad this problem of yours really is."

"My lunch break is coming up," Kat said.

"I'm sorry I can't. Cory and I are about to head out." She glanced at her watch and opened the door to find Cory standing there poised to knock. "In fact, it looks like I'm out of time."

"At least tell me what you're wearing."

"What?" Wendy coughed in surprise.

"Cory's standing there, isn't he?"

"Yes."

"I'll let you go then. As long as you promise I'll see you tonight."

"That I can do." She ended the call and stepped past Cory. "Everything's loaded?"

"Just waiting on you."

They walked to the battered white catering van, Wendy testing how long Cory could go without commenting. She was content to savor the details Kat had shared with her and enjoyed the fantasy of taking advantage of Kat's primed body.

Three minutes later, he blew out a frustrated breath. "You sure are flushed for someone who was in the refrigerator that long. You were talking to Kat, weren't you?"

"Maybe."

"Look at your face! That's a yes! When did you sleep with her?"

"Cory!"

"C'mon. I've been listening to *Kat this* and *Kat that* for years, but now that you've slept together, nothing?"

"What am I supposed to say? That I didn't want the night to end and that I nearly called in sick today, and it's taking all my resolve not to drop you at the event, ditch you and drag Kat into the nearest empty room?"

Cory laughed. "Whoa! Whoa!"

"See? That's why I didn't say anything because there's just too much to say."

"The two of you have your wedding all mapped out?"

"Who said anything about a wedding?"

"This much time you've waited, she's a planner, you're a caterer...You could get married next week."

"But I don't know if you're free."

Cory took his eyes off the road for a moment and smiled hugely at her. "Am I invited?"

"Where are we going again?"

"It's in Universal City, and you're changing the subject."

"I don't want to miss the exit."

"You worried?" Cory's voice was quiet with understanding, which she appreciated.

She *was* worried. She and Kat were so new that it seemed silly to project. But at the same time, she had known Kat for so long and had always hoped, hadn't she, that Kat would want to share her life with Wendy. She'd never had the courage to ask Kat if she would ever consider marrying again. Wendy remembered Jeremy asking if she herself would ever marry. His wedding anniversary was approaching, and she wondered how he and Evan were doing.

She recalled what she'd said to Jeremy, that she didn't mind being alone until she found the right person. And now that she had found the right person, she didn't want to be alone again. That's what Cory had triggered.

"I've never felt like this before. When we did that first wedding at Kat's house, her dad told me that life is sweeter when your heart has a companion. I would have said my life was sweet enough, but now…"

"You want more."

Wendy nodded. "I want more."

"Hopefully, she does too."

The call that Cory had interrupted zinged through Wendy again. For now, she would savor the fact that Kat wanted more of her.

* * *

Kat lay in Wendy's arms later that evening, much later than she usually stayed up. Her appetite for Wendy proved larger than she imagined possible. Wendy traced Kat's skin, hip to shoulder and back again. Kat loved this time, loved Wendy's calm, warm hands on her. Her touch was the perfect combination of confidence and questioning. Her hands asked *here?* And Kat's body answered *yes* every time.

"Thanks for letting me come over tonight. I know you had a long day."

"You're kidding, right? No day is so long that I'd say no to this," Wendy said.

"Like I said, I just can't seem to get enough of you."

"You won't hear me complain about that. Did you get enough tonight?" Wendy asked sleepily.

Kat's hand drifted in lazy circles across Wendy's tummy. "Nope. Not yet." She paused on Wendy's breast.

Wendy smacked her hand away. "You want more now?"

"As tempting as that sounds, I don't think I can have more now. But I can't seem to stop touching you."

"I love your hands on me. You sleepy?"

"Not yet. I'm thinking."

Kat heard Wendy's sharp intake of breath. "Thinking?"

The post-orgasm buzz just beginning to fade, Kat marveled at how good she felt in her body. "Just thinking how much I love being right here in your arms. Thinking you'll have to show me that trick you did with your tongue."

"You liked that?"

"So much."

"Anything else on your mind?"

"Just how much I want to stay here tonight. Would that be okay?"

"You're in luck. There happens to be a vacancy I kind of hoped you'd fill."

"Done. You booked tomorrow?"

"Let me check the calendar."

Kat pinched Wendy's hip.

"Looks like you could have this spot again."

"I'd like that."

"Me, too."

Kat could feel Wendy's muscles loosening with sleep. "Sweet dreams," she whispered, thinking about how Wendy had made so many of her dreams come true.

CHAPTER TWENTY-SIX

One Year Later

Arm in arm, Kat and Wendy walked up the long drive. "You seem nervous. Are you sure it's okay for us to celebrate our anniversary here?"

"It's perfect," Wendy said. They stopped on the front porch. "This is where we had our first kiss."

Kat leaned into Wendy who looked even sexier tonight with her curls framing her face instead of pulled back for work. "You didn't mind my suggestion?" Kat asked, tugging gently at Wendy's tie that she'd picked out to match her red dress.

"Not at all. I'd feel underdressed without it because you're absolutely stunning in this." She ran a finger underneath the spaghetti strap of Kat's dress.

Kat savored the shiver of desire. She captured Wendy's lips in a kiss that briefly made her regret letting her mom talk her into celebrating together. "Your kisses just get better and better," she murmured. Just as she was about to kiss Wendy again, the door opened.

"Enough, enough already," Travis said.

Kat snatched one more kiss before embracing Travis. She only got the hint of a squeeze before he turned his attention to Wendy.

"I think we're almost ready to serve," he said, leading the way to the kitchen.

"It smells good in here!" Wendy said.

"Come see how good the crepes are turning out! I'm pretty sure the butternut squash is done. Will you check it? And I haven't steamed the spinach yet."

Kat watched Travis and Wendy confer, thinking about how much her life had changed in the last year. Where it had once felt strange to drive here to see Travis, it was now part of the rhythm of her weekends. Wendy often joined her and offered cooking tips to Travis and Clyde. Her good works had paid off.

"I'd give you a hug, but…" Clyde held a pan in one hand and expertly poured the crepe batter.

Kat squeezed his shoulder and surveyed the kitchen. The counters nearest the range had neatly chopped green things. The counter next to the oven, however, was littered with flour and powdered chocolate. "Where's the cake?"

"Your mom is decorating it in the dining room," Clyde said.

Kat wrapped her arms around Wendy and said, "I'm going to go help her."

Wendy delivered a quick kiss and swiftly turned back to the crepe assembly line.

Kat found her mom in the next room piping ganache on a tall chocolate cake. "Hi, Mom. Oh! The cake looks awesome!"

"I hope it cuts okay. I didn't know the mousse in the middle was going to make it so slippery. But slippery is good, right?" She smirked.

"Mom…"

"What? This is my chance to live vicariously through you!" She finished placing fresh strawberries around the base of the cake. "Do you think we should drizzle them with the leftover ganache?"

"No. The berries are supposed to cut the sweetness."

"Like ice cream," Millie said. She wiped her hands on the white apron she wore over her ubiquitous purple shirt.

"Not quite."

"Okay. Now that that's done. Come on! I have some things for you." With surprising agility, Millie climbed the stairs without her cane.

"I told you we're not exchanging gifts!" Kat said, following her mother.

"Well this doesn't count because I'm giving this to both of you."

"I have veto power."

"Of course. I can return anything."

Kat accepted the first bag of many piled on Millie's couch. She hoped her mother had been shopping mostly for herself. "A pound of chocolates from See's?"

"You said she loves chocolate."

"But you made that whole cake!"

"Nobody can have too much chocolate!"

"I approve. Is that it?"

"We're just getting started!"

Kat accepted a bag filled with wrapped objects. "Who needs a heart-shaped plate and matching red glasses?"

"Not you?"

"No."

With a shrug, Millie piled the rejects on the couch. "How about this?" She handed Kat a smaller bag.

"What is this? Some kind of…edible massage oil?"

Millie beamed at her.

"Mom!"

Millie's smile disappeared. "Inappropriate?"

"You think?"

"Oh." She glanced at the next bag. "Then I guess the massage wand is out."

Kat covered her face. "I'm going to pretend I didn't hear that."

Millie looked at all the bags. "You're only taking the candy?"

"I'll take the massage oils."

"Great! Let me know if you change your mind about…"

Travis's booming voice saved her. "Dinner!"

Downstairs, the table was extended with the leaves Kat had forgotten even existed.

"You and Wendy get to sit here." Travis pulled out a chair.

Clyde held up his glass for a toast. "Let love be expressed," he began.

"Let joy abound," Millie finished.

"Let's eat!" Travis added.

* * *

"Is that hollandaise sauce?" Millie asked helping herself to some asparagus.

"It is. When Travis said the menu included asparagus, I asked if I could contribute."

"Have I mentioned how glad I am that my daughter is dating you?" Millie asked, passing the plate to Kat, who took one spear and went to the refrigerator for a dollop of mayonnaise. "You're going to pass on this lovely hollandaise sauce your girlfriend was so kind to make?"

"Baby steps," Kat said. "What's in the crepe?"

"Butternut squash, pecan, steamed spinach and some feta," Travis said. "Wendy's recipe."

Kat took a bite, and Wendy waited for her reaction. "Good. Sweeter than I expected."

"Like life." Wendy lifted her glass toward Clyde, remembering again his words about how sweet life is when your heart has a companion. She took a deep breath hoping that she had made the right decision about tonight. Clyde smiled at her, bolstering her confidence.

"What's that about?" Kat asked.

"Something after dinner," Wendy said. She furtively checked her pocket.

Kat and Travis exchanged a look, and then she said, "Not right after dinner because I have something to show you."

"Everything is delicious. I'm sorry that Drew and Marie couldn't make it," Millie said.

"They were very apologetic that it didn't work out and wanted me to thank you again for the invitation." Wendy reached under the table and squeezed Kat's thigh. In truth, they were free, but Kat had said that it felt weird enough to be celebrating with her family. She'd asked if Wendy felt okay telling hers to expect an invitation to a simple dinner soon. Knowing she wanted to sneak Kat away from everyone after dinner, Wendy happily agreed to explain that she'd like them to decline this time. It would have been difficult to leave the two couples alone.

As much as she tried to stay engaged in the lively dinner conversation, she kept losing track of the threads Kat and Millie wove from memories and movie lines. Clyde insisted her silence validated his frustration with their tangent-riddled conversation, but in truth she was lost in rehearsing what she wanted to say to Kat.

Even with the dishes cleared and Kat taking her hand and leading her downstairs after Travis, she was still caught up in her thoughts. Kat sat her on the steps and stepped behind her drum kit. Travis already had his guitar and was waiting for Kat to set the beat.

Kat radiated happiness just as she had years ago when they'd played "Head Over Heels." "Okay, sorry we don't have any trumpet, but I hope you like our version."

"I'm sure you guys rock," Wendy said.

She could see Kat take a deep breath and begin the song. "I used to think maybe you loved me, now baby I'm sure."

Wendy smiled at the opening lyrics though she didn't recognize the song until Kat and Travis got to the "Walking on Sunshine" chorus. She happily joined in, and as she'd anticipated, Kat and Travis sounded awesome. When they finished, she clapped and said, "That was fantastic! I didn't even know you guys were learning a new song!"

Kat bit her lip and rested her drumsticks in her lap, shy as always about the praise Wendy gave her singing.

She stood and extended her hand to Kat. She'd rehearsed the words she wanted to say so many times that she was beginning to worry that she would forget the order. "Come with me for a minute?"

* * *

Kat wouldn't cry. It wasn't like she and Wendy had talked about marriage at all, but for her to not even say a word about the lyrics she'd changed in "Walking on Sunshine" hurt more than she had expected. Travis knew and had reached for her, but she was already pulling inside herself. The words she'd offered Wendy cycled round and round, her intent so clear that Wendy could not possibly have missed it.

Her mom was counting out the good china plates while her dad washed the dishes. Before she could say a word, Kat held up her hand and shook her head. She grabbed her white wrap and draped it across her shoulders. "We'll be right back."

Thankfully, neither said anything as they passed through the kitchen.

Evening softened the landscape, and night-blooming jasmine perfumed the air. Kat admired the yard as she always did, noticing the pansies her father had planted. Wendy took her hand and led her down the porch steps toward the pool yard. It was only at the gate that Kat saw Jeremy and Evan's bridge spanning the water again. "Is this what that look was between you and my dad at dinner?"

"What do you mean?"

"Are he and my mom renewing their vows? Why wouldn't they have asked me for help?"

"Your parents? No. This isn't about them. I asked your dad to help me because I had something I wanted to ask you, and this seemed like the best place." She tried to lead Kat to the bridge, but Kat remained rooted by the gate.

"You didn't say anything about my lyrics."

"Lyrics?"

"To the song. I rewrote a whole verse, and it's like you didn't even hear it."

"It sounded the same to me."

"I used to think maybe you loved me, now I know that it's true. I don't want to spend another day, not one without you." She paused and waited for Wendy to understand. She tried a few more lines. "Now I don't want you to feel put on the spot, but this love that I have for you ain't ever gonna stop."

"I'm sorry." Wendy looked at the bridge and back to Kat. "Wait. You wrote those lyrics?"

"Yes. I wanted to talk about the rest of your life and whether you'd be interested in spending it with me." Kat held up her right hand with the engagement ring she'd selected for Wendy. She pulled it off her finger and held it to her. "I thought you'd notice when I was playing the drums. I had it all worked out, that you would hear the lyrics, see the ring and ask what it was doing on my finger. Then I'd ask you to marry me."

"Oh! I ruined your plan." Instead of holding out her left hand to receive the ring, Wendy dug in her pocket and extended its contents to Kat. "See, my plan was to bring you out here after dinner and ask if *you* would marry *me*."

"So I ruined your plan!" Kat clapped her hands over her mouth, her eyes glued to the ring in Wendy's palm.

"I'm sorry I didn't hear the lyrics. I don't want to spend another day without you, either. I was so worried about remembering what I wanted to say."

"Which was…?" Kat stepped closer to Wendy.

Wendy took Kat's hand. "For starters, we have to be in the middle of the bridge." She led the way, stopping to face Kat once they reached the middle.

"And then you were going to say…"

Wendy stood there staring into Kat's eyes. "I only remember the 'Will you marry me?' part."

Kat extended her hand. "Yes, a thousand times yes." Once Wendy slipped the ring onto Kat's finger, she admired the set of the simple diamond. "I didn't know how you'd feel about marrying a girl with a past," she whispered.

"Your past will always be part of who you are. A mother. An awesome drummer. A sister and a survivor. I counted once and came up with eight lives. Cats get nine lives, right? I wasn't sure you'd want to share your ninth with me."

"You weren't sure? I thought I was pretty clear about how much I want you." Kat kissed her deeply.

Wendy responded to the kiss, stepping forward and running her sure hands along Kat's curves. "Haven't had enough yet?"

Kat loved the way their kisses could make Wendy gasp. She nuzzled Wendy's neck, enjoying the spices that lingered on her skin. "I'll always need more of you. I can't seem to get enough of you. I may never get enough. Would that be okay?"

"I think I could live with that."

"Me, too. I think I could live a long, long time like that."

Bella Books, Inc.

Women. Books. Even Better Together.

P.O. Box 10543
Tallahassee, FL 32302

Phone: 800-729-4992
www.bellabooks.com